# Getting Tyson

This book is a work of fiction. Names, characters and incidents are products of the author's imagination and any resemblance to identifiable characters, persons, situations, locations or events is entirely coincidental unless otherwise so stated

PENPOWER*Writing*
www.penpowerwriting.com

Dec. 2016

To Adam

With Best

Wishes.

Peter.

# GETTING TYSON

A novel
by

# P K DAVIES

# CHAPTER ONE

# VALHALLA

*The great hall of immortality in which the souls of warriors slain
heroically were received by Odin and enshrined*

Tiles were the Victorians' reinvention. In the buildings
destined to be monuments to their munificence and
confidence in the absolute of Empire, tiles were the wallpaper
of their vision, almost indestructible, a marriage of art and
technology, a statement of their self-belief and a message to
future generations. They adorned the floors and walls of their
municipal buildings, their museums and the great houses of
their captains of industry. But their technological perfection
could not hide forever the defects of the material on which they
were built and the tiles of the east London morgue were no
exception. Grouting had disintegrated and dirt had penetrated
to the mortar beneath and the glazed edges of the clay had
succumbed to the harsh treatment of abrasive cleaners and had
chipped, forming jagged lines to which the dirt now clung,
undisturbed by modern cleaning standards. The wooden
benches on either side of the corridor were equally neglected,
still functional but unloved and scratched by the feet of bored
children wondering why a parent was so distressed. This was
no Valhalla and beyond the security
doors of the corridor, the attendant and pathologist were no
Valkyrie either, their plastic aprons were not shimmering chain
mail of gold or silver, their latex gloves were not oiled with
incense of myrrh and their masks were as unforgiving as their
eyes. This was Hades and they were the handmaidens of the
damned. It was no place for heroes.

The two bodies were tabled almost together, charred black and indistinguishable from each other except for the police-issue shoes on one of them which had bizarrely escaped the intensity of the fire and showed a strip of recognisable flesh above them.

"That's where a beam fell across her," the pathologist explained, following the direction of his interest. "You'll notice the other woman's finger tips escaped complete tissue destruction. We think she was probably trying to lift the beam from the WPC. You can see from the photos she was slumped across the other woman's body."

He ignored the photographs the pathologist proffered and continued to stare at the charred, skeletal remains of the policewoman.

"Was she wearing anything around her neck?" he asked.

The pathologist showed him a necklace in a plastic envelope, the gold of the patterned pendant melded to a single structure.

"Can I keep it?" he asked. The pathologist looked beyond him to the other officer who nodded agreement.

"We have enough DNA and teeth to identify them," the pathologist told them. "That is, if they are in your records, of course." she added.

Inside he smiled grimly, knowing only one of them would be in any records and vaguely wondering who his daughter's companion was in her last, horrendous moments of life. He continued to stare at the body even as his hand took the plastic envelope and put it in a pocket.

"Is this your first fire victim, Chief Superintendent?" the pathologist asked him.

"No," he answered. "But it's the first one from my family." As hard as he tried to find any connection between the near skeletal remains in front of him and the little girl who had been the delight of his life nothing came to relieve the iced numbness he felt in both his mind and his body. He turned away from the table and left without another word. The other officer nodded their thanks to the pathologist and followed his colleague.

Outside, the Chief Superintendent was leaning against a wall, trying to breathe in the air as if he had just climbed a steep hill. His companion touched his arm in a helpless gesture of empathy.

"I'm sorry, Mike. And I'm sorry there isn't a better word."

Chief Superintendent Mike Prosser nodded. "What have you got, Geoff?" he asked

"Not a great deal at the moment. But we're working at it."

"Have you made any connection between the explosion and the business at Billingsgate?"

"Not yet. But we haven't ruled one out. We know Janet had been in the Billingsgate truck but we don't know when or how she got from there to the house in Stepney."

"What about the house?"

"It was rented. We haven't traced the tenant yet."

"Who owns it?"

"Dave Tyson."

The Chief Superintendent turned, his eyes showing he was still alive.

"You chaps must know him," the other officer said.

"Oh, yes. We know him," he answered grimly.

# CHAPTER TWO

# A MATTER OF LAW

The BMW was doing seventy miles an hour, sitting comfortably on the winding access road which swept past the golf course from the suburban streets and joined the arterial road which was the busy route from London to the Kent coast. A tunnel of trees accentuated its speed as the light-beams reflected from the trunks like marker posts on a ski-run and the driver, sixteen-year old Danny Murphy, was screaming his excitement but his passenger, Robbie Birch was becoming less convinced about his friend's ability to control the vehicle.

"Slow down, Danny, we're on the wrong side of the road," he advised.

"There aint nuffink comin', we'd scc the lights," Murphy responded.

The road rose ahead of them, inclining upwards progressively in order to cross over the busy dual carriageway which now ran parallel to their course. The incline slowed the car but not enough for the inexperienced driver to safely negotiate the sweeping turn onto the road-bridge which suddenly leapt at them out of the night.

Big Dave Tyson, six-foot five, eighteen stone, was sitting comfortably in his Range Rover listening to The Beach Boys, his huge, tattooed forearms supporting the light touch of his fingers on the steering-wheel. He was in a good mood, having successfully wined, dined and fucked a young female whom he had interviewed that afternoon for a vacancy in one of his London strip-clubs. As he turned onto the road-bridge at less than twenty miles an hour, he could have no idea, not even if he had been ultra psychic, that his life was about to change forever.

He was well onto the bridge when he saw the sweep of headlights on the trees ahead but he was unprepared for the BMW being on his side of the road as it made the turn, its off-side tyres burning and screaming a protest against the abuse of their limitations.

Tyson pulled into the side, almost against the low steel barrier that protected pedestrians on the narrow pavement. He stopped the Range Rover and closed his eyes, perhaps praying, for the first time in his life, that the BMW would miss him. He was wrong.

Although Danny Murphy had recognised the inadequacy of his driving by braking and aiming the BMW away from the inevitable collision, he failed to prevent it crunching into the offside of the Range Rover which stalled the engine and activated the airbags in both vehicles. Murphy was small for a sixteen-year-old, and instead of protecting his chest, the console airbag cushioned his face and pushed him lower into the driving seat and as he was not wearing a seat-belt, he slid downwards almost under the steering column. Robbie Birch, being taller and the same age, reacted to the accident more conventionally, making contact with the airbag with his chest and starting the deflation process which hissed nitrogen gas into the car, causing the boys to panic out of their shock. Robbie managed to reach past the side-impact bag and open the nearside door.

"Danny, you all right?" he asked urgently.

"Yeah," came the reply as Danny struggled to climb back into the driving seat, then he had to negotiate past the obstacles in his way to the nearside of the car as the driving door was crushed against the Range Rover.

"Come on, get out of here," Robbie ordered as he almost fell out of the car onto the road.

Big Dave Tyson also had his difficulties. His large frame

had immediately started the deflation process to the airbags but as he too was unable to use the driver's door, he had to untangle his body and legs from the airbags and then manoeuvre across the central console to get to the nearside of the Range Rover.

Outside, Robbie Birch saw the trees at the end of the bridge and ran towards them, fear driving his legs. Danny eventually managed to scramble his way out of the car but before he could follow his friend, Big Dave Tyson had crossed the road and had a firm hold of his collar.

"Come 'ere, you little git," he snarled.

Danny struggled to free himself but it was an unequal contest until he squirmed sideways, corkscrewing to face his assailant, and managed to land a hefty kick to Tyson's shin. The big man yelled his pain above the hum and roar of the fast-moving traffic below but did not let go of Danny's collar. In severe pain, with his free hand he took a grip on the youngster's trousers behind his crotch, and with a bear-like roar he lifted Danny in one snatch up to his chest and then, with a deep intake of breath reminiscent of a weight lifter's technique, he jerked the boy upwards and launched him over the railings onto the dual carriageway.

From the safety of the trees, Robbie Birch saw the incident with the reaction of a child watching a horror movie. Danny's scream descended, undiminished in volume until he landed on the bonnet of a Ford Focus doing sixty miles an hour in the centre lane. He bounced upwards before his head smashed into the windscreen. The Ford slewed sideways engaging the back of a lorry in the nearside lane and then swerved one ninety degrees and was hit by a sports car travelling at eighty in the outside lane. The sports car somersaulted over the Ford and burst into flames. Behind, vehicles swerved and braked and crashed into each other, the carnage soon stretching several hundred yards down the carriageway.

Tyson leaned forward onto the railing of the bridge and looked down at the headlights scattering in all directions to the sounds of collisions and screeching tyres, then he calmly straightened up and took out a mobile phone and dialled the emergency number.

" Hello. Yeah, I wanna report an accident," he said.

Robbie Birch thought he could be sick as his stomach convulsed, but nothing came up. From his position he could not see the dual carriageway but the sounds were suitably expressive for him to imagine what had happened to his friend. He started to run, at first staggering drunkenly before his legs recovered from the assault on his nervous system. He eventually stopped when he was free of the trees and brambles and started the long walk home, now aware of the many scratches to his body and the enormity of his secret.

Detective Superintendent Michael Prosser had already been up two hours and it was only seven am. He held his fourth cup of coffee and stared through the window of his single-bed flat in South East London onto the tidy entrance court two floors below. It was raining, and if his eyes had been capable of adjusting their focus he would only have seen the reflection of his gaunt, fifty-five-year-old face staring back at himself. But what he saw was a long, narrow garden and two children playing cricket. Janet was bowling aggressively and her younger brother, James was wanting to back away to leg but stoically remained in front of the wicket as his father had taught him. With a Larwood-style action, Janet hurled the ball towards her brother and followed it forward with a raucous "Owzat?" as the ball hit James painfully on his pad. Prosser smiled, the smile growing until it stretched his face and squeezed a tear from his eye. He took a deep breath and shook himself at the sound of the door-buzzer. "Coming, Val," he said into the intercom.

Detective Inspector Valerie Franks looked at him as they queued to filter across the A 205 which was already heavy with commuter traffic heading for the Thames crossings.

"You haven't slept again have you?" she said. "You can't go on like this, Mike," she insisted "I'll sleep with you if it will help," and brought a smile to Prosser's face.

"Our lives are fucked-up enough without adding another complication," he answered. "But, thanks anyway Val."

"You're welcome," she said and wondered if her divorce had constituted the description Prosser had applied to her life. Sure, she had drifted from day to day since her ex had moved to Dubai with his young PA but it had left no emotional baggage. Perhaps that was the fuck-up.

"Did you hear about the accident on the Kent road last night?" she asked. "It sounded horrendous."

Prosser hadn't heard, choosing to sit staring blindly at a film rather than listening to any news items.

"I'm not sure I want to get my driving-licence back."

"No, you've got used to having me as a chauffeur."

They didn't speak for some time as they started moving at a steady forty miles an hour until Mike Prosser suddenly said," It's the anniversary next week." She knew what he meant and knew *anniversary* was not an appropriate word but she just nodded as there was nothing she could say that she hadn't said many times before to make him feel better. Then he surprised her. "Val, thanks," he said. "For everything."

She smiled at him but felt again the pain of his demotion from chief superintendent for the drink-drive offence almost as much as he did but there was no way she could

8

feel the pain of its cause. If she had been a different person she would only have appreciated that his humiliation had been the catalyst to her own promotion to DI but if the new Chief Super had thought that would buy her loyalty to his draft from another district he had been wrong; it had brought everybody in the section closer to Mike Prosser despite his uncompromising leadership when a job was to be done.

"Have you heard from James?" she asked.

"He Skyped me a week ago. He's okay."

Val franks knew it was good to keep the conversation going.

"Is he still in Sydney?"

"No. He's moved to Perth. Got a good offer from another company."

"That's good," she said without conviction.

When they arrived at the police station everybody seemed to be in a cheerful mood and when they entered the CID room they were greeted with inexplicable grins. Mike Prosser looked down at his flies and found them securely fastened. "What?" he asked. Nobody offered an explanation. "Are you going to tell me why you're all grinning like Cheshire cats or are we going to play bloody twenty questions?" he demanded.

"Big Dave Tyson," DS Greening said.

Prosser's face became more gaunt. He sat on the edge of a desk and his voice reflected his expression.

"Okay. I'm sitting down. Tell me."

DS Greening told him Tyson had reported the horrific accident on the Kent road. "Three people dead and six in hospital."

Prosser nodded. "I know Tyson isn't a Good Samaritan. there's more to it than that. There always is with Tyson." Greening told him about the witness.

9

"He saw Tyson throw the boy off the bridge?"

They all watched Prosser struggle with his emotions. He stood up and took off his coat. "Someone get me a coffee." When he had the coffee he sat at one of the desks and took out a pen. "Tell me everything," he said to Greening.

Greening told him how sixteen-year-old Robbie Birch had come into the Station at six o'clock that morning and told the desk-sergeant how he and Danny Murphy had stolen a BMW and of the consequences.

When he had finished writing the bullet points, Prosser fired questions at his sergeant. What time was the emergency call made? Where was Birch when he saw Tyson throw the boy from the bridge? Why had it taken him eight hours to report what he'd seen? Does the boy's mother know he's at the Station? Where are the two vehicles involved in the accident, and "Does the kid think Tyson saw him?"

Greening explained it had taken the boy two hours to walk home, that his mother worked in a night-club and didn't finish until two am and that she was still asleep when the boy decided he couldn't keep his secret any longer and came into his nearest police station – which was theirs. He was sure Tyson didn't see him – "Or he wouldn't have reported the accident would he?" he added cheekily.

"So, it's possible Tyson doesn't know about the other boy?"

They watched as a smile almost eased the severity of Prosser's face, they all knew what the news meant to him.

"Right," he said. "Where's the boy now?" He was told WPC Jordan had taken him for breakfast. "Good. That's good. Did Tyson make a statement?" He was told he was scheduled to come in at ten am to do so. He was given the preliminary report from the Traffic people.

"The boy tried to get away from me and jumped over the pavement barrier. He must have caught it with his foot and just, sort-of took off and went over the railing." he read aloud. "Like bloody Peter Pan,"and he flapped his arms to everyone's amusement. "Okay. Val, find the boy and take him to an interview room. Andy, call his mother, she'll be doing her nut if she wakes-up and finds him missing – but don't give her any details. Susan, contact Tyson and confirm he's coming in to make that statement. Thompson, call the car pound, I want those two vehicles cocooned until Forensics have got to them. Everybody, we all know how long we've been waiting for this. I don't want any gossip outside this room. Nobody must know about the witness until we've charged Tyson. Susan, get on to Traffic and get as many details as you can from them. Please God, we've got the bastard at last."

He walked into his office and was followed by Val Franks. Prosser hung up his coat and sat at his desk.

"Some clever bastard said vengeance is a dish better served cold. Well, my inside is ice. Is that what you wanted to know?"

"Will you interview him?"

"Of course. Does a lottery winner give his ticket away? Don't worry Val, Kasparov couldn't beat me on this one."

"What do you want me to do with the boy?" she asked.

"Love him tender. Make him feel important – and keep his mother at arms length."

She found Robbie Birch still in the canteen with the WPC. He was easy to like, gauche and skinny with warm eyes and clean hair. She introduced herself. "But call me Val," she told him. Yes, he'd enjoyed his breakfast; eggs, sausage, bacon and beans and two rounds of toast. They took him to an interview room. Prosser watched the proceedings through the viewing panel.

"So, Robbie, about this accident," Val Franks began.

"It weren't no accident. It were murder."

Prosser smiled to himself. DI Franks read the notes the WPC had taken from the boy over breakfast.

"You say you clearly saw the man from the Range Rover, lift your friend Danny and throw him from the bridge?"

"Just like a sack of rubbish," Robbie added.

"Why do you think he did that?"

"Because Danny give 'im a hefty whack on his shin."

"And you think that hurt him enough to kill Danny?"

"Course it did, Danny 'as steel caps on his shoes, ee does Irish dancing. Ee's faster with his feet than anyone with their hands. Ee used to get bullied because ee was small but when ee wore his knee-breakers everyone left him alone."

"So you think Danny really hurt him?"

"Yeah. Course. I hope ee broke 'is bleedin leg."

Val Franks hoped so too. "Where did you get the BMW? It's okay, we don't care about a stolen car."

Robbie explained how they were walking back from the park and a geezer was unloading boxes from his car and taking them into a shop. He'd left the engine running and the boot open. As they got near, the man took another box into the shop and before Robbie knew what was happening, Danny had slammed the boot of the car and jumped into the driver's seat.

"So I jumped into the passenger seat as Danny drove off." He then explained everything that happened right up to when he ran for the trees and saw the man grab Danny.

"Could you describe the man? Franks asked.

Without hesitation Robbie gave a description. "Ee were huge an' bald an' wore a belt with a  big metal buckle."

"You could see that well from the trees?"

"Yeah, there are lights on the bridge. I didn't want Danny to take the car.

"Why was that.?

"I was supposed to be home before Mum went to work."

He explained his mother worked nights in a club and left at nine and didn't get home until two in the morning.

"Was she home when you got back?" No. "Does she know you're here?" Yes, because he left her a note. "When did you decide to come in and report what you'd seen?" Robbie explained how he couldn't sleep, how he kept seeing his friend flying over the bridge.

Val Franks explained how he would have to help them write down all he'd told her. "Don't worry, Robbie. We'll get the man who killed Danny."

While Val Franks was preparing Robbie's statement, Prosser was told the boys mother had arrived. Mrs Birch was a woman not much older than DI Franks and had once been attractive but now looked worn and tired beyond her age. She was aggressive as soon as Prosser entered the room.

"Where is he? Where's my boy?" she demanded to know.

Prosser assured her Robbie was fine, that he'd had a good breakfast and was just a bit tired and stressed.

"What's he done, why's he here?"

Reluctantly she sat down at Prosser's bidding. He started to tell her how the boys had stolen a car.

"That Danny," she said. "He's no good. Always getting Robbie into trouble."

"Not any more." He told her what had happened to Danny. Even Mrs Birch, who thought she knew everything about bad happenings, was shocked.

"That's murder," she said. "Poor Danny. His Mum will be beside herself." Prosser agreed that was likely "Have you got the man wot done it?" she asked.

Prosser told her how the man had reported the accident himself, not knowing Robbie had seen what he'd done.

"So, you see, Mrs Birch, Robbie witnessed Danny's murder."

"Will he have to go to court?"

Prosser explained the process after they charge the man. "Even though Robbie will make a statement, the defence have the right to question him."

Doubt showed on her face. "I don't know. I don't like to think of him having to go into a witness box."

"Mrs Birch, we have been trying to get this man for years. He's the very worst kind. He's into drug trafficking in a big way. He has sex clubs that exploit vulnerable girls. He operates a prostitute ring and he has people killed. But this is the first time we have a witness who actually saw him kill someone himself. Robbie can put Dave Tyson down for the rest of his life."

Mrs Birch's face brightened. "Semtex?" she said.

"Semtex?" Prosser queried.

"That's wot we called 'im at school cos he 'ead-butted people." Instinct told Prosser he should be concerned.

"You went to school with him?"

"Course I did, he lived round the corner from us."

The concern grew in Prosser's stomach. "Does he know you now, do you have any contact with him?"

She explained he moved in different circles to her.

"They say ee's got a big mansion somewhere in Kent. I 'aven't seen im in years, an' I don't want to."

Prosser felt relieved. "Yes, he's got a lot of money from making a lot of lives miserable. You know the sort of kid he was, he just got worse as he got older. Now, with Robbie's help we can put the bastard where he can't do anyone any more harm."

Mrs Birch frowned then looked up defiantly. "No," she

14

said. "I don't want Robbie involved."

"He is involved. He's a witness to a murder."

"And that's why I won't let him get involved any further. Do you think for one minute Semtex will let him give evidence? Don't be stupid. I don't want my Robbie getting killed like poor little Danny."

Prosser explained how they would protect him but Mrs Birch snorted her disdain. "Protect him? Tyson's got coppers in his pay," she spat.

Prosser swallowed and closed out the jibe. "He won't be able to hurt Robbie or anybody else any more," he argued. "With his record he'll get twenty-five years at least. He's already done time for assault, theft, possession of stolen goods. The courts know what sort of man he is."

"You'd have to put all his cronies away with him to protect my Robbie. No. I'm sorry, I know what he's like but I won't let Robbie give evidence."

"And I'm sorry too Mrs Birch. Robbie came to us voluntarily. He's now making an official statement. He wanted to do what was right and we'll do everything we can to see he's kept safe."

"He's only sixteen. You have to get my permission even to use his statement."

"You're wrong. He is compellable. We can provide a solicitor for you who will confirm that."

"Then I want to see him. I'll talk some sense into him."

Prosser said they would explain her concerns to him after he had given his statement. "We'll call you then."

"You can't stop me seeing him," she shouted as Prosser got up and opened the door. "You're going to kill my boy," she screamed as he left the room

Prosser went into the interview room where Val Franks was helping Robbie compose his statement. He managed a friendly smile although inside he was not feeling as

15

confident as he looked after the confrontation with his mother. He sat on the edge of the table next to Robbie.

"Robbie, I'm Detective Superintendent Mike Prosser and I'm in charge of the team that is going to help you put the killer of your friend, Danny in prison. I've just spoken to your mother. She doesn't want you to help us."

The boy looked at him as though he was stupid and the DS could feel Val Franks' concern without looking at her.

"Why not?" Robbie asked.

Prosser explained that she was afraid.

" What's she got to be afraid about?"

"She knows the man who killed Danny. She doesn't want you involved. She knows how dangerous he is."

"Too right, he's dangerous. Ee's a bleedin psycho. Look what he did to Danny. He needs locking up."

"That's right, Robbie. And you're the only one who can get him locked up."

"So what's Mum on about? He killed Danny."

"We can take you into protective custody," Val Franks said quickly. The boy looked puzzled.

"We can do that, Robbie. Val is right," Prosser agreed.

"What's that mean?" Robbie asked.

"We can put you somewhere safe, with a temporary guardian. It would be in an ordinary home but no one will know where you are or who you are."

"Can't I  go to school or see my friends?"

"Do you like school?" Prosser asked.

Robbie explained he was about to do his GCSE's. "I want to do well cos I want to get into the air force."

"That's good, Robbie. It's important to have a goal. You won't be able to attend school but we can arrange for you to keep up your school work with one-on-one tuition."

"Will I have my own room?" the boy asked.

"Don't you have your own room at home?"

"No. I have to share it with my brother and he plays on the computer all the time. He drives me nuts."

Prosser asked about his family and was told the brother was two years younger than Robbie and there was a younger sister, Caron, who was six.

"I look after her while Mum's at work," he told them.

"Every night?" Val Franks asked. Robbie nodded.

"Where was she when you and Danny went to the park?"

"She was at home – that's why I had to get back before Mum left for work. She'll kill me for not getting back."

"No, she won't," Prosser assured him. "She's just thankful you didn't get hurt. But she won't want you to help us. You're all we've got, Robbie. If you don't help us that man who killed Danny will get away with murder."

"Will I have to go to court?"

Prosser told him he would have to give evidence despite making a statement. "We'll ask the judge to consider your written evidence and not subject you to cross-examination but I'm afraid the defence will probably insist on it."

"I don't mind," Robbie answered. "It will be cool going to court. I've never been to one."

"And I hope you never will have to again," Prosser told him. "So what do you think, Robbie. Can we depend on you to put the man who killed Danny in prison or will you do what your mother wants?"

"No way, I won't change my mind. I want to see that geezer pay for what he did to Danny."

"Good lad. You'll make a lot of people very happy by telling a judge just what you saw – and we'll see you don't come to any harm. So, Robbie, are you sure?"

"Yeah. I'm sure."

"Okay, you can see your mother as soon as DI Franks has finished with you and after that Val will take you to one of our cells and get you some blankets so you can have a sleep while we sort out somewhere for you to stay. How does that sound. Is that okay with you?"

"Sounds good," Robbie agreed.


Big Dave Tyson didn't arrive until 11am. He was accompanied by his legal counsel, Marcus Swift. It has been said that barristers are would-be actors with all the insecurities and frustrated egos of that profession and Swift could have been the prototype for that opinion. He was large, not large like Tyson, more from too many good lunches, and he wore clothes which emphasised his largesse, physical and emotional. Depending on his mood rather than his environment, he wore dark-striped suits or chequered three-piece tweeds, always with bright ties and socks and always with a brightly patterned pocket handkerchief exploding from his breast pocket. He could just as easily be mistaken for a course-bookie as for a theatrical agent and his background was equally flamboyant. A brilliant scholarship winner for a place at an Oxford college, his extra-curricular associations with some of their criminal clients eventually became too frequent for the comfort of the Middle Temple law-firm who had recognised his abilities and even used his dock-worker antecedence as a token of their liberal values at many drinks parties. Without their support, Marcus found other firms less attracted to the cocktail of his personality and propensities and the trickle of work acting for his criminal drinking companions soon became his bread-and-butter and his academic knowledge and courtroom articulation the bane of prosecution lawyers.

Via the internal monitors, Prosser had watched the two men arrive. He noticed how Tyson had difficulty walking and almost hopped as he tried not to put his left foot on the ground. He watched Swift sharing a joke with the desk-officer and noted how his earlier statement to Val Franks, that his inside would be like ice, proved predictable. He answered the call from the desk officer.

"Thanks. Put them in Room Four," he said.

Immediately Prosser heard Swift protest.

"No. Not an interview room, if you don't mind. My client is here only to give a statement. We only require a table."

"Put them in the waiting-room," Prosser told the officer.

The room was not monitored, which Prosser knew Swift had recognised and did not want the interview to be recorded. Prosser took a uniformed officer with him and went down to greet the man he knew had been responsible for his daughter's murder.

"Ah, Chief Superintendent," Swift said as he offered his hand. "Oh, forgive me, you are no longer that are you? Such a shame. Such a waste. Regardless, it is a pleasure to see you again."

"The pleasure is all mine Marcus," Prosser answered shaking hands. "Hello, Dave. Have you got a problem with your foot? "

Tyson was sitting with one foot held out, resting on the heel. "It's me bloody shin," he mumbled."

"Was it hurt in the accident?"

"What d'you fink? Bloody kid could have killed me."

"Unfortunately, he only killed himself. And two others – and there may be more."

"Good heavens!" Swift looked concerned. "That is tragic. Who would have thought a thing like that could happen?"

"That's the trouble with fatalities, Marcus, if people thought, most of them wouldn't happen."

"Too true. Too true." Swift agreed and nodded his head in a suitably philosophical manner.

Prosser knelt next to Tyson.

"Let me look at that leg, Dave. It could be serious," he

said and started to fold down Tyson's sock. Tyson attempted to bend his leg away but Prosser had a firm hold on his shoe.

"Why d'you want to look at it?" Tyson said aggressively.

"Because, if it was done in the accident you may want to claim damages for it."

Tyson looked at Swift for guidance but none came other than a raised eyebrow.

"Yeah. Yeah. That's right," he said.

Prosser folded down the sock and saw the ankle had been bandaged roughly with what resembled a piece of torn cloth. "It's been bleeding," he told Tyson. "Who bandaged it for you?"

"I did it meself."

Prosser began to unwind the bandage carefully. Marcus Swift smirked. "I am impressed Superintendent. You are maturing into a kind man."

"I'll have to watch that, Marcus. Can't have my reputation tarnished." He looked at the wound, the blood had dried around the broken skin and there was extensive bruising along the tibia. "That's a nasty blow. I'm pretty sure that would have cracked the bone. We'll have to get a doctor look at it for you."

"Don't worry. I'll 'ave it looked at when I leave 'ere."

Prosser rewound the bandage then pulled a chair up to the table. "Tell me about this accident."

"Dave gave a statement to the uniformed officers who attended the scene," Swift told him.

"Yes, he did. I have it here," Prosser opened a file. "Let me see; you say you got out of your car on the passenger side because you couldn't open the driver's door."

"That's right," Tyson agreed.

"How long did it take for you to get out?"

"Ow would I know? I wasn't lookin' at me watch."

20

"Let me help," Prosser tried. "You had to unfasten your seat-belt, presumably get past the airbags and then climb across to the other side of the car. That's not easy for a big man like you. What do you think, three, four minutes?"

Tyson showed impatience. "I don't know. Yeah, three, four minutes. What does it matter?"

Prosser ignored the question.

"And then you say you went around the back of your car and started to cross the road to the other car and you saw a kid get out of the BMW. You did say a kid, didn't you?"

"He looked like a kid to me."

"So you saw him quite clearly?" Prosser asked deliberately.

"Course I did. The bridge is well-lit."

"Lit well enough for you to identify that the other person was young. How young, would you say?"

"Jees! I don't know, He was a kid, fifteen, sixteen. He was a teenager. That good enough for you?"

"That's fine. So we know that as you came round the back of your car and started to cross the road you saw this teenager. You then say you yelled at him and he attempted to run away. Which way did he run?"

"Back the way he drove onto the bridge."

"Towards the trees?"

"Wot trees?"

"I believe there are trees at the beginning of the bridge."

"I s'pose he was trying to reach them to hide then."

"How far from them were you when you caught him?"

"You are taking an extraordinary interest in the trees, Superintendent," Swift said, sensing a motive for the questions.

Prosser ignored him and waited for an answer.

"Bout firty or forty feet I s'pose. We was right in the middle of the bridge. Wot's it matter?"

"And then you say you grabbed hold of the lad but he twisted out of your grip and tried to jump the barrier. What barrier?"

"There's a low pedestrian barrier. I suppose because it's not much of a pavement. The kid tried to jump over it and caught it with his foot. He sort-of jumped in the air and hit the top of the railings and fell over. It's all there, as I told the traffic people."

Prosser was silent for a moment. He looked at the floor and then back at Tyson. "And that's all you want to say about it? You're sure there's nothing you want to add?"

"Like wot?"

"Like how you came to damage your tibia so badly."

"Me shin? I must 'ave 'it it on the barrier as I tried to grab the kid, to stop 'im goin' over the flippin' railings."

"You would have had to have hit it really hard to crack the bone – I'm sure we'll find it is cracked. How would you have done that?"

Tyson's anger began to show. "I don't bloody know. It all 'appened so fast I can't remember. I know it bloody hurt."

"Perhaps the kid kicked you," Prosser suggested

"How could he do that? He just shook himself out of me grab and started to run for it."

"You are sure he was alone?"

"Course ee was. I didn't see anyone else."

"But if it took you three, four minutes to get out of your car isn't it possible there was someone else in the BMW and he got away before you saw him?"

Marcus Swift  got to his feet.

"Well, that's all very interesting conjecture, Superintendent. My client has made a statement and he has nothing more to add to it. He will happily sign what you have there."

Tyson began to struggle to his feet.

"Sit down," Prosser barked at him so forcefully that Tyson fell back onto the chair and Swift turned back with an indignant look

"I haven't finished yet," Prosser continued, his affability abandoned. "As I was saying, If someone else was with young Danny Murphy in the BMW he could have got out before you did and from the trees you have identified, saw you pick Danny Murphy up and throw him onto the motorway."

Tyson's mouth twitched weakly. "That's ridiculous. Why would I do a terrible fing like that?" and he tried to laugh.

"Because Danny Murphy kicked you with his steel-capped  shoes hard enough to crack your tibia." Prosser hissed.

"Superintendent, my client has been co-operative and acted as a responsible citizen. He reported an accident. He is the victim of that accident. Your animosity towards him is well documented but suggesting he threw someone onto a motorway is stretching incredulity beyond even your imagination," Swift protested.

"You may be right," Prosser responded. "I try not to use my imagination too much, Marcus. I prefer to rely on facts and it is a fact that we have a witness who saw your client pick up Danny Murphy and throw him off that bridge, causing his death and the deaths of others."

"What witness. You're bluffing?" Tyson responded.

"When you were a young tearaway, before you got into drugs and prostitution, did you ever steal a car on your own?" Prosser asked him. "Of course, you didn't. You did it to show off with your mates. Well, nothing's changed, Dave. If you hadn't been so slow getting out of your car you would have seen another lad with Danny. A lad who watched what you did to Danny from those trees. That's why I was so interested in them. Marcus, I'm charging your client with the murder of Danny Murphy and the manslaughter of others."

"I wish to speak to my client in private," Swift said.

"Fine by me, Marcus. This officer will lock you in this room until a charge-officer will come and read your client his rights and then he will be remanded in custody."

"Marcus? Do something," Tyson said desperately when Prosser had closed the door behind him and they heard it being locked. "You've got to get me out of this."

"Is that right. Is that how it happened?" Swift asked. Tyson shrugged. "The kid broke me flippin' ankle. It 'appened so quick. 'ow did I know there was two of 'em?"

Swift bit his lip to stop the expletives that had formed in his brain spitting out of his mouth. "Do something? What can I do? If they have a witness you've already convicted yourself. You agreed the bridge was lit well enough for you to identify the boy. You have said you were only thirty to forty feet away from those trees and you have agreed it took you several minutes to get out of the car. And they have said the boy you apprehended was wearing steel-toed shoes. They will insist on an x-ray of your ankle and that will be compelling evidence that you had sufficient provocation to do serious harm to the boy. You tell me what I can do, Dave."

Tyson stared at the ground but found no answer. Marcus Swift paced around him until he stopped and said, "You will have to go to hospital for that x-ray."

"What you thinking, Marcus?"

"There is no way I can get you bailed on a murder charge – and certainly not with your record. When they take you to the hospital that may be your only chance to escape."

"They'll have an escort on me tighter than a bullion truck. They'll 'ave me in and out before I could arrange anyfing. You've got to find that witness they said they 'ave."

24

"They will put an exclusion order on his identity, even on his statement. We won't know who he is until the trial."

"So what the shit am I going to do?"

"We know who the victim is. It shouldn't be too difficult to find out who his friends are," Swift said thoughtfully.

"Good thinking, Marcus. I knew you'd find something."

"Then what – don't answer that. I don't want to know."

Tyson whispered. "Then we can leave it to Jason, he'll know what to do. You find that witness and Jason will do the rest. You do that, Marcus and you can name your own price for this one."

"Don't be silly, Dave. I would have to go and live in Belize to enjoy it. If anything happens to that witness they will be all over your businesses and your bank accounts like a rash – even the Swiss ones. And I don't want to be mentioned in any of them."

"Awright then. The 'ouse, Beaumont. You've always loved my 'ouse."

"It's a beautiful house," Swift agreed

"You get me out of this an' Beaumont is yours."

"That's the prize of your life of crime."

"No bovver. Spain suits me fine. It's yours, Marcus. If I walk away from this, Beaumont is yours. I promise."

"I shall make out the papers," Swift said

When Prosser returned to the squad-room everybody turned towards him expectantly. "We've charged him with murder," he said triumphantly to much celebrating. "But, let's keep our heads and build a good coffin before we bury him, he's escaped before. Thompson, call the CPS and ask them for their best person to work with us on this, we don't want any technical mishaps. Richard, liaise with Forensics and ask the right questions. Meakin, talk to the owner of the BMW – do we know who that is?" He was told it was a Mr Chandri. "Right, get a

25

statement from him, and Val, talk to Childrens Services and see if they can find a safe house for Robbie and see how they can advise us about talking to his school without telling them why he won't be attending. Make Robbie your pet project."

"What about his mother?" Val Franks asked.

"I'll talk to her again and hope she'll co-operate."

Prosser took the buoyant mood of the Section home with him that evening and the little flat seemed more comforting than depressing. There was a moment when he almost reached for the cupboard where he used to keep his whisky before he had told himself he would never touch alcohol again, but he opened a biscuit tin instead and switched on the coffee percolator. When he walked into the living-room his two children, Janet and James, smiled at him from the wall cabinet as they always had. He smiled back at them and said, "We've got him, Janet. We've got him." The telephone didn't ring but he grabbed it suddenly as though it had. He dialled. "Edna?" There was silence from the other end apart from a slight movement of air. "We've got him, Edna. We've got the bastard." There was only the sound of a receiver being replaced.

DC Thompson followed the motorbike into the underground car park. The rider was dressed in red leathers and wore a red and black helmet and, like most men somewhere inside, Thompson felt the anguish of not being able to be that rider and leave his family and mortgage behind and speed into the country on a winding, empty road to nowhere. He hadn't seen the outfit before and he asked the security man who it was. "From the CPS," he was told. By the time he had exchanged a few pleasantries and wound down to the car park the rider had already dismounted and had abandoned his boots and unzipped the leathers and wriggled out of them and stood brazenly wearing black panties and a red and black bra. She then took off her helmet and shook away from her face thick curls which caught the yellow light and sparkled like wet autumn leaves. She didn't turn at the sound of DC Thompson's car crunching into a pillar or at the loud "Fuck," that escaped from it. She exchanged the leathers for a white blouse and light-grey suit from the panniers and then slid into a pair of red-leather, high-heeled shoes. She had completed the operation and was walking towards the lift by the time DC Thompson had extricated the car from the pillar. He stared first at the damage to the light console and then at the shapely hips swinging away from him like a mirage in the yellow-lit, smelly, dingy reality of the police station's garage.

Dominique Harcourt was French and pronounced her name "Aarcoor" as French people would, which confused most people hearing this pronunciation and then recognising the spelling as something more familiar. "That's English," was a usual accusation. "No. That is French," Dominique would insist.

She was directed to the CID section by a gaping-mouthed desk sergeant and there she was greeted by many similar expressions.

"I'm looking for DS Prosser," she enquired reasonably but was met with silence until Val Franks looked up.

"Hello. I'm DI Franks," she said.

Dominique smiled as brightly as her shoes.

"Dominique Harcourt – from the CPS."

"Oh, hello. Sorry, we weren't expecting…"

"A woman?" Dominique suggested teasingly.

"No. No, we have plenty of female solicitors."

"I'm a prosecutor," Dominique corrected her.

27

"Really?" DI Franks was recovering her faculties.

"We were told you wanted help with the Tyson case."

"We certainly do. That's great."

The door behind them swung open loudly as DC Thompson crashed through it.

"You should have seen what I just saw. This bird," he began and then saw his mirage was standing partly hidden by his inspector. He stumbled awkwardly to a stop as everyone stared at him and then followed his eyes back to Dominique as though watching a tennis match.

"What sort of bird was that, Thommo," someone asked. "A Great Tit?"

"Let's go into my office," Val Franks said and led the way to the far end of the room. She turned at the doorway and looked back. "Okay, boys, put your tongues back and get on with it." Inside her office she pointed to a desk. "You can work there if that's okay, Dominique."

"Thank you," Dominique said and took off her jacket and draped it carefully over the back of a chair then unbuttoned her sleeves and rolled them neatly away from her wrists watched with fascination by Val Franks.

"Should I meet DS Prosser?" Dominique asked.

Val Franks told her he was out but would soon be back. She picked up a folder and took it across to Dominique's desk. Chanel drifted up to her as she put the folder on the desk and leaned forward next to the Frenchwoman.

"I've copied everything we've done on the case so far," she began as she opened the file.

The door opened and DC Fowler smiled at them. "Anyone like a coffee?" he asked. They both shook their heads and he retreated under their steady gaze.

"Has Tyson got previous?" Dominique asked.

"Not for a few years. Not since he got rich and could afford a lawyer like Marcus Swift."

28

"I've heard of him."

"I'm sure you have."

The door opened again and DC Thompson walked into the room, staring at Dominique whilst holding a folder in the air, vaguely in Valerie's direction

"That's the preliminary forensic report on the motors," he said, still staring at Dominique.

"Hello. I'm over here," DI Franks told him. "Thank you. Thommo. Goodbye." The two women watched him back out of the office, hitting the edge of a desk as he went.

"Do you always have that effect on men?" Val asked.

"Not on real men. Only on wannados, unfortunately."

"And we've got a few of those around here."

"Don't worry, they never do what they wannado."

"I should hope not. Dominique, forgive me, but you look very young to be a prosecutor. Don't be offended, it's a compliment."

"No offence taken. I've got used to it. At uni I got all the silly little girl parts in the drama group and I was always being asked for my ID in pubs."

"It's a problem I would like to have," Val said.

"No. You're a beautiful woman. I'm just crumpet."

Val Franks put her hand to her cheeks. "I wouldn't mind being that either," she said through her embarrassment.

"I'm sure you were treated like that when you first came on the force. But wouldn't you rather be respected for being a good copper – as I'm sure you are?"

"I'll need to think about that. Then I wanted to be what I am now, but now? It would be nice to be fancied again."

"I take it you're not married?"

"Not married, no partner, not even a cat."

"And not committed either. Don't you love that word? I think it's appropriate in our professions. Perhaps we see relationships like sentencing; how long will we get?"

The women were laughing as the door opened and DS Prosser entered. He stared at Dominique.

"My God! I asked the CPS to send us their best shot."

"Mike." Val tried

"Silly of them." Dominique had risen to greet the DS but put her hand back by her side. "They must have thought an Honours degree from the Sorbonne, a Cambridge First and membership of Lincoln's Inn might have been up to your standard. Should I go now?"

"Have you ever handled a murder case?"

"No. But my job here is only to see you have done yours properly and legally collected sufficient evidence for a successful prosecution. In that context murder is no different from shop-lifting."

"This is not just a murder case, it's Dave Tyson's murder case. Do you understand how much we want Tyson?"

"No. And what you want is not important. The Court may take account of the accused's record for sentencing but to a jury the facts are on trial, not Dave Tyson."

Val Franks watched the exchange, noting the passion in Dominique's green eyes matching that of her boss.

"I'll tell you a story," Prosser said and pulled a chair to Dominique's desk, sitting on it the wrong way round and leaning on the back with his arms. Dominique sat before him, her head on one side, a patient, expectant expression on her face. Prosser told her the story. Two years previously the Drug Squad were trying to get a handle on Tyson's trafficking. They knew he was behind a regular supply operation because their informants and minor dealers all had connections either with his many properties or known associates but they could not get anything directly on him. Then they discovered a known associate of his, a Dutch fruit and veg importer who was suspected of laundering Tyson's drugs profits, owned a

30

small Estonian company that had a fleet of refrigerated trucks carrying Baltic fish and food supplies. The fruit and veg trucks had been routinely inspected several times without a result so when the connection to the Estonian company was made, the Drug Squad asked their Dutch colleagues to check them out without arousing too much suspicion. A routine check with sniffer dogs found nothing and then, when the driver was having his papers checked they ran a heat-detection camera on one of the trucks and it showed a positive result. The Dutch let the truck carry on and alerted the Border Agency at Harwich. The Border Agency, working with the Essex police delayed the driver by asking him to open up the truck for inspection. The Dutch had already reported no sign of an access point from inside the truck to a secret compartment, so while the driver was attending the inspection at the rear, a search was made of the driver's cab and on lifting up his bunk they found five pairs of legs extending under it from the refrigerating motor compartment. The women were all teenagers. It was known that Tyson's pole-dancing clubs were fronts for organised prostitution and a decision was taken that the truck should be followed into London to find the destination for the women. They had no time to arrange for a tracker to be put into the vehicle so a WPC stripped off her jacket and equipment and joined the women in the hidden compartment with her mobile phone left on so a tracking operation could be organised. Before it reached its destination the truck made one stop on the M11, it was a usual place for a meal break for the Harwich traffic but it was there for less than fifteen minutes. The tracking showed it then continued to Billingsgate fish market. When the reception unit located it there was no driver and no women found and the WPC's mobile phone was on the driver's seat. At the same time there was a gas explosion in a house in Stepney less than half a mile away.

"There was no connection made to the truck until two female bodies were recovered from the burned-out house. They had been locked in an upstairs room. One of them was the missing WPC. The house was owned by Dave Tyson. That's who Tyson is." Prosser finished his story and watched Dominique's face harden.

"Then I hope you have enough evidence to convict him for this murder," she said.

"We do. But if there's the slightest chink Marcus Swift will slide Tyson through it. I don't want that to happen."

"Then if it's okay with you, I'll examine  what evidence there is and let you know if I find a chink."

She opened the file and concentrated on the first page.

Prosser stood up. "Okay, I'm sorry. I was out of order. It's just that you look…"

"Too young?" Dominique looked up at him accusingly

"I was going to say, inexperienced."

"Isn't that the same thing? I'm also French. Are you going to hold that against me too?"

"Let's start again," Prosser said and held out his hand.

"Hello. I'm Detective Superintendent Mike Prosser."

"How d'you do, Superintendent. I'm Dominique Harcourt."

"Call me Mike."

"Dominique – and  I'm a bloody good prosecutor."

"Then I'll let you get on with being bloody good," Prosser said and left the room. The two women looked at each other.

"Definitely not a wannado," Dominique said.

"More a wannadone – preferably yesterday. What he didn't tell you was, the WPC in the truck and burned alive in that house was his daughter."

Dominique's body reacted more expressively than any words she might have chosen.

"He's still suffering. It broke up his marriage – his wife silently blamed him for letting the daughter join the police and he blamed himself. Janet wanted to do what he did – she loved her Dad - and when he couldn't persuade her to change her mind they compromised by her going to live with her grandmother in Suffolk and joining the Essex force. As the marriage went to pieces he drank and then his son emigrated to Australia and his wife left to live near her mother in Suffolk. Then he was pulled-over by an unmarked patrol car and found to be over the limit. He was disqualified for a year and demoted from chief superintendent. So, that's why this case is personal."

Later that afternoon Dominique had gone through the evidence file. She noted Forensics had confirmed four different sets of prints in the BMW and had matched two sets to Danny Murphy and Robbie Birch. But they also recovered female DNA from hairs found on the rear seat.

"I presume one of the set of prints will belong to the owner, Mr Chandri," Dominique said. "But what about the female hairs? Do we have a match for those?"

"We asked the owner, Mr Chandri, about them. He said no one had been on the back seat, his wife always sat in the front and he had the car valeted every weekend."

"Perhaps he has a lover," Dominique suggested.

"That's what we thought – but uniform, who got his statement, reported he was a little fat man about sixty."

"Sex doesn't stop at sixty – or because you're fat. There's someone for everyone."

"That's comforting to know," Val Franks answered.

Later, Dominique sat back and made a summary of the evidence they had accumulated thus far.

"Every thing's strong," she said. "But it all hangs on your

witness. Without him there is no case. How safe is he?"

Val explained he had agreed to be taken into protective custody despite his mother's opposition. She explained how the mother had known Tyson for years and knew what he was like and was afraid for her son's safety.

"That's your biggest problem. If the mother knows where Robbie is and complains too loudly, the  Defence could find him too. That might be dangerous."

Val Franks agreed. "We've had to get a Restraining Order to stop her seeing Robbie unsupervised before the trial. She doesn't know where we're hiding him."

"Is he sixteen? The age is important too."

"He said his sixteenth Birthday was in April and his mother confirmed that – and so did Social Services. They've known the family for a few years."

"That's good. If he is sixteen his mother can't stop him giving evidence or you using his statement. Would it be possible for me to see the accident site?"

"You are thorough aren't you?" Val Franks smiled.  When would you like to go?"

"Now – if that's possible?"

"The traffic will be terrible at this time in the evening and It will be getting dark by the time we get there."

"That's good. It will be similar conditions to when the accident occurred."

"Okay. I'll tell Mike he'll have to get another lift home."

"I've got a motorbike in the garage, if you direct me I can find the place."

The vision of the very feminine Frenchwoman on a motorbike brought a smile to Val Frank's face and when Dominique explained what had happened to DC Thompson the smile became hilarious laughter,

"I'll drive you then drop you back here.  By that time the garage should be quiet. We don't want any more damage."

Val parked in a pull-in against the trees where Robbie Birch had hidden. They walked back onto the bridge, which was now busy with a steady stream of traffic. Many flowers were tied in the centre of the railings from where Danny Murphy had been thrown. Dominique studied the plan of the accident site that Traffic had supplied. The two women discussed the positions of the relative vehicles, then Dominique walked back to the trees. She found a path which led immediately off the end of the bridge into the wooded area with shrubs and brambles on either side. She could see Val Franks clearly. She walked back to the detective. She confirmed Robbie would easily have seen what happened..

"Enough to convince a Jury it was definitely Tyson?"

"Yes. But he won't have to because Tyson has already admitted he was the driver of the other car. All we have to convince a Jury of is that Robbie could see clearly what happened on the bridge – and that isn't a problem."

Dominique crossed the road to where the collision was marked on the plan. She pictured the physical progress the occupants of the two cars would have made to vacate the vehicles and timed the mental process.

"It must have taken several minutes for Tyson to extract himself from the Range Rover and cross the road."

"What about his defence that the boy caught his foot on this barrier and fell over the railings?" Franks asked.

"It might be possible. But the injury to Tyson's leg and Robbie's contention that he saw Danny kick Tyson is Probable Cause. If the Jury visit here I think the evidence to support Robbie's statement will be overwhelming."

They leaned on the railings and looked down at the speeding traffic below. "Can you imagine the last moments of Danny Murphy's life?" Val Franks asked.

"Horror for eternity," Dominique answered.

Her companion looked sideways  then gave a cry of pain. "What?" Dominique asked quickly.

Val held her neck stiffly. "Something went in my back." Dominique took her by the shoulders and eased her up and away from the railings. "Sit here," she said and lowered her onto the pedestrian barrier. "Now, hold your arms out." She put her arms under the DI's and round to her front and linked her hands behind the detective's neck then she suddenly pulled upwards and back. There was a crack and a pained cry from Val Franks.

"There, that should be okay now," Dominique said. Val moved her back carefully and then stood up.

"That's amazing. The pain's gone. Who taught you that?"

"My Mama always told us, first know your body and then you'll know your mind."

"You'll have to thank her for me."

"I wish I could. She died when I was young."

Involuntarily and uncharacteristically, Val Franks put her arm around the Frenchwoman's shoulders. "I'm sorry."

"Valerie, you'll have to get some exercise or you're going to have serious back trouble."

Val Franks smiled at the use of her name, the French pronunciation making it sound especially attractive which she had never before thought it was.

"I know," she agreed. "I keep telling myself that climbing stairs and jumping in and out of cars all day keeps me fit, but I know it doesn't. It just  uses  up all  the caffeine I drink to  keep me going."

"Then we will have to change that. Where do you live?"

"Greenwich," Valerie answered. "And you?"

"Near Canary wharf."

"Posh," Valerie teased.

"Expensive and barren. Do you know Millwall Dock?" Valerie said she did. "Meet me there on the Thames Path by the sailing club at 6.30 tomorrow morning, Have you got trainers and a track-suit?"

"Yes, almost unused. We're not going jogging are we? I hate jogging."

"You'll see," Dominique replied with a secret smile.

At six-thirty the following morning Val Franks parked her car by the sailing club and walked towards the quay. She saw Dominique outside one of the boat-houses talking and laughing with a man. Her immediate instinct was to turn and retrace her steps but Dominique saw her.

"Please, not water," Valerie said as they met.

Dominique took her hand and led her down to where the man was now holding a training skiff against the pontoon.

"No. I can't do this," Valerie protested but Dominique kept a firm grip of her hand.

"Yes you can," she insisted. "Close your eyes if you want to. Turn around. Now put your left leg out."

She steered Valerie's foot into the skiff, causing it to rock and Valerie to moan. She stepped into the boat and guided the policewoman onto the stern seat and sat behind her.

"Now you're okay," she said. "Merci Bob." Bob pushed and the boat slid away from the pontoon. Val moaned continuously. "Take hold of the oars," Dominique instructed. She leaned forward against Valerie's back and reached around her to guide her hands onto the oars. "Keep the wrists level, keep your head up and your eyes on that building at the far end. Now ease forward in the seat and then back. Forward, back, forward back. Don't reach, keep your elbows in."

They made steady progress with Dominique guiding Valerie's arms and counting the time until Valerie realised how far into the middle of the wide stretch of water they were and immediately crabbed and fell back into Dominique's thighs. Dominique kissed her head before pushing her upright and screaming with laughter.

The Mercedes slowly motored into the council estate, past the high-rise blocks with their balconies loaded with bicycles and domestic rubbish and washing lines waving their bunting above them. Past the walls of graffiti and groups of youths with their Bull Terriers, jostling each other and singing to ghetto blasters. Some of the youths eyed the Mercedes and buzzed it on BMX's. Jason opened the window and told them where to go and his size and scarred face told them not to argue. Beside him, Marcus Swift squinted through half-closed eyes and his expression was as though they were about to be penetrated by a sharp needle. They progressed to a more recent addition to the estate where blocks gave way to rows of maisonettes some with little gardens in front. Swift studied a plan and guided Jason to a cul-de-sac.

"There, that must be it," he said and pointed to a terraced maisonette with flowers and messages tied around the fence bordering a tiny front garden.

"All right," he said as Jason stopped the car. "Wait here."

He got out and strode up to the house and rang the bell, he knew Jason was not capable of doing what he was about to do. The door was opened by a small, tired-looking man who opened it just enough to peer around it.

"Mr Murphy?" Swift enquired with a deferential stoop as though to lower himself to Mr Murphy's level.

Murphy quickly took in Swift's expensive suit and the bunch of flowers extended towards him.

"Yes," he answered suspiciously

"Mr Murphy, my name is Chandri. I was the owner of the car your son stole, when they had the accident."

Murphy mumbled something and was about to close the door when Swift's large hand fell against it. "Don't be alarmed, Mr Murphy. I'm not here to complain." Murphy allowed the door to be pushed wider.

"What do you want?" he said.

"First, I want to say how very sorry I am about your son. It was a terrible thing to happen and I am deeply sorry." He offered the flowers which Murphy took from him.

"Thank you. That's very understanding of you."

"I cannot begin to imagine how your wife must feel."

"She's not up to seeing anyone," Murphy apologised. "But I'll tell her what you said."

"I want you to have this," Swift said and handed Murphy a thick envelope. Murphy looked inside and the tiredness leapt away from his face.

"What for?" he gasped. "This is a lot of money. Why do you want us to have it?" his voice became suspicious.

"Only because I feel partly responsible for your son's death. I should not have allowed my car to be stolen. I should have been more careful and locked it."

"I'm afraid Danny was a bit of a chancer, even when he was little. He snatched an ice-cream off a baby in a pram once – an' he was only four. I give 'im a right wallop. It's all right Mr Chandri, we're not blaming you. There's no need to give us anything." He offered the envelope back.

Swift waved it away. "I want you to have it. I am a business man and I know the cost of things. It will help with Danny's funeral."

"It's very decent of you."

"Not at all. It's the least I can do. Did you know the other boy who was with Danny by any chance?"

"Yeah, of course. He lives over there, number fourteen." Swift looked across to where Murphy pointed.

"I must call on them and see if he was injured in any way. I don't even know the poor boys name."

"Robbie Birch. He was okay, thank God," Murphy said.

They shook hands. Swift got back into the Mercedes. "Robbie Birch. Number fourteen," he said to Jason.

It was a few days later that Mrs Birch went over to see how Mrs Murphy was and learned of the visit of "that kind Mr Chandri." She immediately became suspicious when the money was mentioned and the "posh car" and then the description of Marcus Swift whom she recognised from the local publicity concerning the many court appearances of her one-time school acquaintance. She had seen Robbie twice since his custodial protection had been arranged. She had been unable to persuade him to leave well alone and have nothing to do with giving evidence. "You'd better learn that minding your own business is the only way to survive in this world," had made no impression on her son nor had, "You'll end up like Danny," desperately thrown at him with anger at his intransigence. Secretly, Robbie was rather enjoying the attention he was getting from Val Franks and the Childrens Services officer and he was very happy with the accommodation they had found for him in a volunteer emergency foster home with an elderly couple who had only been told that he was being protected from an abusive parent and were dutifully sympathetic. So Robbie, who had only known step-fathers and boyfriends with various deficiencies of character, was reluctant to relinquish his moment of comfort and self-respect for his baby-sitting-house-chores existence and argumentative relationships with his mother and brother. Their meetings were arranged and supervised by Val Franks and when Mrs. Birch realised that nothing she could say would change Robbie's mind, she had to find another way to protect her son from what she considered to be his inevitable destruction. It was not difficult for her to find an address for Marcus Swift and to arrange a meeting. When she rang the bell of his office near London Bridge her body and mind were in turmoil of conflicting emotions. Her body almost trembled and her stomach noisily articulated her nervousness but her mind drove her forward with aggressive determination which was demonstrated by her first words to Marcus Swift as she was shown into his office.

"You're the man wot gave that money to Jerry Murphy."

"I don't know what you are talking about," he told her.

"You are Dave Tyson's solicitor, right?"

"I do represent Mr Tyson from time to time."

"And that bloke wot was with you was Jason wasn't it?"

"Mrs Birch," Swift began but was soon interrupted

"Don't play friggin games with me. I know you an' Jason got Robbie's name from Jerry Murphy. I've known Dave Tyson a bloody sight longer than you an' I know the way he operates. So don't waste my time."

Marcus Swift realised charm was no defence against an irate woman. "Please tell me what you want from me."

"I'm 'ere to save my boy," she answered

"Save him from what?"

"You're playing games again. I want you to tell Dave that before he sends any of 'is gorillas like Jason after my Robbie there's something he ought to know."


Dominique Harcourt and Val Franks were at their desks when Mike Prosser came in and asked how they were getting on  Val Franks gave him a summary of their progress and Dominique said she was typing-up the prosecution evidence for a trial hearing.

"The only thing we have not been able to finalise is who the hairs on the back seat of the BMW belong to."

"Is it important?" Prosser asked

"I can't see any significance at the moment."

"So, the evidence is watertight is it?"

"Conclusive," he was told

"Good. Excellent. Fantastic. Great job, both of you. Thank you." He turned to Dominique. "Have you noticed how Val is glowing lately? I think she's hiding someone from us. Too busy to give me a lift these days."

"It must be the thought of putting Dave Tyson in gaol," Dominique suggested.

"I haven't seen you glowing, Mike," Valerie said.

"I'm saving it for when he gets a life sentence. Go for it, Dominique. let's get the bastard into a courtroom."

After he'd left, Val Franks put her hand to her face

"Glowing?" she asked

"He should see your bum," Dominique replied


Three days later the whole of the squad room looked expectantly at Dominique Harcourt as she entered. She stopped near the door, conscious of their stares. Mike Prosser was discussing something at the far end of the room. Val Franks was taking a phone-call but put the receiver down when she saw Dominique. Prosser walked some way towards the Frenchwoman.

"I don't like that look on your face," he said.

Dominique nodded. "Nor do I," she agreed. "The Defence have requested a pre-trial hearing due to new evidence. They say the evidence may prejudice our case."

There were many different expressions both vocal and physical at the news but all of them, in some way, showed astonishment. "What new evidence?" Prosser demanded.

"Swift wouldn't disclose it until they have verified its authenticity. But he's requested a  High Court ruling."

Prosser kicked a desk. "I knew it. I bloody knew it."

Val   Franks   came   down   the   room   and   looked

sympathetically at her friend, feeling her misery.

"Can they do that?" she asked. "Don't they have to give us the new evidence?"

"Eventually, of course. But they have a right to choose their point of disclosure."

"And what does this High Court hearing mean?"

"It's just like the magistrate's hearing. A High Court judge will examine the evidence the Defence will present and decide whether or not it alters our case for trial."

The Hearing was soon arranged. Marcus Swift and Dominique Harcourt were seated before a clerk and behind them Val Franks and DS Prosser sat disconsolately in the otherwise empty courtroom. They stood as Judge Harris entered.

"Who are you?" he asked of the two detectives.

"We are the prosecuting officers," Prosser explained.

The Judge asked if the Defence had any objections to their presence and was told by Swift that he was always delighted to educate the police in matters of the law.

"Good. Then you can start by educating me," the Judge responded. "Having read the indictment I cannot think of a clearer case for trial. On what grounds are you challenging, Mr Swift?"

"I would refer the court to the Human Rights Act 1998, Article 6 (3) Unterpertinger v Austria," Swift responded.

"Indulge me," the Judge replied

"A ruling by the Convention in 1986 m'lord," Dominique interrupted. "It confirmed the right of a witness not to have to give evidence against a close family member. But I cannot see what relevance the ruling has to this case."

"I congratulate Ms Harcourt on her knowledge of the Human Rights legislation," Swift began

"No need, her father is an Appeal Judge in Strasbourg I believe. Is that not so Ms Harcourt?"

"It is, m'lud." and Dominique knew, behind her, Val Franks and Prosser were looking at each other in surprise.

"Then I am sure my esteemed prosecution counsel will know that the Unterpertinger ruling also confirmed that where a prosecution witness exercises their right not to testify against a family member, any written evidence they have provided is deemed inadmissible on the grounds that it cannot be challenged by cross-examination," Swift said

"Relevance, Mr. Swift?" the Judge asked

"The relevance, m'lud is that the prosecution case for a murder conviction relies entirely on the evidence of one witness and that witness is the son of the accused."

Swift smiled in the silence that filled the courtroom.

"Ms Harcourt? From your stupor it would seem the prosecution has no knowledge of this information."

"No, m'lud. Nor do I believe our witness is aware of it either. Has the Defence got supporting evidence for such an astonishing declaration?"

Swift waved a piece of paper towards the clerk who took it from him and gave it to the Judge.

"A birth certificate for one Robbie David Birch naming David Tyson, the defendant, as Father."

"Ms Harcourt?" the Judge enquired as he handed the certificate to the clerk to carry to Dominique. She read the document and seemed to see it with difficulty.

"Why has the Defence presented this evidence without previous disclosure?" she demanded helplessly.

Swift explained they were only able to verify the evidence themselves two days previously as the prosecution excluded the identity of their witness. The Judge suggested they had good reason.

Dominique recovered her faculties. "M'lud. It is my contention that Article 6 cannot apply here because the witness is not aware of his relationship to the accused and, as it now stands, he is under no stress by testifying against a father of whom he has no knowledge. The essence of the Unterpertinger case and Article 6  is to protect a witness from undue stress by having to testify against a close family member. Our witness is neither close to his father nor even knows who he is," she argued. "M'lud. the Defence is not obligated to hide the relationship now established between the prosecution witness and the accused, and if we were, surely it would breach my client's Human Rights," Swift countered.

"Ah, yes, the accursed Human Rights," the Judge smiled. "I have to concur with that argument, Ms Harcourt. I cannot agree your witness should not be informed of his relationship to the accused – and  I am sure, even if I could agree, that you are unable to guarantee the relationship would not be leaked at some stage, either before or during the trial and if it were during the trial it would do irreparable damage to your case and to the witness. Am I not right Mr. Swift?" Swift bowed his acquiescence. "I cannot ignore the implications of Article 6. I will have to allow the Defence submission. I presume, Ms Harcourt your case relies solely on your witness?" Dominique reluctantly agreed. "Then I am obliged to examine the witness and explain his rights according to the precedent Mr Swift has presented to the court. It might well be that the witness will not exercise his right not to give evidence. I'll see the witness in my chambers at three o'clock. Will you please arrange his attendance Detective Superintendent – and Superintendent, under no circumstances must the witness be told of this disclosure. If that happens I will declare no trial. Is that understood by everyone?" They all acknowledged and the Judge began to rise but Marcus Swift had not finished.

"M'lud," he said. "This news has been of equal shock to the defendant as it is likely to be to the prosecution witness. He has always maintained that he is the victim of an accident and it troubles him greatly to discover his own son was involved. He had no knowledge of having a son until a few days ago and he is appalled by the possibility of going to trial without ever speaking to the boy. He pleads for the opportunity to do so before the witness commits him to a charge of murder."

"M'lud, it is unthinkable that the witness should be subjected to such emotional blackmail," Dominique protested.

Judge Harris took some moments to consider their opinions. "I'll allow it. But under my supervision. Clerk, arrange for the accused to be brought to my chambers along with the witness but be sure to keep them away from each other. Three o'clock everyone."

DS Prosser left the courtroom quickly, without a word to Val Franks. She understood his feelings and knew he had made the right decision to find his way back to the Station by public transport rather than cover Dominique with his bile. Val Franks was less accusatory. "How could we have missed that?" she asked as they walked out together.

"It's my fault," Dominique confessed. "I didn't check his birth certificate. I should have done that to confirm his age. I relied on what was in the file."

"We knew his mother had the three children by different fathers – Social Services told us that much," Val admitted. "They knew the family, they knew who Tyson was – there's been enough publicity about the case. Why didn't they alert us? But, I suppose we should have realised then it was a possibility. After all, Robbie's mother told us she knew Tyson when they were kids."

They chose a café and nibbled their sandwiches mostly in

silence, each with their thoughts of the implications if Tyson escaped the judgement he deserved. Val Franks thought of what it might do to Mike Prosser but Dominique's thoughts were more practicable.

"If Tyson escapes, Robbie won't be safe," she said. "If there is no trial, Robbie could change his mind at any time and still give evidence against his father, even if he decides now that he won't. Tyson will know that."

Val Franks realised how right she was. "And we can't explain that to Robbie before he sees Tyson."

At three o'clock precisely, Robbie Birch, attended by an officer of the court, was seated in the chambers behind the courtroom when Judge Harris entered. He signalled for Robbie to sit as he began to rise and then he pulled another chair next to the boy's.

"May I call you Robbie?" he asked.

Robbie nodded, intimidated by what was happening to him and worried by the refusal of his escort to answer any of his questions on the way to court

"My name is Judge Harris and it is my job to assess whether the evidence you have given to the police is sufficient to send the accused to trial for murder. Do you understand, Robbie?" Robbie again nodded in answer. "Good. Do you know why you have been brought here?"

"No, sir. I asked why but no one would tell me."

"Good. Robbie, have you any idea who your father is?"

"He's dead."

"How do you know that?"

"He was killed in an accident when he was in the navy." He wondered why he was being asked about his Dad.

"Then we have a problem if that is what your mother told you. Is it possible she didn't tell you the truth?"

"Why? Why would she lie about it?"

"It's what single mothers sometimes do, I'm afraid. We

47

sometimes lie to our children to protect them."

The Judge watched Robbie struggling to comprehend this information. "In my job, I learn a great deal about human relationships which sometimes leave me quite shocked – rather as you seem to be now. It is then my job to seek out the truth as best I can. Robbie, three hours ago, the defence counsel for Mr Tyson brought evidence that Tyson is in fact your father."

Robbie's reaction was to leap out of the chair and for a moment look threatening so that the court officer stepped forward but the Judge put up his hand to assure him it was all right. Robbie eventually found his voice.

"No. That's not true. That can't be. My Dad's dead. That's crazy stuff wot you just told me."

"Sit down, Robbie. Please?" Robbie resumed his seat. "As incredible as it may seem, I'm afraid it is true. I have seen your birth certificate." Robbie buried his face in his hands as though to make the information go away.

"I understand this is very difficult for you, but I have to proceed in the case against your father and to do so I have to consider carefully certain facts of law. A man is accused of murder."

Robbie suddenly looked at the Judge defiantly.

"Yeah. That's right. He murdered my friend, Danny. I saw him," he almost yelled.

"Calm yourself, Robbie," the Judge told him. "I know that's true. I have read your statement. It is very clear and precise and would undoubtedly convince a jury to bring in a guilty verdict should the case go to trial. But you are the only witness. What you said must be the truth."

"It is true," Robbie told him. "Why would I lie?"

"Very well. Now I have to tell you of your legal rights given this new evidence that the accused is your father. Because he is your father, it is your right not to give evidence against him if that is what you choose."

Robbie looked at the Judge as though his words had suddenly taken all the anguish from his body.

"You mean, I won't have to go to court?"

"Not if you choose not to give evidence."

"Wot about my statement, wot I told the police?"

"I'm afraid your statement would not be allowed either if you could not be cross-examined during a trial."

"Then no one would be charged for Danny's murder?"

"Not for murder. It is very likely the prosecution would still bring a manslaughter charge against your father but there is nothing to support a murder charge except your evidence. You must think very carefully before you decide what you want to do."

"I dunno. I dunno," Robbie whined and looked distressed.

"Would you like to speak to your father?"

Panic showed on Robbie's face. "Wot? Now? Here?"

"Yes. He has asked if he can speak to you. But you must not talk about the case. You understand?"

Robbie nodded and the Judge gestured to the attendant who left the room. "I will remain here with you," the Judge assured Robbie.

"Wot can I say to 'im?"

"You don't have to say anything, if you don't want to."

The door was opened and Tyson was brought in handcuffed, with two prison officers escorting him. The Judge went behind his desk and gestured for the officers to put Tyson on the chair opposite to Robbie. Robbie's body swayed away as though trying to put more distance between them.Tyson grinned at him

"Allo Son. This is a turn up ain't it? Who would 'ave fought this could 'appen?" Robbie nodded without looking at the man's face. "Robbie ain't it? Yeah, I should 'ave known. Your mum's little bruvver was called Robbie.

Ee was killed by a motorbike when ee was a baby. Some maniac 'it his pram at a zebra crossin'."

Robbie showed some interest.

"You didn't know that did yer? Well, why should you. Your mum's good at not telling you fings. Me neiver."

"Wot d'you mean?" Robbie asked

"Well, you frinstance. She never told me abaght you."

"You mean, you didn't know about me. Not ever?"

"No, course I didn't. I only found out a coupla days ago."

"Yeah? Is that the truth?"

"Well, sort of. I knew she was pregnant but I give her some money and thought she'd taken care of it – you know? We was only kids, about your age. We didn't know nofing in them days. Not like now, every kid knows everyfing 'bout them fings. I fought she didn't want a baby at her age. When she told me I fought we'd agreed abaght it. I bung er some money an fought that settled it. I suppose she just wanted to keep the money an 'ave you too. But she never told me."

"You never knew about me?"

"No. Like I said. I fink it's great 'aving a son, we could 'ave 'ad a lot of fun togevver."

"Haven't you got any kids?"

"Yeah. Twin Girls."

"Where are they?"

"At 'ome in Kent. Got a nice pad over there, huge garden, tennis court an' a big swimming pool. Ere, Robbie, ave you ever bin to Spain?"

Robbie shook his head. "Went to the Isle Of Wight once, with the school," he said.

"You'd like Spain. I've got a great place over there. Ere, you could go there, ave a nice 'oliday, take your mum. My man, Jason would arrange it. It would do you good to get away from all this business. It was an accident Robbie."

"Do not talk about the case," Judge Harris interrupted.

"Sorry, Judge." Tyson apologised without taking his eyes off Robbie. "Funny you taking that car. I used to skin motors when I was your age. Like farver, like son, eh?" he laughed. "That's ow I got started as a mechanic. I was a bloody good one too, 'ad me own garage once."

"I think that's enough time for you to have introduced yourselves," the Judge decided. "Is there anything you want to say to your father, Robbie?"

Robbie looked at Tyson who smiled encouragingly, then Robbie looked down at the carpet and shook his head.

"Then you can take the prisoner away," the Judge told the officers who helped Tyson from the chair.

"Awright, Son?" Tyson asked. Robbie nodded. "It's bin great to see you, you're a good kid. Look after yerself."

Robbie watched as the officers took him away and he continued to stare at the door after it closed behind them.

"Robbie, we're going back into the courtroom where you will be asked whether or not you wish to proceed with your evidence in this case. Are you ready to do that?" Robbie nodded.

Mike Prosser had returned when Robbie and the Judge entered the courtroom and the clerk told everyone to rise. Robbie was told to enter the witness box.

"Robbie," the Judge said. "This is a court of law and anything you say here must be the truth. I am not going to put you under oath but I want you to think carefully before answering any questions, and you must only say what you truly believe. Do you understand?" Robbie mumbled his assent. "Good. First I will address the counsellors. I have spoken in private with the witness and advised him of his rights under Article 6 of the Convention On Human Rights together with the principles inherent in paragraph 3 (d) which allows family members to refuse to give evidence against another close member of the family. I have also allowed the accused an audience with the witness in my presence in order to acquaint themselves with each other but not to discuss in any way the case pertaining." He turned to Robbie. "Now, Robbie, I'm going to ask you a question and you must answer it. Robbie Birch, do you wish to give evidence in a court of law against the accused in that you saw him commit an act of murder? It is your right not to give such evidence if you do not wish to do so. What is your answer?"

Robbie looked across the room to where Prosser and Val Franks were sitting, then he looked back at the Judge, a pained expression on his face.

"No," he cried and put his hands over his face.

The word pierced the consciousness of all except Marcus Swift with varying degrees of pain but to everyone it had the finality of a fire-curtain descending in a theatre.

Marcus Swift attempted to increase the pain by asking the Judge to order the immediate release of his client as the prosecution now had no means with which to pursue the charge of murder. Judge Harris brushed his request aside, telling him it was not within his jurisdiction to do such a thing, adding, "It would seem there is still a strong case of manslaughter against your client which, I am sure, the prosecution will address."

Mike Prosser chose not to return to the police station after the hearing and Val Franks was relieved as she too could not face the reception they would get when breaking the news of their disaster. Giving Prosser a lift home, she argued a strong case for a manslaughter charge and forced a note of optimism into her voice but she soon abandoned her efforts at the continued silence from her boss and when he left her with no more than an almost inaudible

"Thanks" her depression increased.

The hearing had been on a Friday afternoon and over the weekend Valerie's anxiety was fed when her calls to both Prosser and to Dominique were unanswered. She knew she could not risk visiting the Detective Superintendent but she had no such doubts when she called at Dominique's Canary Wharf apartment. She rang the bell and waited some time until someone from the building emerged and informed her she had seen Dominique leave on Friday evening on her motorbike.

Val Franks had not realised how anxious she had been at her colleague's silence, until a rush of adrenalin ran through her when Mike Prosser walked into the squad room on the Monday morning. The Chief Superintendent, who had been on an inter-force seminar, was holding a post-mortem.

"Mike, so glad you're here," the senior officer said. Val Franks looked at her chief closely as he parked himself on a desk next to her and she could smell his stomach as he cleared his throat and attempted to sound normal in greeting the Chief Superintendent. The uniformed officer was a fast-track promotion, some ten years younger than Prosser, and had been swept in from another force when Prosser had been convicted of drink-driving. Taking the senior station officer from the uniformed branch was a way of mitigating Prosser's pain at his demotion but it had not been easy for the new chief facing the silent hostility of the tightly-knit CID squad. Surprisingly, Mike Prosser had shown no resentment towards him, accepting his punishment with almost masochistic enthusiasm.

"I was just expressing everyone's horror at the unexpected turn of events," the CS told him. "What we have to decide now is where we go from here. How do you see the situation, Mike?"

"As the cock-up it is," Prosser responded. "We've got bloody egg all over us. We knew Robbie's mother was just short of a whore and we knew she had a relationship with Tyson going back to their childhood. Social Services had her on their books for years and we were aware of her hostility to Robbie giving evidence. Why the hell didn't any of us, including Miss Hardcore, see the possibility of the connection between the two?" The sobriquet for Dominique bringing much laughter from everyone but Val Franks.

"Quite," the Chief Superintendent commented. "But, we have to decide what we should do now. Do we drop the charge of murder and go for manslaughter? After all, you may not know this, but another victim died in hospital over the weekend. That's four deaths other than young Murphy's. We know Tyson caused it but if we can't use Robbie Birch's evidence can we make a case that, by trying to apprehend Danny Murphy, Tyson caused him to fall into the traffic with the obvious consequences?"

Val Franks said she thought they needed a legal ruling about a manslaughter charge from the CPS.

"Not from Miss Hardcore," Prosser said. "I knew she wasn't up to the job as soon as I saw her. I should have dumped her then."

Val Franks choked back her anger. "That is not fair. She did everything she could – and you can't accuse her of not knowing the law. She was up to the mark with Marcus and argued the case well – especially what was suddenly thrown at her. It's not her fault she didn't know that Tyson was Robbie's father."

"She should have checked everything."

"And so should we," Val Franks almost shouted.

"All right. Calm down," the CS said. "We're all upset by what's happened. What we do now is what I want to know. Has anybody got any constructive suggestions?"

"We go for the manslaughter charge," someone answered. "That must be worth ten years."

There was a general murmur of agreement.

"A jury would convict on that," someone else added. "You've only got to look at Tyson and show them a picture of little Danny and they'd soon put two and two together."

"And there's the steel-toed shoes and Tyson's broken leg. It should be easy to convince a Jury that a confrontation between Tyson and Danny took place," Val Franks said. "Manslaughter should be easy to prove."

"Mike?" the CS asked. Prosser took a moment to answer and when he did his voice was quiet and threatening.

"Look at the evidence. In his statement, Tyson said he didn't know how he got his leg injury – he assumed he must have hit it on the barrier. Do you think Marcus Swift won't find a good reason as to how he got that injury?"

"Like what?" Val Franks asked

"Like falling out of the wrong side of a high Range Rover in a dazed state after an accident onto a steel crash barrier." Prosser looked from Val Franks to all the other faces as though challenging them to argue, no one did. "Without Robbie there's no one to dispute anything Swift will come up with. Our only chance is to persuade Robbie to change his mind before he goes home."

"It's too late for that, Mike," the CS told him. "Marcus Swift acted straight after the hearing on Friday and served a release order on Childrens Services."

"What I would like to know," a young female detective constable said before Prosser could respond. "Is how did Tyson get to know Robbie was his son?"

There was a general silence and it was obvious no one else had posed the question. A light came into Prosser's bloodshot eyes. "You're right, Bridget. You're damned right. Why didn't we ask that question? There's only one way he could have found out. There's only one person who knew who Robbie's father was"

"Robbie's mother," Val Franks said to general agreement.

"Why didn't I see that," Prosser scolded himself. "She was ready to do anything to stop Robbie testifying in court. She told Marcus Swift. That's why he acted for her to get Robbie released. She's done a deal with the devil. She thinks Robbie is safe. How stupid is that? As Miss Hardcore said, Robbie can change his mind and give evidence against his father anytime. Tyson knows that." He stood up. "I'm going to talk some sense into her."

"Mike. I can't let you do that. If you approach her she will throw a harassment charge at us."

"If we don't do anything Robbie will end up like his pal Danny. We may still be able to persuade her that giving evidence is the safest thing for Robbie." Prosser argued.

"I hope you're wrong about his safety but there's nothing we can do about it. It could even jeopardise furthering our case against Tyson and I doubt that you could persuade her to change her mind now. We have to pursue the manslaughter charge with what we've got. Val, can you liaise with Ms Harcourt?"

"I don't know where she is. The CPS told me this morning that she'd taken a few days off. I kept ringing her over the weekend but her phone was turned off."

"All right. Val, get back to the CPS and ask them to send someone else. I have no doubt that Marcus Swift will file a bail application. We'll need the CPS to fight that one."

As the meeting broke up  Prosser took Val Franks aside.

"Val, can you take me to the Birch's. I've got to speak to Robbie."

"No, Mike," Val answered. "You heard what the CS said.

You don't need any more trouble – nor do I."

Prosser felt the hostility on her face.

"Okay, I'm sorry for what I said about your friend. I'm still bloody angry about what happened."

"So are we all. You're not the only one to care, you know," she said and walked away, leaving him staring after her, another layer of anguish in his eyes.

# CHAPTER THREE

# A QUESTION OF JUSTICE

Val Franks went every morning to the sailing club hoping Dominique would suddenly appear, but Bob told her she had not been seen for several days. It was on the sixth morning, a rainy, misty, chilly morning, that Val was standing under an umbrella scouring the stretch of water from the road. Through the rain-mist she could see a single sculler, a black etched shape, riding the middle of the water, approaching from the far end of the half kilometre reach and she was surprised by the feeling of excitement and relief that went through her body. She ran back to her car but by the time she had parked and walked towards the pontoons, Dominique was stepping out of the skiff and Bob had come down to take it out of the water. When Dominique looked up and saw Val standing by the clubhouse, her arms folded, unsmiling, she walked slowly up to her, apprehension in her eyes. They regarded each other for a moment until the suggestion of a smile showed on Valerie's lips. Dominique put her soaked body against Val's raincoat. Val stood motionless and then unfolded her arms and hugged her back. After showering and changing, Dominique joined her in a nearby café.

"I went to see my tutor at Cambridge," Dominique explained. "I wanted to hide. It's the first time I've experienced failure."

"You didn't fail. You did what you could."

"I should have checked everything. That was my job."

"We all failed in that case. Who could have guessed that Tyson was Robbie's father. What are the chances of that happening?

"The possibility was there. I should have seen his birth certificate. I relied on what I was told. But I should have checked everything myself. It was a basic failure."

"Your being too hard on yourself. We all make mistakes. What did your tutor tell you?"

"She didn't. She just opened another bottle of wine."

"I could have done that for you."

Dominique looked at her friend and reached for her hand

"Valerie, I'm sorry. I'm so selfish. Of course you were suffering too – and Mike."

"He's one step away from meltdown."

"God! It was so selfish of me. I thought you wouldn't want to see me, but I should have been thinking how you and Mike would feel. I don't want to do Law any more."

"Now you're talking shit. Dominique, you're going to be a great advocate. You held your own against Marcus in that courtroom. You were terrific considering what was suddenly thrown at you, Nobody is blaming you – well, except Mike, but then he's blaming everybody. We need you. We can still get Tyson on the manslaughter charge. Go back to work and come back to us."

"What about Robbie?"

"He's gone home. Mike wanted to persuade his mother that he was still in danger but the Chief Super wouldn't let him. He said she could bring a harassment charge if we went near Robbie again."

"He's probably right. But I could try."

"She might listen to a woman. Give it a go, Dominique. If you succeed, even Mike will love you."


Dominique was grateful for the anonymity of her cycling leathers as she motored slowly through the estate looking for the Birch's house. Mrs Birch answered the door with six-year-old Caron peering cheekily around her mother's restraining body.

"Yes?" Mrs Birch asked aggressively.

Dominique introduced herself. Mrs Birch had difficulty in

associating a leather-clad female with a lawyer and waited for more information.

"I was wondering how Robbie was getting along?"

"Who wants to know?"

"I do – and so does DI Franks. She looked after Robbie when he was with us. We are all concerned about him."

"We've got a new car," young Caron interrupted and pointed to a bright blue Toyota. Dominique's brain quickly made connections.

"Don't interrupt," her mother told Caron

Dominique gave Caron her dazzling smile. "It's a lovely colour," she told her.

"Is that your motorbike. What sort is it?"

"A Ducati."

Caron looked disappointed. "Not a BMW?"

"Not a BMW."

"Does it go very fast?"

"Over one hundred and fifty. Do you like motorbikes?"

"Anything that goes fast," her mother said.

"Can I have a ride on it?" the girl asked. Her mother told her not to be silly and to be quiet.

"Sometime. I'll have to get a helmet to fit you, though," Dominique said. "What's your name?" Caron told her.

"That's a nice name. I'll tell you what I'll do, Caron. If your mother agrees I will come round with a child's helmet and give you a ride." Caron jumped around excitedly and even Mrs Birch had to smile.

"Robbie's, fine," she said as Dominique winked at her.

"The police don't think he is safe even though he has chosen not to give evidence against his father."

"They wouldn't. They just want to get Tyson any way they can. They don't care about Robbie."

"That really isn't true. Everyone is horrified at what Tyson did to Danny and those other innocent people.

They don't want him to do the same thing to Robbie."

"Tyson won't harm him."

"How can you be sure? Tyson knows Robbie can change his mind about giving evidence any time. I think we should explain that to Robbie. Can't I speak to him?"

"He's gone to Spain," Caron told her.

Dominique looked quickly at Mrs Birch.

"He needed to get away," she mumbled. "I thought a holiday would do him good."

"Tyson has a place in Spain hasn't he?" Dominique asked. "Surely he hasn't..." she didn't have to finish the sentence; Mrs Birch's discomfort gave her the answer.

"Do you still have a relationship with Tyson?"

"A relationship. Are you serious? Tyson got me pregnant when I was fifteen. My father disowned me and threw me out of the house. I went round to see Tyson and his father called me a little tart and threatened to kill me if I went near his son again. If it hadn't been for my Nan I would have been on the streets. When Tyson got flash with his cars and clubs and I was pregnant again and desperate because Caron's father had done a runner, I went round to see him. I had no money, nowhere to live. I thought he could get me somewhere in one of his properties. He wouldn't even see me. One of his bouncers pushed me into the street. Do you think I would have a relationship with someone like that?"

"Then, I don't understand, Mrs Birch."

"Course you don't. You've never had to struggle everyday of your life to stay alive have you? to keep going because you've been lumbered with three kids an' no fathers."

Dominique looked at Caron and saw the concern in her face. She looked coldly at Mrs Birch.

"I haven't. But how will keeping Tyson out of jail help?"

"I got him to admit in court he's Robbie's father didn't I?

Now I can bleed the bastard for sixteen years maintenance. That's just a down payment." She pointed towards the Toyota. "Now Robbie can get anything we want from him."

"Not if he's dead?"

"That's not going to happen. Tyson likes the idea of having a son. You're right, Robbie has gone to Spain to Tyson's place an' me an' the kids might go there too when they've finished school. Now Robbie's safe and doesn't have to hide like he was a criminal any more."

"I hope you're right," Dominique said. "I really hope so."

There are probably more people in Britain who have never flown than have. There are probably more people who have never been abroad than have. There are probably more people who have never been to the seaside than have. Robbie Birch qualified for all of those statistics except the last – and his school trip to the Isle Of Wight almost didn't count as, by the time they got there after a ferry breakdown, they had to return and the trip was only memorable by how many kids were sick either on the ferry or on the long coach ride home. Now suddenly, Robbie's deficits were rectified in the space of three hours. He had been amazed by Heathrow Airport, the sight of the great machines landing and taking-off and taxiing and the thousands of people and the shops with their expensive goods ripe for nicking. He had started off being amazed by Jason's Mercedes, the tan-leather seats and thick carpeting and the surge from the six cylinders as it accelerated into the fast lane of the M4, and when they were airborne he was amazed by the carpet of soft clouds they seemed to skim over until they suddenly disappeared and there was sparkling water and tiny dots that moved upon it. Then land and the Pyrenees, so clear and breathtaking with snow peaks and vultures circling at great heights although Robbie had no idea what they were. Then the bays and beaches of the Costa Brava and soon they were landing at Malaga with a surge of power that brought a huge smile to the boy's face.

His escort, Jason was not child-orientated. In fact, if Robbie had been so inclined, he might have thought Jason had emerged from the womb as he was. But his inability or disinclination to talk suited Robbie as it did nothing to interrupt the visual and emotional feast he was digesting. Somewhere in the turmoil of his mind there were many questions he wanted to ask but images of Danny, his laughter, his cockiness, his unpredictable ways, kept flashing into his head threatening to spoil so many pleasures and he was reluctant to return to reality. "Later, Danny" he told himself.

The villa was in the hills above Marbella. They motored up the winding country road past other houses, softly pink in the evening light, their heavily tiled roofs blood-red amongst green blankets of foliage, with palms and tall pines rising above them like markers of a recent past. Behind high gates Dobermans and Rottweilers protested their presence and Robbie thought he was in a movie – the kidnapped son of Michael Caine; half-expecting to be dragged from the car and handed-over to Gene Hackman who would cut-off his finger with a smile, telling him it wouldn't hurt.

But when the car pulled onto a winding drive and stopped beside a porticoed entrance to a single-storied building, they were met only by an old man called Jesus. If Robbie had seen the name written without hearing the Spanish pronunciation, he might well have believed he had arrived in heaven when they entered the building into a marbled hall. Before him was a long room, walled by full-length glass with a terrace beyond with urns laden with bougainvillea and jasmine and beyond the terrace more terraces, a swimming pool and gardens and beyond the gardens a panorama stretching to the sea where a great ball of sun seemed to be turning it into a stew of glistening colours. It was not a single storied building, it descended in terraces from the road and housed eight bedrooms and a cottage in the grounds and if Robbie was able to get the sun's view of it he might have likened it to half of a wedding-cake. Robbie walked to the windows and stared beyond them as though mesmerised by the retiring sun. The old man cackled behind him and said something in Spanish to which Jason responded and made the man cackle even more.

Robbie turned and looked at them. "Is my dad rich?"

Jesus cackled louder and Jason managed a smile.

"You could say that," he answered. "Come on, I'll show you where you sleep."

He led the way to a lower floor and opened a door into a bedroom. Robbie stared at the bed which would have filled the living-room of their maisonette in South London. He went into the ensuite bathroom and stared at the corner bath sunk into the marbled floor, at the basin and the shower and the toilet and the heavy, traditional Spanish rugs, at the many bottles and jars and the towels heavier than any coat he'd worn. Jesus had entered the bedroom with Robbie's bag and started to take his spare trousers, shorts, two shirts and three T-shirts from it to hang in the walk-in cupboards but Robbie quickly stopped him, unconsciously embarrassed at the contents. Jason stood near the doorway. "This awright then?" he asked. Robbie could only nod, he wasn't certain he still had a voice. "Right then. 'ave a wash an we'll see you up top for some supper," Jason told him and disappeared with the cackling Jesus. Robbie closed the door behind them and then ran at the bed, soaring onto it like a swallow and yelling into the goose-down duvet.

Supper was English sausages, chips and beans cooked by Jesus' wife, Maria, who spoke some English and fussed around Robbie like a childless woman. After the meal Jason watched Robbie touring the gardens.

"It's amazing," was Robbie's verdict when he returned. "An' the pools amazing. Can I 'ave a swim tomorrow?"

"Course you can. That's what it's there for."

"Great. I love swimming. Do you use it?"

Jason pulled a face "Naw. Don't like water much."

"Can't you swim?" Robbie guessed instinctively.

"Course I can," Jason answered defensively but Robbie wisely decided not to persist with his advantage.

That night, with the air-conditioning switched on, Robbie slept better than he had ever done in his life. When he wakened the next morning and jumped out of bed, he rushed to the window to reassure himself the previous evening had not been a dream. He saw everything was still there, dazzlingly brighter in the strong sunlight, and he could now make out the boats in the marina which seemed to ride taller than the buildings around it. The sea was an aquamarine ribbon then the blue of the sky with only a darker line marking their separation. He saw Jason sitting at a table on the terrace reading a paperback and sipping from a cup and he could see a basket of fruit and pastries next to him and he suddenly felt hungry.

He showered longer than he meant to as it took him some painful experiment to find how to adjust the many taps. He put on shorts and a T-shirt and joined Jason on the terrace. Maria fussed about him again and made him some tea as he tucked into the pastries. As he ate and drank, the questions began to flow; how long ave you known Dad? D'you know his other family? What are they like? Wot does ee do for a living? Is ee married? Ow many cars 'as ee got? Jason answered patiently – considering someone in the paper-back was about to have her vagina filled with hot tar – but not always truthfully.

Robbie eventually ran out of questions and there was a period of silence until his impatience got the better of him. "Wot we doin today, Jase?" he asked. Jason sighed and closed the book. He told Robbie Jesus was taking his wife to town to buy fresh fish and he was probably taking one of the cars into the garage to have the brakes repaired. "But you can stay here and do some swimmin'."

"Great," Robbie enthused. "Can I ring my mum later? She doesn't get up till about ten cos she works at night.?"

"Course you can. Oo takes your bruvver an' sister to school then?"

"I do. But they're okay goin' alone, the school's near an' they don't 'ave to go through the estate."

After breakfast Robbie could wait no longer to get into the crescent-shaped pool. He was a decent swimmer because the school had used a local baths for years until the council finally closed it because they didn't have the money to refurbish it. Jason watched from a distance as Robbie swam up and down and across, did somersaults in the water and jumped and dived in various ways and somewhere deep inside his brain, the few good moments of Jason's childhood flashed into his consciousness. Later, Robbie called his mother and breathlessly told her what an amazing place it was and how amazing the flight had been and described his bed and the bathroom and the flowers and the sunset and the toothless Jesus and how he was going to spend hours in the pool. "It's amazing," he concluded before remembering to ask how Caron was.

"She misses you," his mum told him. "So do I. But you

enjoy yourself Robbie and don't get into any trouble."

Robbie laughed. "There's no trouble here, Mum."

He was still in the swimming pool more than an hour later when Jason took a call on his mobile from Marcus Swift.

"Hello dear boy," Marcus began. "I spoke to Dave last night. We've got a bail hearing scheduled for Thursday. No, there shouldn't be a problem. Yes, they are pursuing a manslaughter charge but I think we can deal with that. How is the boy getting along?" Jason told him he seemed to be enjoying himself. "But I don't know 'ow long I can nursemaid 'im wivout doin' me 'ead in." Marcus made several constructive suggestions to amuse Robbie, knowing what Jason was like when his head was done in. "Dave gave me a message for you. He told me to tell you the weather was going to change and it's going to rain. Have you any idea why he is suddenly a weather forecaster?" Jason only said, "I'll prepare for it."

After the call Jason watched Robbie for a few minutes and then descended to the swimming pool. Robbie saw him standing on the side wearing shorts and flip-flops.

"Come on Jase. Let's see you do a few lengths then."

Jason stepped into the pool and waded towards him.

"You're supposed to swim not walk," Robbie laughed.

Jason reached him and suddenly shot out an arm and grabbed Robbie's hair, then his other hand was equally fast in taking Robbie's wrist and bending it behind his back. He pushed him under water and held him there despite his kicking feet until he struggled no more. He then let him go and watched as Robbie floated face-down before giving him a push so that the body gently bobbed to the deep end. Jason got out of the pool and walked through the house and climbed into the Ferrari. Robbie's moment of heaven had gone.

When the news of Robbie's death reached the CID room in South East London a heavy silence descended and seemed to stupefy everyone's brain for the rest of the day. Phones were answered, questions were asked, files were exchanged, notes were taken with the minimum of action, comment or conversation. People went about like automatons. There was no chat, no laughter no emotion.

The news had been relayed to them by a Captain Hernandes who had liaised with Mike Prosser on several occasions, sharing information about the many East London criminals who had fled to his parish. Dave Tyson had long been flagged-up to him by Prosser and others but he had been unable to uncover any criminal activity by him during his regular trips to Spain. But now that a dead boy had been found in his swimming pool Fernandes wanted to hear more about his visit than what Jason had told him. The first question he had posed was why Tyson was not at the villa and when he was told Tyson was in prison his nose twitched enough for him to call Prosser directly. Mike Prosser had not been there to receive the call but one of his officers supplied much of the information  he required.

"On the face of it, it was an accident," Hernandes had reported. "The boy drowned. There were no marks on him to suggest he fell into the water. The housekeeper and her husband were not there and Jason had taken a car into a garage to have the brakes checked. The garage confirmed that and the time. It was the housekeeper and her husband who found the boy."

When Prosser was told, he phoned Hernandes. He told the Spanish officer about the Tyson case.

"So it is good for Tyson that the boy was drowned?" was Hernandes' conclusion. "Okay, I will dig a little deeper."

"Confiscate Jason's mobile," Prosser suggested. "Tyson is still in gaol and would only be allowed a local call. I would like to know if Jason talked to anyone here after arriving in Spain."

It was late afternoon when Hernandes got back to him and told Prosser they had checked Jason's phone but he had only received one call. "He said it was from Tyson's solicitor asking how the boy was getting on. But here is something interesting, Mike," he went on. "The garage said there was nothing wrong with the brakes except the brake-fluid reservoir was almost empty – but they didn't find a leak anywhere. They also said the driving seat and the carpet was wet."

"Like someone had driven it after getting out of a swimming pool," Prosser said.

"Exactly. Do you want us to hold Jason here? I don't think we have enough evidence to charge him."

Prosser agreed there was no point in holding Jason in Spain. After he put down the phone he immediately made a call to the Governor of Tyson's prison and told him they would be very interested to know if Tyson had called Marcus Swift and if so what was said. The next day the Governor called him back to say Tyson had made a local call but there was nothing unusual in the conversation except, he quoted, 'Tell Jason the weather is going to change and it's going to rain.' Prosser thanked him. He stood up and kicked the waste-paper bin across the office and yelled through closed teeth enough for everyone to stare at the glass partition separating them from his office. Val Franks knocked and walked in, half-expecting to be told to fuck off. Prosser sat at his desk and put his head in his hands. "The weather's going to change. It's going to rain. Is that a normal comment to someone in Spain?" he asked his CI.

69

"Sounds like a code."

"Of course it's a   code. 'Kill the boy' that's what it meant."

He told her of Hernandes' call. She could think of nothing to say.   Hernandes' information had added nothing to what they all knew to be true; Robbie had been murdered.


Mike Prosser stood on the other side of the road, staring at the 1930's double-fronted semi-detached house. A new wall had been built in the front and the old bushes removed and replaced with a raised, planted border. The drive had been paved with multi-coloured stones right down to the garage and the house had been painted and the old windows replaced with double-glazing. It was still early and no one was yet departing for work. He stood holding a bouquet of flowers from a hand that hung downwards from his sagging shoulders. The front-door of the house opened and a man stood there, wearing a red tie with his smart white shirt and blinking behind glasses at Prosser on the other side of the street. The man walked to the gate and called softly so as not to disturb the neighbours.

"Can I help you?" he enquired. Prosser crossed the street.

"We used to live here," he said in way of explanation.

"Ah!" the man exclaimed. Prosser stared  past him into the hallway beyond the now open front-door.

"We've done quite a lot to it since we moved in," the man said, to alleviate the embarrassment he was feeling.

"I can see," Prosser responded, still staring rudely past the man. "Is the back lawn still there?"

"Well, not exactly. My wife's a keen gardener. We've changed it somewhat. Would you like to see?" he asked with sudden enthusiasm.

"Yes. Thank you," Prosser answered

The man led the way down the path and through a side door next to the recessed garage. Prosser followed him through the door and stood next to the man who was now beaming expectantly. The garden had been landscaped professionally with raised planting areas snaking sinuously between paved walks and a patio. At the end of the long, narrow garden, an old hedge separated a small area now used for composting. A swing hung from a large Sycamore tree.

"I see you kept the swing at least."

"Yes, we've just got our first grandchild. We thought she will enjoy it. Did you have it put there?"

"No, I put it there myself." Prosser turned and quickly walked out of the garden back to the driveway. "Thank you," he said "Give these to your wife. Enjoy the house. We did." He thrust the flowers into the man's hand and walked quickly away. The man stared after him with a worried look on his face.


        Val Franks arrived at the police station and was called aside by the desk-sergeant. "DS Prosser signed a car out of the pool half an hour ago." he told her. "The gateman said he was driving it himself."

The implications of the news were obvious to both of them and her reaction justified the sergeant's trust. "Did he say where he was going?" she asked with some urgency. The sergeant said not. "But isn't Tyson being released on bail today?" he asked.

"Oh, Christ!" she exclaimed and started to make her way back towards the garage calling her thanks as she ran.

The prison was set well back from the road with a wide area of grass bordering its length and an approach road leading through it to the great oak doors set in the castle-like wall. Mike Prosser sat in a car parked on the far side of the main road that ran past the gaol. There were several cars between him and where the drive up to the prison entrance joined the road and the car opposite the entrance he had recognised as Dave Tyson's Range Rover. He had a good view of the entrance and had already recognised Marcus Swift and Jason standing outside. Eventually a door in the great gates opened and Tyson stepped out. He spread his arms and walked towards them and hugged them in turn then the three men began to walk towards the road, laughing and jostling each other. Prosser started the engine of the car and as the three men reached the main road and started across it towards the Range Rover, Prosser hit the accelerator and the car leapt forward with a scream of tyres. The noise made the men turn and they froze in the middle of the road, staring like rabbits, unable to move, but it was not Prosser's car that mesmerized them, it was another car that overtook it on the kerb on the wrong side of the road before it swung in front of Prosser's car forcing him to make an emergency stop.

The men stared as Val Franks got out of her car and walked back to where Prosser was squeezed breathlessly against the front-impact bag. She opened the door and looked at his staring eyes and wondered if he was going to have a heart attack. Tyson wanted to know what the fuck that was all about, but only Marcus Swift had recognised Val Franks.

"I think the Met might have a new agenda," he said.

"Let's get the fuck out of here," Tyson commented and led the way to the Range Rover.

When Val Franks thought Prosser was all right, she parked her car and walked back to him. "Get over," she ordered. Prosser limply obeyed, climbing across to the passenger seat.

She drove in silence, controlling her temper until she felt

calmer. "You've really fucked yourself now," she said eventually. Prosser made no reply. At the entrance to the garage, she spoke to the gateman. "You saw me take this car out earlier, right?" The gateman looked perplexed. "You did, didn't you?" she persisted.

"Oh, right. Yes ma'am. I remember now."

"Good." She drove into the garage. She looked at her boss who was slumped into the seat looking as though he was asleep. "For God's sake, Mike, take a holiday. Go to Australia  and visit James."

"Don't tell me what to do," Prosser responded but showed no physical intent to match his voice.

"Someone needs to," Val responded. "Look, I know what day it is, I know how you're hurting but that's no excuse to lose it like that. You're no better than Tyson."

Prosser turned on her. "Watch it, Val. I'm still your DS."

"Yes. Dip Stick," she responded. She got out of the car and slammed the  door  before walking away.


Dominique watched from the wall as Val Franks sculled alone, energetically moving the boat in a series of forward jerks. She applauded as her friend stroked into the pontoon "Bravissimo!" she cried and ran down to hold the boat as Valerie scrambled onto the pontoon.

"You did it. You went out there alone." She gave the policewoman a hug and kissed her on both cheeks.

"You were on fire. But you had too much energy for the boat. You have to control it. It's all about rhythm. You have to  feel  it through your bum, stroke it forward like riding a horse."

"I've never ridden a horse."

" like making slow love then."

"That neither."

"Oh, Cherie. You have led such a useless life," the

Frenchwoman said, pinching Val's cheek. She smiled but Dominique could see it was an effort.

"I think you have had a bad day. N'est pas?"

"You could say that." Val Franks answered.

"Then don't bother changing. You'll come back to my apartment, have several glasses of wine and something to eat and then you can tell me all about it If you want to."

Although the two women had become friends they had socialised only in bars or cafés and at work and as they entered Dominique's penthouse studio apartment they each sub-consciously acknowledged their relationship was about to change. For Dominique it was the risk of exposure, she lived alone and everything in the apartment and how it was used was an expression of who she was. For Val Franks it was the responsibility the invitation placed on her. Did she want to be closer to Dominique. Did she want to know how she lived, to see her bathroom, what she ate, what she read, whether she was tidy or a slut? Did she want to discover something about her friend she might not like?

Dominique was typically practical. "There's the bathroom," she said, not giving Val a chance to do any more than glance around the room. "Have a shower and by the time you're finished I will have something for us to eat. Do you want to take some wine in with you?"

"No thanks," Val laughed. "I don't like it watered."

When she emerged, her hair loose and shining damp, Dominique had set a lasagne and a bowl of salad on the table and was pouring a light Pinot into large goblets.

"There you are," she smiled. "You look like Alice in Wonderland like that. I hope you like lasagne."

"I love Lasagne, and I'm suddenly very hungry."

"I'm not surprised. You were rowing like a gladiator out there. Who upset you?"

Gradually, Val told her about Robbie's death and Mike Prosser's attempt to kill Tyson. When she'd finished, her friend was fascinated, horrified and then demoralised. They took the second bottle of wine and sat together on the large settee that faced the full-length window with it's view of the river and South London and the distant hills. Robbie's death had physically upset Dominique.

"I warned his mother," she said. "That poor woman."

"It was her fault," Val replied

"She was only trying to protect him; it's what any mother would do, isn't it?"

"And making Tyson pay," Val reminded her.

"Yes. But can we blame her? We have no idea what we would do in the same situation. Oh, that evil man. All those people dead, all that suffering in so many homes because of him. And Mike, being driven to such madness. I feel like killing Tyson myself."

"That's how Mike feels. It's two years to the day that his daughter was killed."

"Burned alive." Tears suddenly filled Dominique's eyes.

"Hey," Val said. She put her arms around Dominique who stuck her face into her shoulder. Val held her in a way she had not held anyone since her mother had had a stroke and died in her arms three years earlier.

"We have to get him," Dominique said strongly, untangling her face from Valerie's shoulder. "I think he could escape the manslaughter charge. We have to find another way."

"That's what Mike thought," Val reminded her.

"No. That was crazy. We have to be more subtle than that. There has to be another way."

Val still had her arms around the Frenchwoman, their faces were inches apart and Dominique's eyes, still moist, were as pleading and as innocent as a child's.

"Would you like to sleep with me?" she asked.

Val Franks looked into the green eyes, so near to her own and almost felt the Chanel in her nostrils. "Flesh on flesh," she said. "I've almost forgotten what that feels like."

"Like this," Dominique said and pressed her lips gently onto Val's as her hand slipped under the policewoman's shirt.

Mike Prosser was into work early. "Bridget," he said to a WPC. "Can you get me the Constable File?"

"The Harwich case? That was handled by Poplar."

"Yes, I know that. But the file was copied to us."

"That was only the report, sir," the girl corrected him.

"Yes. Will you get that for me please."

When he had it on his desk, "Operation Constable" was a one hundred and fifty page report compiled from the Essex Police, the Border Agency and Poplar CID. Prosser had read it several times before and he knew every detail of it. It was Janet's own idea to climb in with the females and keep her mobile phone open. The Essex police force had then set up a tracking operation and had followed the truck at a safe distance as far as Leyton when they handed over to the Met. The truck's destination was known to be a food outlet called Quiros in Billingsgate fish market. After Janet had been put into the truck it had stopped only the one time on the M11. Janet's partner, WPC Carol Gibbs, had followed it at a safe distance. She had not pulled into the rest-stop because she was not in an unmarked vehicle and had waited for the truck to resume it's journey after a fifteen minute break. The Essex force had called off their surveillance when the truck was signalling it had entered the metropolitan area and was on course to Billingsgate. The Met had called in extra police

76

during the night, including two from Prosser's station, and had their officers located around Billingsgate Market. The truck had been located by irate drivers honking for it to move forward. It had no driver and no one else was in it. Janet's mobile phone was found on the driver's seat.

A search was immediately begun to find the driver and it was as the police units were searching for him that the explosion occurred in near-by Stepney and all available units were ordered to attend the fire. Old man Quiros, the fishmonger, was yelling to be allowed to unload the truck before the fish went off and the officer in charge eventually gave permission and the truck was then taken away for forensic examination.

There had been no reason to connect the explosion to Operation Constable until the bodies of the two women were found and DNA evidence confirmed one was of Slavic antecedence, possibly Russian, and the other was Prosser's daughter. Further enquiries discovered the house was owned by Dave Tyson but rented to a third party whose name was inevitably found to be false and the renter untraceable. Evidence from the neighbours confirmed that women came and went to and from the house and some of the neighbours thought they had heard a vehicle in the street but only one person had seen it.

Prosser was reading the report when Val Franks knocked and entered his office. He kept his eyes down.

"Are you all right?" she asked in an unsympathetic voice. Prosser nodded, leaving the tension between them. She had reached the door, "Val. Thanks," he said but didn't look up from his desk.

She turned back to him. The Operation Constable Report was familiar to her as it was to all the CID officers.

"You're still not letting go," she said. "What else is there to find? We've been over it so many times. It's driving you crazy, Mike. Please, give it up."

"I can't let go until I know what happened," he said

"You know what happened. We all know what happened."

"Do we? Do we know how they knew the truck was under surveillance? How did they know Jan was in it?"

"They found out at the rest-stop, I know what you think; you want to think there was an informer, but even if you're right how are we going to prove it?

"Have you ever asked yourself why they blew-up that house to kill the girls? And why only Jan and one other?"

"The other girl wouldn't play ball. She spoke English and Jan warned her what was going to happen to them."

"Why do it by causing a gas explosion. Jason's handy with a knife, why not do it that way? "

"I don't know Mike. We'll probably never know. Not unless we can get Tyson or Jason on a murder charge and they want to plea-bargain. Why do you think they blew up the house?"

"I don't know. But I know there's a reason and I'll find it."


Mike Prosser walked out of Poplar tube-station and crossed the dock road into Billingsgate fish market. He had been there once before, he had visited all the sites connected to the case, mostly in a daze of unexplained curiosity, perhaps hoping for some explanation of his daughter's death to come leaping into his mind and fill the ever present void that separated them. The market stalls were closed but the Quiros' shop was still open.

A young woman in a white hat and apron was taking the few pieces of fish that had not been sold from the slabs and packing them into the freezer room behind the counter. She smiled at him, showing lovely white teeth behind her lipsticked mouth and somewhere in his body something murmured like an old memory.

"What can I do for you Luv?" she enquired.

"What's in these pots?" he asked pointing to small plastic tubs on top of the counter thinking they might be the cheapest thing to buy.

"That's smoked Baltic Perch roe. Lovely on toast with a drop of horseradish. How many would you like?"

"Only one," he smiled

"Live alone do you?" she asked teasingly. The banter continued as Prosser took out his wallet to pay. The girl noticed his Warrant Card in the other half of the wallet

"You a policeman. Know Barry Jarvis do you?"

He knew Detective Inspector Jarvis very well and was not surprised that this pretty girl knew him too.

"Does he come in here?"

"He's a regular. He loves our smoked Vendace"

"Never heard of that," Prosser said. The girl explained it was a fresh-water fish but the sea variety was found only in Estonia. Prosser noted the place-name. "Perhaps I should try some," he said.

"Sorry luv. We won't have any more in until our next delivery – and we keep it for special customers."

"Like Barry Jarvis. Is he special?" Prosser smiled.

"You're a bit naughty, you are," the girl replied

"Does all your fish come from Estonia?"

"That's our main supplier."

"How often do you have deliveries from there?" he asked innocently. "I'd like to try some of that Vendace."

"Every four weeks. We'll have one next Friday – but you'll be lucky to get any vendace."

"I know. I'm not special."

When Prosser got back to his office he phoned Paul Richmond, a Drug Squad officer based at Harwich. Richmond had worked with his daughter and they had met socially when Richmond had come to London. He

79

was aware of the date. "I sent Edna a card," he said.

"That was nice of you," Prosser told him. "Paul. Have you ever got a handle of any sort on Tyson's trafficking?"

The drugs officer said they hadn't and went through the various efforts they had made to do so. Prosser told him about the latest incidents involving Tyson.

"He's a target for us too, Mike," Paul answered. "He can only make his sort of money from being a major supplier, but we haven't found his source yet."

"Can your dogs sniff-out drugs packed in ice?"

"Depends. It's more difficult and if there are other strong scents they might miss them. Why are you asking?"

"Did you do a search on the Estonian trucks?"

"I thought they were all about people-trafficking. But, yes, we did a physical that night with Jan. We took out a few crates and nearly got frost-bite, but we found nothing. Why are you still interested in the Estonian trucks? It's unlikely they would risk using them again for trafficking. I thought that avenue had closed."

"There are still unanswered questions about that night." Paul, like Val Franks, knew Prosser would never accept that those questions could not be answered.

It had been a corner house of a typical three-storied Victorian terrace that had survived the blitzing of East London and the development frenzy of the sixties and eighties. The area had been left to the floods of West Indian and then Bangladeshi immigrants, too far out of the City to be financially viable and too deeply enmeshed with rental restrictions to be improved. There was a parade of grubby shops further along the terrace and a pub on the other corner. Mike Prosser looked at the roofless, floorless façade of the stricken house. What remained of the walls were boarded on the ground floor and the upper windows were vacant, showing the night sky through them to the other side of the house. He had been there several times before, leaning his head against the boards that protected the crumbling brickwork, forcing his senses to make the connection that he so needed but which never came.

"Terrible fing it was," a voice said beside him.

Prosser turned and looked at an old lady leaning on a shopping trolley and he vaguely wondered why she had a shopping trolley at that time of night with only a corner shop nearby. She nodded to the stricken building

"Went up like a doodle-bug. I was just about to go to bed when it 'appened. All me winders came in. There was glass all over the floor an' on me bed."

"Do you live here?" Prosser asked

"Just there across the road, above that shop," she said and pointed to the opposite pavement directly behind them.

"It's not a very wide street. I'm not surprised the explosion broke your windows. Did you see the truck that was here before the explosion by any chance?"

"It weren't no truck, it was a van and a car." she said.

Prosser's antennae quivered. "Are you sure?"

"Course I am. I saw them."

"What did you see? It must have been a bit frightening?"

"I was just goin up to bed and looked out of the winder when I 'eard a motor. There was a van with its back doors open. I saw a lot of women's feet under the doors, the van was blockin the door of the 'ouse, see. They were getting into the van. Then this big car arrived and someone got out and sort of dragged a woman out an' I fink they took 'er into the 'ouse. Then the van an' the car drove off. I 'ad just got me frock off and been to the lav and was putting on me nightie when, bang! I was thrown on the bed an' the winder glass came all over me an' the cat jumped right on top of the wardrobe."

"Did you tell the police all this at the time?"

"Course I did. Are you a copper?"

Prosser ignored the question. The woman looked at him slyly. "Knew one of the women did you?" she asked.

"Yes, my daughter."

"I fought they was all foreign women over there. Well, they was all someone's little girls, poor lambs. We knew wot was goin' on there. The girls used to be picked up every night an' brought back in the mornin'. Taken up West I dare say. "

"In a van. Was it the same as the one you saw?"

"It looked the same. But wot do I know?"

"I don't suppose you ever saw the registration?"

"Why would I? I 'ad no reason to."

"Do you remember anything about the car?" "I couldn't see much of it 'cos it was further along from the van, but it looked big an' posh."

"Had you seen it around here before?" he asked.

"Naw. It wasn't the sort of motor you see round 'ere."

What time did all this happen?"

"Bout one o'clock."

That's late. Do you always go to bed so late?"

"Always 'ave. Used to work nights at the Q an me body's never got used to not going there."

"The Q?" Prosser queried.

"The pie-factory. You know, '*Q pies are worth queuing for*' she mimicked musically. "You must ave 'eard of em. They supply all the local football grounds."

"What about the men. Did you see them?"

"Not really, they 'ad the van doors open in front of the 'ouse like I said and that 'id 'em. But the one oo came from the car wiv the woman was tall an' the one oo closed the doors of the van when it left was sort of short

82

'an fat – but I only saw 'im for a moment."

Prosser thanked the woman and made his way home. So it wasn't the truck that dropped them off - and why wasn't that in the Report? The next morning he made a call to a detective sergeant who used to work for him but was transferred to the Poplar station. He asked the man about the officers on duty on the night of the explosion.

"Who was in charge on the ground?"

"DS Jarvis," the man replied.

"Can you check something for me Colin? Do it quietly. Can you see if there was anything about an interview with a woman living opposite the explosion?"

Colin remembered. "Yes. I interviewed her."

"Did she say anything about seeing a van and also a car?"

"Yes. She said she saw a van and a car."

"It only says a vehicle in the Operation Constable Report. We all assumed it was the truck."

"I filed the interview with her. The guvnor didn't think she was reliable. I thought she was a bit pissed when I talked to her. She rambled on a bit. It was only when we spoke to her again that she mentioned the car."

Prosser remembered the chinking of bottles in the woman's shopping trolley "And her description of two of the men?" he asked

"It wasn't much of a description. From her flat I don't think she could see as much as she said. There's only one street light and that's at the end of the street and her place is in the middle. I went back there at night to interview her in the flat and check it out. If the van was outside the house she couldn't have seen much beyond it and if she saw anyone it could only have been a silhouette. I did report everything."

Prosser thanked him and told him to keep the conversation to himself. He rechecked the report after speaking to Colin and confirmed there had been no detailed description of the vehicle seen at the house, only that a witness had seen one but was unable to identify it. There was also no mention of a car. Prosser knew very well how unreliable witnesses are, frequently changing their descriptions when reinterviewed. But the evidence that the girls had been put into another vehicle meant they knew about Janet's infiltration before the truck reached London. He had asked himself many questions about Operation Constable but it was only now, two years almost to the day, that his brain was beginning to ask the questions that he had been incapable of seeing before, questions that other people should have asked.

It is said it takes at least two years for the body to adjust from a deep trauma, perhaps his was making that adjustment – although his attempt to settle the Tyson problem two days before had hardly been demonstrative of any such adjustment in his emotional state. He felt no better about Janet's death than he had when it happened, less numb perhaps but no less vengeful, and he was now more convinced than he had ever been that there had been an informer somewhere along the route.

Robbie Birch's funeral service was held in the local crematorium and as DS Prosser stood beside Val Franks, Dominique Harcourt, a uniformed officer and the Childrens Services Officer who had handled Robbie's case, he thought of the irony that such a beautiful, tranquil area had been created for the dead in the midst of the depressing housing that was designed for the living. It was a sparkling day, as fine a morning as had been Robbie's last experience of his brief life, and the funeral was well attended with Robbie's school friends making the majority of mourners. Their young bodies and lively movement made Prosser smile as he remembered such a day when James and Janet were chasing each other amidst the saplings in Sundridge Park and a grass snake had sent them screaming to their mother.

He had steeled himself to come, it was in such a place that Janet's short life had been finally remembered by her many friends and colleagues. He knew she would have been scathing if anyone had suggested she should have been buried, but now, especially now, having a piece of ground over which to talk to her and to touch would be a bridge across the void of silence that distanced her presence increasingly as in a rear-view mirror.

The mourners were still filing out of the service, mingling together, silently pleased that it was over. Mrs Birch, with Caron and her brother, was thanking them for attending.

Prosser knew that he, of all people, should understand what Robbie's mother now felt but he could not help the feeling of anger towards her rather than the sympathy she needed and he would have left before she reached them but Val and Dominique lingered, feeling it appropriate to speak with her, and when she finally arrived at where they were standing he knew his instincts had been correct.

"Come to gloat 'ave you?" she asked Prosser, looking challengingly into his eyes. Prosser returned the animosity.

"No, Mrs Birch. We came to pay our respects to a decent young lad who did not deserve to be murdered."

Mrs Birch's face crumpled but before the tears came Dominique was quick to step forward. She bent down and smiled at Caron.

"Hello Caron. Do you remember me?"

"Have you got your motorbike?"

"No. I couldn't get on it in this skirt," Dominique laughed. "But I haven't forgotten I promised you a ride."

"I didn't see Robbie's father here," Prosser said provocatively. "His affection didn't last long."

"All right. All right. I should have listened to you," Mrs Birch spat and the tears fell down her face.

Val Franks put her arm around the woman's shoulders. Mike Prosser turned away and the Childrens officer and the uniformed officer started to follow him.

"He's angry. Take no notice of him," Val Franks told Mrs Birch who wiped her tears and nodded.

"He's right, though. I'm bloody angry too."

"Of course you are, we all are." Dominique told her. "Did Tyson pay for the funeral?"

"I wouldn't take anything from him. I sold the car," she explained, knowing Dominique would understand. "Would you ladies like to come back with us, I've laid on some food for a few friends? You'd be very welcome."

"Sorry. I've got too much to do," Val Franks apologised. "There were nearly three thousand crimes reported in our district last month and I seem to have most of them waiting on my desk."

"Mummy, when are we going to take these flowers," Caron asked, tugging at her mother's hand.

"We've got to get back," Mrs Birch said. "We've got Robbie's friends coming to tea. We"ll take them later."

"But you promised," Caron said petulantly

"What does she want to do?" Dominique asked

Mrs Birch explained how she wanted to take the flowers and put them against the railings on the bridge where Danny fell to his death.

"She thinks Robbie and Danny will see them."

"What a nice thought," Dominique said. "We could take her, couldn't we?" she said to Val Franks.

"I must get back," Valerie said. "But you can take the car, I'll get a lift with Mike and the others."

"What sort of car do you have?" Caron wanted to know. Dominique told her it was a sports car and they would have the hood down and Caron got excited.

"Is that all right, Val?  Do you mind?" Dominique asked as Val Franks offered her the car-keys.

"Of course not. You seem to have got yourself a friend."

"Is it okay with you Mrs Birch?" Dominique asked.

"Of course. It's very kind of you. Come in and have some tea when you drop her back."

In the car, Dominique smiled sideways at Caron who seemed to be in heaven as they drove, her curls blowing wildly about her face. They parked in the same place that Val had used on Dominique's first visit just beyond the trees. As Dominique helped Caron out of the car, holding her hand tightly, she noticed how much of the girl's hair had been left on the back of the seat.

"You need some vitamins, young lady. "We'll get you some fresh orange juice  on  the way  home."

"This is where Robbie hid and saw the man throw Danny off the bridge," Caron  said as they  reached  the trees.

"How do you know that?"

"Robbie said he hid in Dora's wood. He was scared in case her ghost was still here." She explained that Dora was a little girl who disappeared and her body was discovered in the wood. "They  never found who did it."

"That's awful. And Robbie told you that is where he hid?"

"Yes. They came round this corner on two wheels." Caron prattled on, reciting almost word for word what happened just as Robbie had described it in his statement. The astonished Dominique pulled her to a stop.

"How do you know all this?"

"Robbie told me," Caron answered and was tugging to resume their walk but Dominique held her back.

"When did he tell you, Caron?"

"When he got home after the accident."

"Were you awake when he got home? It was very late wasn't it? What time was it when Robbie got back?" Caron seemed uncertain. "Why were you awake?" Dominique persisted," but Caron only looked puzzled.

Dominique let go of the girl's hand, she bent low and held her shoulders, forcing her to look directly into her eyes.

"Caron, were you in that car with the boys?"

Caron looked as though she was about to cry.

"It's all right if you were. You can tell me, I'm not going to tell your mother, I promise"

"Only at first," Caron said, shuffling her feet and looking at the ground.

With persuasion she explained she was with the boys in the park. "We came out an' saw the man taking things from the car into the shop. He'd left the engine running and Danny jumped in as we was passing. Robbie shouted at him to get out an' he wouldn't get in but I wanted a ride an' I jumped into the back and then Robbie had to get in too. It was my fault." she said and started to cry.

Dominique hugged the girl to her thighs. "It was Danny's fault," she told her. "It was his idea, not yours. Were you with the boys when they had the accident?"

Caron told her that Robbie made Danny drop her off near home. "Robbie had to drag me out of the car. I always wanted a ride in a BMW."

"And that's why you stayed up until Robbie came back?" Caron nodded. "And then he told you what happened?" Caron agreed. They walked to where the flowers had been placed against the railings. They were now dead and Dominique gathered them up and took them to the trees, then she helped Caron tie the bouquet to the railings and watched as she put her hands together in prayer.

"Please, God. Make Danny and Robby happy together

and not let them get into any more trouble. Amen."

When they got back to the house people were still there. Dominique declined an invitation to join them as Caron busily told her mother how great Val's sports car was.

"She's just crazy about cars," her mother said. "If she was a dog she would chase them." She thanked Dominique.

Dominique asked if it would be all right if she returned and took Caron out on her motorbike as she'd promised.

"Of course you can. That would be really kind. She misses Robbie. He looked after her when I was at work. I don't know what I'm going to do now..." she began to weep again. "I'm sorry, I miss him too. I'll have to get a child-minder somehow – but I have to work tomorrow and I can't trust the other boy to look after her. One of the neighbour's girls said she would baby-sit but she can't start until next week."

"Can I help?" Dominique offered. "I haven't got a case at the moment. I could help for a few days."

Mrs Birch resisted, not wanting to put her to the trouble, but Dominique was persistent and it was agreed she would come at seven the next day.

"I'll make you a cottage pie. It was Robbie's favourite."

When Dominique returned Valerie's car to the police station she gave her an envelope. "Can you get these hairs DNA'd urgently, cherie? she asked and before Valerie could ask any questions she was already walking away.

"Will I see you tomorrow?" Val called after her.

"No. I'm baby-sitting," Dominique called back

*Baby-sitting*? Val Franks said to herself.

The next evening Dominique arrived at the Birch's house and was greeted enthusiastically by Caron.

"I've brought you a present," Dominique told her. Caron pulled a little box from the paper bag she was given and her eyes opened wide as she took a model BMW from it.

"Wow!" she said. "And…." Dominique gave her another box. "A Range Rover," Caron squealed.

Mrs Birch looked at Dominique who held her gaze. "Isn't that kind," Mrs Birch told Caron. "Take them into the other room, Caron and be careful. Don't break them."

"I won't. They're my best ever presents," she told them. The two women looked at each other.

"Do you hate Tyson as much as we do?"

"Of course I do. I would kill him myself if I could."

"Good. We'll find another way," Dominique told her.


It was several days before Val Franks saw her friend again. They met at the Frenchwoman's apartment "Where have you been?" Val asked. "I was worried."

"Baby-sitting. I told you. Have you got a DNA match for those hairs yet?"

"They're the same as those on the rear seat of the BMW." Dominique's face expressed her inner elation and she clenched her fists and closed her eyes.

"What's it all about?"

Dominique hugged her. "We've got another witness."

Val's amusement disappeared. "I need a drink," she said.

Over dinner she listened to Dominique's report before she asked the important questions.

"Do you think Caron is capable of going to court and testifying against Tyson?"

"She's a bit of an actress. Yes, I'm sure she can do it."

"What about cross-examination, a courtroom is a scary place for anyone, let alone a six-year old?"

"She would be allowed a video link. She would like that, she'd think she was on Television."

"It all sounds too good to be true. Why didn't Robbie tell us Caron was in the car with them?"

"I should think it was because he didn't want to get into

trouble with his mother," Dominique answered.

"Would she be up for it. I could understand her not wanting to after what happened to Robbie."

"She said she would kill Tyson herself if it were not for the children."

"We'd have to protect Caron – and the rest of the family. We'd have to find them a new home."

"Surely that wouldn't be a problem, would it?

"No. But Mrs Birch would have to be prepared to live somewhere else."

"She would love to move away from London."

"So she does know about Caron?"

"Yes. We've discussed it."

"Even before we had the DNA on those hairs?" Valerie asked and hated herself immediately for being a policewoman.

Dominique noticed the sharpness of the question which reflected for a brief moment in her eyes.

"Once Caron had told me she was in the car with the boys, I knew the hairs would be hers. If you examine the front seat of your car you'll find quite a few on there too. That's why I had them checked," she said just as sharply.

Then they both laughed as they realised they had succumbed to their professional lives.

"Once a copper always a copper," Val said.

"And perhaps I can't get rid of the lawyer in me after all."

"I'm glad to hear it. Will you stay with the CPS?"

Dominique sighed. "I don't know, Valerie. I'm still feeling a bit humbled by what happened. I just want to get Tyson for what he's done to everyone. But I don't know how I will feel when we've done that and this is all over."

"Do you ever know how you will feel?"

"Yes. Nearly always."

"I'll drink to that," Val said, but not with confidence.

91

Mike Prosser was surprised to find his wife, Edna in his office. In thirty five years of marriage she had never been in any of his police stations. She had attended official functions sometimes but had always distanced herself from his profession regardless of the fact he had been in the force when they had married. But she had not expressed particular vehemence against his job until their daughter, Janet, had told them she wanted to be a policewoman. Then years of suppressed loathing had surfaced as an unpleasant and irreparable shock to Mike Prosser. So it was with a degree of trepidation that he entered the office having been warned of her presence.

She was a large woman, seemingly to have taken any surplus fat from her husband during their years of marriage. She was dressed immaculately, as always; a lightly woven wool suit with matching leather handbag and shoes, her hair permed and tinted and her eyelid colour chosen to match. She wore two diamond rings and a double-string of pearls. She was studying a wall of photographs as he entered.

"You look terrible," she told him after she had sat opposite in the small conference corner of the office. She refused tea unless he could provide a proper cup. "I couldn't use one of those mugs," she added, nodding towards one containing unfinished coffee on his desk. He offered to send out for something but she again declined. Reading his thoughts, she explained she had come up to town with a neighbour to an exhibition at Tate Modern.

"And you just thought you would pop in," he suggested, trying to keep the sarcasm from his voice.

"Not exactly. I wanted to talk to you about something."

"You do seem to have difficulty using a telephone," he said, remembering the few times he had rung and been met with silence. "So what did you want to talk about?"

"Mother's got to go into a home," she began and went on to tell him how difficult it had become looking after her even though she still lived in her own cottage.

"She disappeared the other day and we found her wandering by the river. She could easily have fallen in."

He wondered if that might not have been a good way to end her problems but he let Edna continue her flow. He half-listened to complaints about local health facilities, useless doctors and the intrusion of new homes in the area and realised he had switched-off completely when he heard her say, "But it's going to cost a lot of money."

"What is?" he asked

"Mother's care home," she told him as though he was stupid. His brain had begun to function. She hadn't come to see how he was, she hadn't come because it was so near to Janet's memoriam – she hadn't even mentioned her. Nor had she mentioned their son, James. She had come to ask him for financial assistance.

"For your mother?" he said.

"Yes," she replied defiantly.

"You want me to help you pay for Jean to go into a private nursing home?"

"Yes. That's what I've been trying to tell you."

"Why doesn't she sell her cottage to pay for it?"

"Because that's in trust for James. You know that."

"Why don't you move into the cottage and sell the house?"

"Don't be ridiculous Michael," she scoffed.

"Why do you need a four bedroom house?" he asked.

"How could I possibly live in Mother's cottage? It hasn't even got a garage."

"You and two brothers lived there once," he reminded her.

"Then I didn't have any choice. Now I have."

"Now you have several," he argued. "You could sell both places, buy something smaller and still honour James' inheritance."

"I knew it was a waste of time coming here," his wife told him and got up to leave.

"Edna, what did you expect me to do?" Prosser protested

"I thought you might draw on your pension."

"To pay for your mother to go into a home while you stay in a large house which I paid for when we separated? I rent a one bedroom flat with service charges for a garden I don't have time to use, after having taken a crash in my salary and pension."

"And whose fault was that?" she asked without shame.

"I used to think it was mine. But now I'm not so sure."

She left him sitting, staring at the wall and wondering if he was really mad. Had he lost his reasoning. Was he so out of step he didn't understand anyone any more? He was tired. He suddenly felt the need to lie down. He fell sideways on the sofa and was soon snoring loudly.

When he wakened he was still in the same position on his side, his legs curled upwards to fit onto the short sofa. It was dark, only electric light filtering weakly into the office from those beyond. He tried to move and groaned as various parts of his body protested the loss of sufficient blood to the muscles. His neck felt as though it would break if he moved it too quickly and his hip creaked like an old door as he gingerly eased himself onto his elbow and moved his feet to the ground. He sat back and waited for the blood to circulate, hoping it would eventually reach his head where a sharp pain went from his neck to his eyes. He moved his back forward to test his legs then straightened them into an insecure standing position. He moved unsteadily to his desk and switched on the table-lamp and looked at his watch. It took several attempts to

94

get his eyes to focus and to discover it read two am, he had slept for ten hours. He tried to remember what had happened to Rip Van Winkle  but abandoned the attempt as his bladder protested it needed urgent attention. He walked into the deserted CID room. The only light was coming through the glass partitions from the uniformed section beyond. He slouched out into a corridor and found the toilets. He splashed cold water clumsily onto his face and neck and then returned to his office to get his jacket. He startled several people as he opened the door into the uniformed section.

"Can anyone organise a lift home for me?" he asked

By the time he entered his flat he was feeling a lot better. His body was functioning normally and after he had showered and had a mug of coffee in his hand his head too was free of pain and his brain was beginning to suggest that it had benefited hugely from the desperately needed time-out. He ate some cereal and had an urge to call James, it would be afternoon in Perth. James was not working from home but he picked-up the call at his office. Initially, he was afraid something bad had happened, it  was a feeling that was constantly lying in his sub-conscious ever since Janet's death and the consequent break-up of the family, but when he realised it was just a social call his nervousness was replaced by one of pleasure which developed to almost one of elation as his father talked easily and lightly about things, asking questions about his life in such a way that James felt able to mention several times his flat mate, Kevin without feeling guilty about it. His father told him how near they had got to putting Tyson away and of his mother's visit and the purpose of it. James was as comfortably bemused as Prosser had been as to why his mother did not move into a smaller house and he said he would talk to her about it. They talked for an hour and ended with James saying he hoped to get home for a holiday the next year and Prosser saying that would make him very happy.

Prosser dressed and even boiled himself an egg and had it with toasted stale bread and listened to the BBC World Service for the first time in months. He had even started to doze again when the buzzer went and Val Franks explained she had called on the off-chance he needed a lift. She had been happy rather than amused like everyone else at the sounds of snoring from his office that had permeated the CID Room all the previous afternoon and into the evening and she had hung a notice on his door for him not to be disturbed. Even the Chief Super had been sympathetic, everyone knowing it was a therapy long overdue. She immediately saw the benefits in his smart appearance and clear face.

"Did Edna's visit have anything to do with it?" she asked.

"Yes. It released me," he said without explanation.

"Mike, I don't want you to get overexcited or go into shock if I tell you something," she said.

"You're pregnant," he suggested

"By divine intervention? It's more dramatic than that."

She told him about Caron being a new witness. When she had finished, he stared ahead, his face tight but not gaunt as it had been for so long.

"Venus is in the ascendancy and Mars is aligned with Jupiter – or something," was his eventual comment and it was some time before he started to ask the questions Val Franks had asked of Dominique the previous evening.

"Okay. Let's take it to the Chief Super," he said as they entered the Station car park.

The Chief Superintendent listened attentively and when DI Franks had answered all his questions, like Prosser had been, he was carefully optimistic rather than elated.

96

"Does Ms Harcourt think we can do this?" he asked and was told that Dominique was confident about everything. Prosser remained silent.

"Right. Let's talk to the CPS and see what they think. I'll speak to the area director myself. But, for now, let's keep this to ourselves.The fewer people that know about the girl the safer. Val, can you quietly sound-out Social Services and see what might be available about putting the whole family under wraps with a view to finding a permanent move away for them? I think I should visit the Birch family and assess the situation myself. We don't want another disappointment."

*Disappointment.* Mike Prosser could have thought of a more accurate word. He should have been annoyed that the Chief Superintendent had suggested no part for himself in the new developments but he was relaxed enough to acknowledge that he was not the right person to visit Mrs Birch and he was surprised that he was not only calm about the prospects of charging Tyson again but was relieved that he could take a back-seat and let others deal with the inevitable anguish another bout of jousting with Marcus Swift would bring. But he was not sure whether this was because he had regained his dispassionate self-control or whether it was because his long practised cynicism expected a new prosecution to fail like all the others concerning Tyson.

Slowly, slowly the bricks were assembled. The Chief Superintendent's visit to Mrs Birch and his meeting with Caron supported Dominique's confidence that Caron would be a reliable witness. Val Franks liaised with Childrens Services to find a temporary home for the family once a trial date was fixed and a permanent home away from London for when the trial was over. Dominique, because of her special relationship with

Caron, was given the prosecution lead by the Director and an arrest warrant for Dave Tyson was prepared. It was after all this had been arranged and during a closed assessment in the Chief Superintendent's office attended by Val Franks, Dominique and Prosser that Prosser was asked what he thought. He had sat and listened without comment which was noticeably unusual and when the CS asked for his opinion it was with a forced note of geniality in his voice, "Well, Mike? What do you think? I think you should be the one to serve the arrest warrant."

Prosser spoilt the enthusiasm. "A six-year old versus Marcus Swift in a courtroom. That's like putting Amir Khan in the ring with Mike Tyson – or even Dave Tyson." They all argued that the girl would be on a video link and would not be in the actual courtroom. "And she's a little actress, she'll love it," Dominique added.

"An actress, is she?" Prosser said and his eyes were so penetrating that Dominique avoided them.

"We could have a mock trial," the Chief Super suggested. "I'm sure Ms Harcourt and her colleagues could organise it so it was like a proper trial."

"I think that is a very good idea," Dominique said. "And I believe Judge Harris would be up for it. I met him after Robbie's death and he was absolutely horrified by what happened to the boy. He even thought he might have been partly responsible for allowing Tyson to meet Robbie."

"What do you think, Mike?" the CS asked..

"A trial without a Judge, without a jury and without Marcus Swift. But why not? it can't do any harm."

Dominique was right and Judge Harris thought it was a sound idea and arranged for his courtroom to be available one evening. Dominique's colleagues also gave their time with some enthusiasm and argued as to who should act as the judge. The video link was set-up in an adjoining room. At the trial a WPC would be allowed to sit with Caron and Val Franks was given that task. Mrs Birch and Caron's brother sat on the Jury benches but would not be seen by Caron. Mike Prosser and the Chief Superintendent sat behind the counsel tables. An eminent QC acted as Defence Counsel. The acting judge over-egged his role somewhat by prolonging the preliminary proceedings leading up to Caron's appearance on the video link and making the girl impatient rather than relaxed by his over-elaborate descriptions to her as to why she was there and what would happen during the trial. Eventually, Dominique stood and addressed Caron.

"Hello Caron, can you see me all right?"

"Yes, Dominique, you look funny."

"I know, but it's what we have to wear, like school uniform." She explained to Caron that she would have to answer some questions from other people but that she only had to answer in her own way. "Take your time, Caron. Just tell us what happened the night your friend Danny had his accident."

"It weren't no accident, It were murder," Caron answered forcibly and Prosser's antennae quivered as he recognised the words Robbie had used to the same suggestion.

"Yes, that's what we think." Dominique agreed. "Can you tell us what happened, Caron, from when you and Robbie and Danny came out of the park and got into the BMW."

Caron told them. She dwelt unnecessarily on what they did in the park and what they were talking about and then became animated as she described Danny slamming the boot and then jumping into the car and how Robbie tried to stop her getting into the back seat but how he had to jump in the front himself as Danny started to drive off. Then her voice changed to a monotone as she told them what happened as they came round the corner and hit the

Range Rover and how she and Robbie hid in Dora's Wood and watched "this man" throw Danny off the bridge. When she had finished to Dominique's satisfaction, the acting judge told her she would have to answer questions from another person who did not believe what she had said was true. "So it's important that you tell him what you believe is the truth when you answer his questions - just as you have told Dominique," he added which, Prosser thought, Marcus Swift would have jumped on like a scrum half.

The QC gently but firmly questioned Caron. What time was it when you left the park? How long did you and Robbie hide in the wood? How do you know if neither you nor Robbie had a watch? What did the accused do after he threw Danny from the bridge? Did you actually see him throw Danny, could he not have been reaching to stop him falling from the bridge after tripping over the crash-barrier?

"Ee picked 'im up just like a sack of rubbish and threw 'im," Caron interrupted and Prosser again noted they were the exact words Robbie had used.

After the QC had cross-examined, Dominique came back and had Caron confirm one or two points of doubt the QC had created. They were about to end the proceedings with smiles of satisfaction and congratulation when Prosser snatched the wig from the QC's head and told the acting judge, "The Defence would like to re-examine m'lud," and went to the microphone. "Hello Caron. Can you see me?"

"You're that policeman," Caron said.

Prosser threw off the wig. "That's right, I'm a policeman. But I'm going to ask you some questions that you may have to answer in the real trial. Is that all right?"Caron told him it was, she was enjoying her moment of stardom.

"Now, Caron. You have told us what happened, but there are one or two things you haven't told us. For instance, you say you and Robbie were in the wood and saw this man throw Danny off the bridge and there was a lot of noise from the road of car's crashing and tyres screaming. Could you see what was happening on the road?" There was a long pause as they waited for Caron's response. "Come, Caron. You must remember if you could see the road or not. You must have wanted to know what happened to your friend, Danny.

"I don't think so because we were in the trees," Caron eventually answered.

"Good. That's good, Caron. Then you saw the man who threw Danny from the bridge use his mobile phone? How long after that did you and Robbie stay in the wood?" Caron couldn't remember because neither she nor Robbie had a watch. "So you stayed a while. Then what happened?"

"Then the man started to walk towards us and Robbie said we should scarper quick like, so we did."

"And then you said that you and Robbie walked home. How long did that take, Caron?" Prosser asked.

"We got in just after midnight."

"How do you know that if you don't have a watch?"

"Robbie said it was midnight on the kitchen clock. He was pleased that mum wasn't home yet."

"So it took you about two hours to walk home."

Prosser turned to the jury benches where Mrs Birch and Caron's brother were sitting – and the boy was asleep.

"We know the distance between the crash site and the Birch's home is nearly five miles along the route taken by the witness. That means that Robbie and his sister must have covered the distance at an average speed of two and a half miles per hour. You must ask yourselves if a six-year old girl could average that, and whether a six-year old girl could even walk that distance."

"Objection," Dominique protested. "M'lud, the Defence is trying to be precise about the time it took for Caron and her brother to get home based on the imprecise information as to how long they remained at the accident site. The witness had no watch and is only repeating what she thought her brother had told her. The Defence has declared her brother's evidence inadmissible. If they now want to allow her brother's statement they will know that Robbie said he ran a lot of the way home."

"Objection," The QC responded. "The Prosecution is attempting to bring inadmissible evidence to the court."

"Agreed – on both counts," the Judge announced

"Okay, Caron," Prosser continued. "So you managed to get home in two hours and you ran a lot of the way. You must be a very fit little girl for your age. Now, Caron, I want you to tell us exactly what happened after the BMW you were in hit the other car."

"Robbie and me got out an' ran to the trees."

"Did you find it easy to open the door on your side of the car to get out?"

"Yes."

"What about the air-bags?" Prosser asked innocently.

Caron's face could be seen frowning and turning sideways to where Val Franks was sitting. Prosser's voice was quickly aggressive

"Come on Caron. What about the air-bags. You said it was easy to get out. How did you get past the air-bags?"

Caron looked as though she was about to cry. She looked sideways towards Val Franks but Prosser was unrelenting.

"Do you know what air-bags are?" he demanded. When Caron didn't answer he insisted. "You don't do you, Caron. You don't know what air-bags are because you were not in the car with Danny and Robbie when it crashed. Were you?"

Caron did cry and when she started she couldn't stop. Val Frank's face appeared holding her cheek to Caron's and then she looked into the camera. "You're a bastard, Mike."

"Yes. That's what I get paid for," Prosser responded. "And I'm a bastard so I can put worse bastards in gaol – but not by manufacturing evidence. If that girl had been in the car she would have known there are side and front impact bags in that model which had deployed during the accident. And," he added with a slow gaze in Dominique's direction, "If the Prosecution had done their homework they would have known that too."

He walked back to the benches and continued to look at Dominique Harcourt but her eyes were closed in the direction of the table in front of her. Prosser walked out of the courtroom leaving a heavy silence behind. He paused in the corridor and leaned against the wall.

"Bugger," he said. "Bugger. Bugger."

Mrs Birch came out of the courtroom, looking furious.

"I thought you wanted to get Tyson," she yelled at him.

"Not like that," he responded.

"What does it matter. We know what he did to Robbie."

Prosser turned on her. "Yes we do. And whose fault was that? If you hadn't told him he was Robbie's father Robbie would still be alive and Tyson would be in jail. "

"He knew Robbie was your witness." she protested. "He would have had him killed anyway if I hadn't told him Robbie was his son. I didn't think even Semtex would have his own son killed."

"How did he know Robbie was our witness?"

"Because Marcus Swift had found out," she said.

Prosser stuck his face almost into hers.

"Swift knew who Robbie was before you told him?"

"Course he did. He found out from Danny's old-man didn't he." She told Prosser how Danny's father had told her about a Mr. Chandri giving him money. "I knew it were Swift from his description. I've known he was Semtex's solicitor for years."

The courtroom was emptying and Caron's appearance with Val Franks ended the conversation but Prosser had learned enough. Val Franks and Dominique ignored him as they joined Mrs Birch and the children. The QC and his colleagues came out talking and laughing together.

"Good work, Superintendent," the QC slapped Prosser on the back. "You could have another career."

During the ride home in Val Frank's car, the Birch family and Dominique were mostly silent until Caron began to recover her normal demeanour and started to chatter as though the previous hour hadn't happened. When they arrived at the Birch's house Mrs Birch invited them in. Val Franks declined the invitation and Dominique was telling Mrs Birch not to worry that they would get Tyson eventually when Caron, who had run into the house first, returned and thrust her hands at Val Franks.

"Look what Dominique bought me," she said and held out the model BMW and Range Rover for inspection. Valerie looked from the cars to her friend and Dominique looked back, a fleeting expression of panic in her eyes. Val Franks turned away from her and walked from the house without a word. Dominique rushed after her.

"Please, Valerie," she called, but Val Franks got into her car without looking back. Dominique turned towards the house and tears already clouded her eyes.

Mike Prosser's driving ban ended the next day. Despite what he had said to his DI about not wanting to drive again he felt a degree of comforting isolation as he went to the garage that had stored his car and he sat in it and started the engine. But it was not like riding a bicycle after a long absence, his eyes and ears were ill-tuned to the chaos and noise around him and his ankle protested as he stepped out into his old parking place.

He was on his second cup of coffee when Val Franks knocked and entered. They had known each other a long time. It had been Prosser who had suggested she should try for the CID when she was in uniform and he was then a Detective Chief Inspector. He had gone to her wedding and helped her drink away her sorrow and anger when she had discovered her husband's affair and he had supported her every word about the pathetic, weak, immature, foot-stinking narcissistic sod when they had separated and finally divorced. She had been equally supportive over Janet's death – as had everyone in the station. And she had tried hard to reason with Edna when she had complained about the years of neglect she thought she and the family had suffered because of his job. She had watched his deterioration with increasing concern up to the final humiliation of his demotion and separation from Edna and the departure of James to Australia. So apologies were not necessary in their relationship and when she flopped on his sofa he got up from his desk and sat beside her.

"How was it?" she asked with little interest in her voice.

"It's been so long I can't remember," he replied

"I meant, the driving."

"Not as good as yours." He waited.

"You were right," she said. "You're always bloody right."

"Usually, not always. How is Miss Hardcore taking it?"

Val Franks looked miserable. "I don't know."

"Haven't you spoken to her? I thought you were friends."

"So did I." Again, he waited, knowing there was more

"I've not taken her calls," she said. Then she looked at him. "She was coaching the girl. She bought her two model cars, a Range Rover and a BMW. That's not right Mike," she protested.

"No. Running Tyson down was a much better idea."

It brought a reluctant smile to her face. "What did you mean when you said Edna had released you?"

"It was like suddenly opening my eyes after a nightmare. I always thought everything was my fault," he explained. "For years I've felt guilty about everything; being a copper, not being interested in pottery, swearing, drinking, hating all the bastards we have to deal with. Just being me. The other day I suddenly realised I didn't like her – and that she had never liked me."

They sat in silence, comfortable with their separate thoughts and their physical closeness.

"There might be another way," he said eventually and he told her how Marcus Swift had pretended he was Chandri and given Murphy money.

"My God! That must be some sort of offence."

"Oh yes. Deception. Bribery. Accessory to Murder. Do you want to come with me to see Murphy? Dig out a photo of Swift and bring it with you."

Murphy met them at the door in a dressing gown. After they had identified themselves he invited them in, apologising for the untidy state of the kitchen. His wife was working. "Thank God she's bringing in some money. My breathing is still bad but I can't afford to stay off work much longer."

They showed him the photograph of Marcus Swift.

"That's Mr. Chandri," he said. "He's a very decent feller."

They explained it was not Mr Chandri and asked Murphy about Marcus Swift's visit.

"How much was in the envelope?" Prosser asked. "It's okay, we have no powers to take it from you," he added as Murphy hesitated to answer. "We need to know whether Swift was trying to bribe you."

"Five hundred quid." Murphy told them. "He didn't want anything. He only asked me about Robbie Birch."

"Have you still got the envelope?" Val Franks asked. Murphy handed it to Prosser, still with some notes inside "Can you let us have two or three notes for DNA testing?" Val Franks asked.

When he had been told of the implications of Swift's deception, Murphy was upset that he might have contributed to Robbie's death – even though the police officers were quick to say they could not prove he had been murdered. The Irishman readily agreed to identify Swift at a later date in an ID parade.

They left the cul-de-sac where two families had had their lives forever scarred and as they drove away, Prosser thought of the other four families who would be suffering in the same way because of Dave Tyson's moment of tyranny. He knew how all of them would feel; they had been sentenced to a lifetime of never again feeling happy.

"How do you want to play it?" Val Franks invaded his thoughts.

"I'm not sure yet.

"Shouldn't we bring him in under caution? That will put a lot of pressure on him. Even Marcus would be worried."

"He can just deny he gave the money to Murphy. Or he could say he must have dropped the envelope and accuse Murphy of lying for keeping it. You know what a clever sod he is. But if his DNA is on the notes it's going to be harder for him to wriggle out of a bribery charge or of being an accessory to murder. Let's wait for the results."

## CHAPTER FOUR

# DECEPTION

Big Dave Tyson's house was set in a high position overlooking a sweeping panorama of the Kent countryside. Marcus Swift had been right to describe it as beautiful. The main skeletal building was of the Tudor period and the brickwork had survived the centuries in remarkable condition and demonstrated the skills of the craftsmen in the tall, twisted patterns of the chimneys and the stone mullioned windows and doorways but it was the Elizabethan additions of the full length windows that looked onto the stone-walled terrace to the rear and overlooked the Weald which distinguished the building from many of its contemporaries. An early fifteenth century tower at one end was all that was left of an earlier building, its crenulated roof and the vallied fall from it's footings reminders of a moated, fortified house that was perhaps appropriate to it's new owner. A medieval barn now housed a heated swimming pool and the luxurious interior fittings of the house defied the quiet elegance and settled peace of the exteriors. Once owned by a pop star, Beaumont's antecedents were no less implausible now than when it was named, supposedly, after a sixteenth century ancestor of the Elizabethan playwright of that name, a bishop who's fortune was made from grazing stolen sheep and cattle and shipping them to the low-countries. He might well have approved of its present owner.

The party was in the way of celebrating Tyson's release from gaol to the bosoms of his family and the many other bosoms that were nakedly flaunted around the swimming-pool. His wife was an ex winner of the Southend-On-Sea beauty contest and had graduated to a middle-page display in Playboy but her outward credentials had provoked her inner abilities to the point of taking an accountancy course and becoming Tyson's trusted manager. Their two daughters were away at boarding school and Francine had no problem in accepting her husband's social predilections, knowing that her position was one of indispensable power given her knowledge of his business enterprises.

When Marcus Swift arrived, the party was well into it's third act and he had to pick his way around several recumbent bodies on the lawn between the gravelled drive and the house, their various noises reflecting the self-imposed exile that a mixture of champagne and cocaine induced. He was greeted enthusiastically and warmly by Tyson and Francine – for whom he had a silent admiration – and even the imperturbable Jason managed a toothy "Awright then?" Francine escorted him to a table and supervised the waiters as they brought him a bottle of good Burgundy from the cellars to compliment the strips of wild boar and Pimiento salad he had chosen. Champagne, he believed was a drink for tourists; quick to its destination with no lasting pleasure.

Francine sat at the table with him. "Thank you, Marcus," she told him, her dark eyes matching the sincerity of her voice. "That was a bloody close call."

"It was indeed," Marcus agreed. "But I'm afraid it did have a price, Francine."

He told her about the agreement he had made with Tyson if he got him off the charge of murder. Francine's eyes lost their sparkle and her no-longer youthful face displayed all the facets of her experiences. But she soon recovered. "Well, what the hell? I don't know why we keep this place anyway, it's far too big and draughty. We rattle around here like the bloody ghosts the girls say they've seen. But what would you do with a place like this, Marcus. You've only got your old mum?"

"And Archie," he reminded her. Archie was his ageing retriever. "I would make it sing again. I would turn the banqueting hall into an Elizabethan theatre and have lots of Thespians to stay. The minstrel gallery would fill the house with Purcell and Monteverdi and I would keep peacocks."

Francine's laughter tinkled like a bell and made her husband turn to a sound he hadn't heard for a long time.

"You're a bloody old romantic," she told Marcus.

"And you are beautiful," he answered quickly. Her expressive eyes acknowledged his uncharacteristically emotional spontaneity before Tyson was at her side.

"What's so funny? You flirting with my wife, Marcus?"

"But of course, why wouldn't I? She is a thing of beauty that will never pass into nothingness once seen."

Tyson swept up the steak knife and held the back of it to Marcus' throat as he gripped his nose. "Because, I would cut you into bits and feed you to my dogs," he said and then he laughed.

"Whatever for? I thought you paid Jason to do that sort of thing," Marcus responded and made Tyson laugh even more. Francine joined the laughter but her eyes did not mirror it.

"Marcus was telling me of your arrangement," she said.

Tyson looked from one to the other with a frown.

"The house," she prompted

"Oh, that?" Tyson laughed. "Good try, Marcus."

"It was an agreement. I have the papers with me."

"Yeah, but that was if you got me off the murder rap."

"Which I believe I did by finding your witness," Marcus countered. "That was our agreement. Nothing less."

"No Marcus. That weren't the agreement. It was if you

110

got me off the murder charge. But you didn't exactly do that did you?"

"I thought I had. Otherwise you would not now be here."

"Yeah but that wasn't your doin was it? If that bitch hadn't told you Robbie was my kid I'd still be in gaol. An' as it is, Jason 'ad to do the business."

"What do you mean?" Marcus asked

"Well, the kid could 'ave changed 'is mind anytime couldn't ee an' given evidence?"

The reality of the statement sent Marcus Swift back in the chair. He looked at Tyson as if he were an apparition.

"Tell you wot, Marcus, you bill me double. You did a good job. I'll give you that." He put his hand reassuringly on the other man's shoulders.

"An keep yer 'ands where I can see em while you're chatting up my wife," he chuckled as he walked away. Francine studied Marcus' face without speaking.

"Excuse me," Marcus said and rose, picking up the bottle of wine and his glass. Francine knew she needed to say something but she could not think of anything appropriate to stop Marcus walking away. It was later that she found the words when she met her husband coming from another direction.

"Dave, you shouldn't have spoken like that to Marcus," she told him

"Yeah. Yeah," he answered and continued walking.

"He knows as much about you as I do," she said.

Tyson stopped and looked back at her.

"You're right," he agreed. "Yeah. I'll ave to fink abaght that won't I?" and he walked on.

In the nearby library, Marcus Swift heard the exchange from the depths of a winged armchair to where he had taken his bottle of wine. The claret lost it's flavour to the acid that surged up from his stomach.

111

It was in the embers of the party, when bodies had collapsed on various settees around the house and bursts of drunken laughter penetrated the night from dark corners that Marcus found Jason sitting alone on a step of the terrace smoking something that did not smell like tobacco. With difficulty Marcus lowered himself and settled next to him. Jason silently offered a smoke which Marcus silently declined It was a fine summer's night and the great beech trees of the park were silhouetted against the night-blue sky and in the darkness of the countryside the stars overhead hung like down-lights. The two men sat in silence as though any sound would disturb the air right up to the stars above them. They were easy in each other's company despite their disparate personalities. They had known each other a long time and in their different ways had empathised their abilities to handle Tyson's needs and moods.

Marcus was reluctant to disturb the spiritual perfection of the moment but the view of the estate, rolling away from the ancient terrace, and the Tudor brick walls behind him, pulled at a yearning somewhere in his body that he had so nearly quieted earlier that evening and the beauty of the scene even fuelled  the  quiet anger that drove him to break the spell.

"Dave told me about Spain," Marcus said.

Jason turned and looked at the other man but Marcus continued to stare into the darkness of the gardens.

"Yeah?"

"It was a shame you had to do that to the boy."

Jason took a long pull on the cigarette.

"Yeah."

"Was he a decent chap?"

"Yeah. He was okay."

Marcus sucked in the night air.

"I suppose Dave's weather forecast was a coded message for you to get on with it?"

"Yeah. It's a code we use sometimes."

"Poor Robbie. But I suppose Dave had to get rid of him."

"Yeah."

They continued to sit for some time in the solace of the night, only the sound of laughter and squeals from the swimming pool occasionally disturbing the air. Eventually Marcus Swift stood up. He brushed his trousers with his hand and rubbed his bottom.

"You must tell me how to get some muscle on my arse dear boy. This fat is inadequate to support my weight on this step."

"Yeah," Jason responded.

"Well, good night, Jason. Sleep well."

"Yeah. You too Marcus."

After the debacle of the mock trial, Dominique Harcourt's emotions had moved from humiliation through desperation and depression to uncompromising resignation. There are moments in our lives when our actions or utterances leap from our sub-conscious and totally shock us as much as those about us and the attempt to persuade Caron to perjure herself was one of those moments for Dominique. The desire to get Tyson had been so intense it nullified the normal reasoning of her considerable intellect and it was only when Mike Prosser had exposed her efforts that she had realised to the full the extent of her culpability. Panic had then seized her when Valerie recognised the significance of the toy cars she had bought for Caron, and Valerie's reaction had hurt more than her self-inflicted humiliation. She had made the many calls to Valerie's mobile in a desperate need of forgiveness. In another world she would have flagellated her body until it shed all the impurities of her blood, but silence had been more effective; she had accepted the severance of their relationship as something she deserved and had even seen it as an inevitable response to who she really was. Out of silence came reformation. She analysed the traumas in her childhood that had crept up and grabbed her when her logic had switched off; her father's many lovers, her mother's misery and early death from a weakened heart. She had eventually reasoned that only Valerie and Mike Prosser had guessed the extent of her deviation and that her legal colleagues would believe only that she had been led astray by a child's imagination.

But she did not flinch from recognising the passion that had made her want to get Tyson at any cost and she knew exactly how Mike Prosser had felt when he had attempted to run the man down. But, like a douche of cold water to a sleeping head, she realised that passion is not a suitable bed-fellow to a legal career, and in her self-loathing she tendered her resignation to the Crown Prosecution Service.

Her apartment was rented on a yearly renewable contract and she gave notice to vacate it despite six-months remaining on the present lease. She arranged for her beloved Ducati to be railed home to the family estate in the Jura and took several items of household usage round to Mrs Birch and bought Caron a bicycle. Her last task was to say goodbye to her ex-colleagues of Kerry, Bryce and Tomkins where she had started her legal career.

She was descending the narrow, winding stairs from the third floor when she met Marcus Swift moving upwards. They stopped and looked at each other, both realising that to pass there would have to be an unacceptably intimate conjunction. Marcus Swift swept off his tweed cap and bowed, showing his thick, silvering hair.

"My! My! Little John, what beautiful legs you have."

"All the better to kick you with, Friar," she responded

"You are full of surprises," Swift smiled. "Your knowledge of English folk-lore is as great as that of constitutional law, and all in such a delightful accent too. I can hardly wait to share a courtroom with you again."

"Then I'm afraid you will suffer boredom waiting for that, Mr Swift," she answered. "I have resigned from the CPS and have no more desire to practise." Swift looked genuinely concerned.

"Marcus, please call me Marcus. Dear lady, why on earth would you feel like that? I had you marked as a comet to higher things."

"Higher things are not high enough to escape the stench below," she said.

For a moment Swift's face reacted to the iron in her inflections but soon assumed the normal mask of unemotional affability. "Then you are the angel that you look. *'Does man, his glassy essence like an angry ape, play such fantastic tricks before high heaven as to make the angel weep?'* he smilingly quoted

*"Beating in the void, my luminous wings in vain,"* Dominique responded.

"Qu'est que c'est?"

"Arnold on Shelley."

"Ah! Not my cup of tea. I would be more interested to know what Shelley might have said of Arnold. But why here, why a visit to Messrs Kerry, Bryce and Tomkins?"

"To say my farewells. I did my Pupillage here and was with them until I joined the CPS."

"How amazing that I knew nothing of such a jewel amongst these dark satanic mills. I must chastise Harry Meadows for not alerting me to your presence."

"And I to yours, forewarned might have been forearmed.

How do you know Harry?" she asked.

"We were at school together. Lewisham Grammar."

He had been retreating downwards as he spoke and had reached the second-floor landing to allow her to pass and they were now standing close so that her Chanel met his Old Spice.

"Does he give you work?" she asked

"They leave me the bits they find too unpleasant to chew. I am their mediaeval dog," he told her cheerfully.

"Does Mr. Tyson not feed you enough?"

"Not as much as you may think. He has the occasional gourmet banquet when I have to swallow more than I wish to digest but fortunately they are no longer as frequent as they used to be."

"How did your angel fall, Marcus?" she asked.

He knew from her voice, she expected an answer.

"Have you had lunch? Would you care to give me the great pleasure of your further company so that you may explain why you are leaving us bereft of your talents and beauty?"

"No. I haven't had lunch, and, yes, I would find that interesting. But don't you want to see Harry first to see what he has for you?"

"Harry can wait. The world can wait."

He led the way down the stairs and as they stepped outside he swept his arm towards the green swathe of grass that formed a quadrangle between the buildings.

"Lincoln fields," he said. "Did you know that here Lord Fairfax and Cromwell camped an army to bring the City to heel and Parliament trembled to their will?"

"And now the pen is mightier than the sword," she smiled

"If only that were true. Brute force still rules, I'm afraid."

They walked into Chancery Lane as he explained how

116

Harry Meadows had failed to get a scholarship as had he. "Life is a giver of talent but not of favours. Society makes the rules and they never favoured Harry – but he has more brain than most of your ex-colleagues."

They reached Fleet Street and he led the way into the Wig and Pen and was greeted warmly by many members of the profession who were normally less ebullient. They were shown to a corner table in one of the warrens of timbered rooms with envious looks stabbing his back. He ordered guinea fowl and she chose a Puligny Montrachet, surprising him that she chose a white Burgundy. "It cuts the sauce," she explained without reason, but she was right, the flavours remained separately complimentary. He asked what part of France she came from and why she had chosen to practice in England rather than there. She told him of her love-hate relationship with her father, of the family estate on the slopes of the Jura, of school in Geneva and of her love for horses and dogs and the countryside. "I read languages at the Sorbonne. I wanted to do law as law and politics had been part of my family life but I resisted because my father was so well known. But after the Sorbonne I decided to compromise and do law here at Cambridge."

"So you wanted to do a bit of slumming to get away from your privileged background while I went the other way?"

"Did you want to get away from your father?" she asked.

"Not at all. I loved my father dearly." He told her how he had died in the local pub from a heart attack while celebrating Marcus' scholarship to Oxford. "He was a docker who loved to read, especially history and more especially Roman history."

"Were you named after Mark Antony?"

"Marcus Aurelius, he thought Antony was a fool."

"To have loved and lost. Isn't that what most people do?"

117

"No. He took me to see Antony and Cleopatra at the Aldwych, just across the road from here, when I was ten would you believe? He derided Shakespeare's romantic interpretation of Antony's relationship with Cleopatra. He explained it was all about politics and power, that Antony made the wrong decisions because he was poor, not because he was in love. 'So never be poor,' he told me, 'Because then you will always lose.'"

"And you followed his advice, no matter who pays?"

"I have never been poor. But I suspect it was the poverty around us when I was a child that taught me that lesson rather than anything Father might have said."

"And to love and to lose?"

"He never told me about that."

"Haven't you been in love? Why do you smile?"

"Because it was a sort of love that got me entangled with Mister Dave Tyson."

He told her how a fishmonger, George Quiros, accosted him in a pub in Leadenhall Market one evening and Dominique's brain searched for the connection to the name she had heard before.

"I had just been given the heave-ho from my chambers and was washing down my tears with a solicitor friend. Quiros must have heard our conversation and came and sat at our table. 'You want a job?' he asked me and made it sound like a threat. I showed only mild interest – and then he showed me a photograph of his daughter, Francine."

He explained that after winning a beauty contest, Francine had got a few publicity spots in local events and had then been persuaded by a local disc-jockey to sign a contract with his agent, a hopeless failed accountant who had visions of becoming the next Brian Epstein. But the agent got her no work and when she picked-up with a photographer and got noticed by Playboy he tried to

118

muscle in on the deal and take over her life.

"It got a bit nasty," he explained. "We had to go to court to untangle it but I managed to get rid of her so-called agent and then I acted for her with a few modelling contracts and publicity launches."

"And you fell in love with her?"

"I suppose I did. But anyone would have," he excused himself. "She was, is, very attractive – not like you, you are class, Francine was lust. I was younger then," he smiled.

"Did you have an affair?"

"No. I am ten years older than her. She has led me on a bit from time to time and I think she was, is, genuinely fond of me. But then she met Dave."

He explained how Tyson had then owned a club in the East End and had met Francine when he was trying to persuade her father to put money into it. Quiros wasn't interested until Francine went with him to the club and saw the potential to make it something else.

"She has  a smart mind, very shrewd like her old-man, and she learned things quickly. She had been to the States and seen what could be done and she persuaded her father to back Tyson so that she could manage the club. She soon turned it into a big, glossy sex and drinks palace and made a lot of money. She went to college and did accountancy and then married Tyson.  Tyson owes all his success to Francine. She  made him what he is."

"A killer of children?"

The words cut noticeably into him. "I didn't know about that," he said. "Until a few days ago. Dave more or less told me. I was horrified. There was no need."

"How did that make you feel, Marcus. Knowing what he had done to that other boy and causing so many deaths?"

"Sick. But you know the game we play, it's called *Prove*

119

*It Or Lose it.* There is always someone else to do our job if we don't want to do it and I have a horror of someone doing it less well."

"I'm sure that would always be the case," she smiled. "Did you do it for Francine?"

He sighed and closed his eyes and looked remarkably vulnerable when he opened them and looked at her.

"I used to. She would kiss me and ask me to help him for the sake of her children. At first it was easy, assault charges, handling stolen goods, minor possession, soliciting. Then it became harder, a rival club owner died in a fire, a drugs runner had his throat cut. I tried to get away but they know that I know too much. I am in a whirlpool. Dave often mentions my mother, asks how she is, worries that I have to leave her alone when I'm working. "What would happen to her if there was a fire," he once said when I threatened to have no more to do with him."

"He seems to like fires. Did he burn those women?" she asked

"I don't know, Dominique. He never does things himself. When you have his sort of money there is always somebody else to do it for you."

"He's not likely to let you go. Do you really think you are expendable, after all you've done for him?"

"If and when it suits him. But I do have insurance."

Dominique looked at him and then reached across the table and touched his hand. "Poor Marcus," she said.

His face almost dissolved as she leaned towards him. Her great, green eyes were separated by a soft furrow and her lips pouted slightly as though they were primed to kiss his forehead.

"You understand?" he asked.

"That we have to do what we have to do? Yes. I suppose I

do understand that. That's why I can't do it any more."

"You are right," he said. "I should sell up too and go to Florida."

"The cesspool of fraud?"

"Is it? I suppose it is. Where is not? Where is Utopia?"

"Here," she said and put the flat of her hand against his heart so firmly that he felt her pulse through his shirt.

"Are you really leaving us and going back to France?"

"I'm booked on an evening train. I have already taken my luggage to the station. I wanted to do a little shopping. "

"How dreadful, that we are never to meet again. I am the Flying Dutchman, destined to travel forever alone. If we are lucky, once in a lifetime do we meet a soul-mate, where two voices, personalities, ideas and inclinations fuse in harmony. It is sometimes for only a moment, like now, and then it is gone into a black universe for eternity."

She looked at him and saw the questions, the fear, the hope and the helplessness in his eyes. She smiled .

"I would like to meet your mother," she said.

They took a taxi and she held his arm as they sat together. He recounted many tales of past encounters, his voice modulating to the nuances of the events even sliding easily into various accents of the characters he described. It was entertainment rare to her ears and the journey to Kennington was one she would remember that ended all too quickly.

His house was in a late Georgian terrace, set back from the road with small gardens in the front. The houses had semi-basements and two full-length windows above a narrow iron-fenced balcony on the first-floor. They had all been gentrified and it was difficult to imagine this had been the rat-infested slum-heap district that had moulded the worlds most famous silent-film comic actor. Perhaps

121

it was an appropriate haven for Marcus Swift. He had not been born there, his childhood and youth were spent in Deptford, not far from the docks where his father worked. He had bought the house in Kennington when the area was still a threat to white affluence and the first thing he had done was to fit steel shutters to the ground floor and basement windows. But there was still the remains of a community of sorts and it was soon known that he was useful to the many inhabitants who frequently displeased the law and it wasn't long before he could remove the shutters and was greeted warmly as he stepped along the Old Kent Road. As soon as they entered the hallway they were into another world. The passageway was parquet floored in shining elm with a Baroque mirror above a crescent-shaped, marble-topped side-table. A mahogany balustraded staircase was carpeted in pale blue Wilton and lit by a small crystal chandelier. Marcus called down the stairs at the end of the passageway.

"Hello Mother. Are you decent?"

"Of course I'm decent," came the reply in a course voice. Marcus led the way down the stairs into a small dining-room in the front and then through a kitchen into a room at the rear of the house which was his mother's sitting room. It had French windows opening onto a small terraced area from which steps led upwards to the garden. Archie, the golden retriever, got arthritically to his feet to greet them and Dominique bent to make a fuss of him. Mrs Swift was sitting near the open window as it was a fine afternoon. He introduced Dominique who bent and shook the old woman's hand and smiled brightly,

"Are you one of 'is acting ladies?" she asked.

Dominique looked to Marcus for an explanation.

"I'm a member of a Shakespeare Reading group," he explained. "No, mother. Dominique is a barrister too."

"Mmm! Clever and pretty," was the woman's comment and her intonation made it sound dangerous. They left Mrs Swift to continue watching Countdown and Marcus led the way back to the first floor.

There were two long rooms, front and back, with a double-spaced doorway between them. The front room was an office-sitting-room cum library. One wall supported full-length book cases and a fine mahogany desk backed onto a window. At the opposite end, two winged armchairs of Sheraton style confronted a marble fireplace which was converted to a coal-effect gas unit. In the back room, which overlooked a small but pretty garden, a Steinway baby grand piano dominated one corner. There was a Knowle settee along one wall and a fine, walnut-framed chaise longue along the other and occasional chairs set at various points near pedestal tables with carved, gilded table lamps and pieces of Meissen china on them.

"Tres charment," was Dominique's comment as she toured the rooms without inhibition. "It is like one of my father's salons in his apartment in Strasbourg."

"Then I am deeply complimented," Marcus smiled. "What may I get you, would you like more wine, coffee, or something stronger?"

"A glass of iced water would be very welcome."

"An excellent choice," he agreed. "Amuse yourself, I have to go down to get it."

Dominique took off her jacket showing the sleeveless, loose fitting silk shift beneath, which was short enough to show some bare midriff above her skirt and loose enough to show the rise of her breasts when she leant forward.

She went to the desk and surveyed it, speed-reading the notes scribbled on sheets of motifed paper. She examined a folder on top of the desk  which seemed to be a case-file, then she opened the full-width drawer.

She was admiring the eclectic collection of books when Marcus returned carrying a small tray with a bottle of mineral water and long iced glasses with a slice of lemon in each. He set them down on a table and poured. He had already removed his jacket and his bow-tie before he returned from downstairs. They chinked glasses and smiled at each other.

"Welcome to my humble abode," he said. "You do me a great honour. But you too are honoured, very few of our profession have entered here – only dreamers like myself."

"What do you dream most about?"

In way of an answer he led her into the back room and pointed to a set of framed theatre programmes.

"From Neville through Olivier, Burton, Gielgud, Jacobi and Branagh. I dream of them and the glories that were."

"You would have made a fine actor, Marcus."

"Would have?" he protested indignantly. "I do. Every time we step into a courtroom we are making the dough from which Shakespeare made such exquisite cake."

"Unfortunately, it's not a play that ends when the curtain falls. The consequences are real and never poetic."

"True, true," he agreed. "But, without the ugly we would not appreciate the beautiful, would we? Look now to ourselves, we met in the most tragic of circumstances, yet here we are celebrating all that is fine in life, good food, good wine, good company."

"Is that enough?"

"What else is there?"

She smiled suggestively

"Ah! Yes. That." he commented without enthusiasm. .

"*That?*" she emphasised. "Isn't *that* the finest dessert to good company, good food and good wine?"

"Perhaps. I am informed it can consummate those things but also that it can be a feast too far; bad for the digestion and can leave an enduring headache."

She laughed and stood on her toes to kiss his cheek.

"Poor Marcus. You've dined with the wrong people. Have you never been tempted. Not even with Francine Tyson?"

"That would be like stealing a mackerel from a shark, the eating would not be worth the eaten."

"Has there not been anyone else besides Francine?"

"There have been one or two moments – but they are so rare they are fossilised in my memory."

They were still standing almost together. Dominique put a finger inside his shirt and moved it playfully.

"And what sort of moment is this?"

"The rarest."

She put down her glass and unfastened two buttons of his shirt, looking up at him with a smile that Leonardo might have envied.

"Then Mr Swift, it is time you collected another fossil."

As she spoke, her fingers pressed against his chest, moving him backwards. Marcus' eyes looked at her disbelievingly.

"Not a feast. Not a headache. A memento of our sharing."

She had continued the pressure on his chest until the back of his knees reached the chaise longue. Suddenly her hand went inside his shirt and pulled outwards so that the buttons parted and sprayed onto the floor. She swept her hands wide, opening his shirt and at the same time, pushed so that he fell back onto the chaise. She continued to smile down at him without parting her lips.

"What would William Shakespeare have to say now?" she asked. He struggled to find a suitable answer and before he could speak she had bent forward and kissed him gently, softly on his lips. "Shush," she whispered. "Even

Shakespeare knew when not to talk." She stood upright and lifted the shift above her head and threw it on the floor. Marcus stared at her breasts which were supported by a half-bra of red and black lace. She then stepped out of her skirt and his eyes went down to the lace panties that matched her bra and barely covered the rise of her pubis. She unfastened her bra, and her breasts, brown and cream rings with deep violet nipples, eased outwards and almost sighed.

"Ah! His voice lingered on the sound like the diminishing harmonics of a muffled bell.

The Mona Lisa smile had remained on Dominique's lips. She expertly unclipped and unzipped his tailored trousers then tugged them forcibly. Marcus bounced upwards from the chaise and the flesh of his stomach wobbled in protest. She put one knee on the chaise between his legs and leant forward so that her breasts brushed his ribs as her lips played about his eyes.

"Oh!" he said and Dominique's smile seemed as permanent as the painting's She pulled down his pants and for a moment her expression wavered as his penis jumped at her like a shocking toy. She took his testis in her hands, like a moneylender weighing a handful of gold, then she leant forward so that her breasts brushed his lips and his penis lay against the rise of her pubis. She caressed it, holding it against her gently thrusting flesh, massaging it rhythmically with the movement of her hips. Marcus lay back, arms stretched wide, his head pulled back almost to his shoulder blades. He made a continuous moan deep in the throat until it grew loud and emitted a cry in a rush of air as it seemed the whole of his body deflated. Dominique slid downwards onto her knees between his legs and smiled up at him. He looked down at her, his eyes clouded, his mouth open for air, then his head fell back with a groan reminiscent of Archie appreciating the comfort of his bed.

Dominique stood and looked down at him. Although his stomach was of a similar shape to a five month pregnancy it was disturbingly attractive as was all of his body. His skin was of a clear, firm consistency and she was reminded of Rodin's drawings of Balzac prior to his sculpted masterpiece and for a moment, only for a moment, she experienced an urge to take off her pants and fall on top of him. But instead, she bent down and kissed his head and left to find the bathroom.

When she returned Marcus hadn't moved, oblivious to the comedic effect of his naked body tied at his ankles by his pants and trousers above the light, brown brogues. His brain was struggling to understand the situation that had consumed him like a lightning strike.

Dominique fetched their unfinished glasses of iced water and sat beside him. She placed his glass against his groin which looked in need of it's cooling effect.

"You have a fine instrument there," she said. "You should play it more often."

He chuckled and put his arm around her shoulders.. "You are an enigma Miss Aarcour. A planetary phenomenon. A comet of astonishing beauty, shaking worlds as it disturbs their orbits in passing before moving away for a thousand years."

She kissed his hand which hung near her breast then lifted his arm from her shoulders and placed it across his stomach She stood up and began to dress, smiling that smile as his eyes followed the enclosing of her breasts.

"Is our moment gone?" he asked

"I have a train to catch," she reminded him.

He nodded resignedly and raised his glass and smiled a sad smile. "Then here's to the next thousand years."

The evening commute was already hazing the summer air as Miss Hardcore walked into the Old Kent Road and raised an arm. Two taxis swept competitively towards her.

Prosser was up early and at Billingsgate fish market by six am. He wore a pair of overalls he had borrowed from the maintenance block. One can smell the market long before one can see it and the smell permeates everything close to the laid-out crates of fish and the slabs where so many varieties from prawns to sharks were arranged in wholesale lots.

Even though it was late by market standards, there were still many customers haggling with traders and the porters were busy taking crates to various vehicles. It was noisy with the banter of Cockney humour and the shouted insults from drivers trying to manoeuvre their vehicles.

The delivery trucks were patiently waiting to filter along the narrow street which wound up from the market onto the flyover to start their long journeys home. Prosser walked along the line of trucks until he saw what he was hoping to find, a white truck with *Estofish* on the side. The Estonian company was imprinted on his memory.

The driver was waiting patiently for the queue of vehicles ahead of him to move and he looked down and nodded as Prosser smiled up at him. The window of the truck was down and Prosser called up.

"You've come a long way."

"Oh yaa," the driver responded.

"How long does that journey take?"

"Three days." The truck in front was not moving and the Estonian driver had lit a cigarette.

"How often do you have to do it?" Prosser asked.

"Every two weeks. Six days away and a week at home."

Prosser hoped his surprise didn't show, the girl at Quiros'

shop had said they had a delivery every four weeks.

"I didn't think there was that much fish in the Baltic."

"We  bring chickens over too, thousands of them."

If Prosser had been surprised before he was now stunned.

"Where do you take those to? We don't do chickens here."
The man  laughed and waved a hand out of the window before pointing in a northerly direction.

"Some factory, over that way.  Near the football ground."

"Do you mean the Q pie-factory?"

"Yaa. That's it. We deliver there every two weeks with the chickens, and here every four weeks with the fish," he said.

Prosser tried to hide his interest. "Not in the same truck?"
The driver  laughed  "We have two trucks. We are rich."

"I'm sure someone is but I'd bet it's not you."

"Yaa, of course. The workers never are."

"You speak very good English. Did they ever find that driver of yours, who disappeared two years ago?" The driver's eyes narrowed.

"Who was that?" he asked suspiciously.

"I don't know. I was here when there was some sort of bother with the police. One of your trucks was abandoned."

"Do you work here?" the man asked.

"Yes," Prosser lied. The man's face relaxed

"Yaa. That was a funny business."

"It caused some chaos. Did they ever find the driver?"

"Yaa. In the dock back home."

The trucks started to move and the driver waved at Prosser who waved back but would rather have hugged the man. He walked out of the main square and crossed the road by the Quiros' shop where he had talked to the pretty assistant. The shop was not yet open and he continued to where he had parked his car. He took off the overalls and put them in the boot then he walked back to the Quiros stall. A large man, quite a bit older than himself, seemed to be the only one serving. Prosser hovered without attracting the man's attention.

The stall was no different from the many others. A small covered area was fronted by a low slab on which the piles of various fish were laid out with ice scattered over them. There were two further bins of ice inside the covered area and a small table and chair next to them. Despite Prosser's casual interest the older man had glanced at him as he served a customer and then the glance became a stare.

"You get Vendace don't you? Prosser asked quickly.

The man  continued serving the customer.

"How much did you want?" he asked eventually

"I was told it was special. I just wanted to taste it."

"We do wholesale," the man told him.

"I didn't know you got that much of it."

The man finished serving the customer and turned to Prosser. Despite his age, he was  quite intimidating.

"We don't 'ave any," he said. "Do you want to buy anyfing else or are you just wasting my bloody time?"

"Sorry. It's just that the girl in your shop said it was special."

"And that's why we don't 'ave any." The man turned his back on Prosser and ended the conversation.

He breakfasted in a near-by café and even had time to read a newspaper. He then walked back to the car and sat in it, dozing until a uniform knocked on the window. He showed the woman his ID and she moved off. It was ten o'clock and he had liaised with his station several times before he saw DI Jarvis cross the road and enter the Quiros shop. He emerged some time afterwards carrying a plastic bag. Prosser got out of the car and waited round a corner on Jarvis' route. He timed his emergence perfectly, charging into the DI forcefully. Jarvis staggered backwards and the plastic bag fell to the ground. Prosser bent and picked it up, noting the long envelope of fish inside. He was apologising when Jarvis recognised him.

"We'll have to stop meeting like this," Prosser said and they both laughed. Prosser handed back the plastic bag and they shook hands. "What are you doing here?" Jarvis asked him.

"I was going to do a barbecue for a few friends this weekend, I thought fish would make a change," he said.

They chatted for a while about routine things, asking about various people, and then Prosser asked what he had bought. Jarvis told him it was a special fish from Estonia.

"Estonia?" Prosser said. "That has bad memories for me."

"I know. It was then I found out about it," Jarvis said. "Old man Quiros gave me some because I let them unload the truck."

"Yes, that's right. Weren't you the operations officer?"

"Well, there was no harm. Forensics didn't want a load of fish in their lab and it was worth a lot of money to the fishmonger. I didn't see any harm in it."

Prosser agreed it was a sensible thing to do. He asked if he could see the fish. Jarvis pulled the envelope with it's plastic cover half out of the bag.

"Doesn't look special to me," Prosser commented. Jarvis told him it tasted better than it looked.

"It's a hefty lump though. That pretty girl in the shop must like you. Is that Quiros crossing over to the shop?"

Prosser indicated the man who had been impatient to brush him away earlier. Jarvis said it was. "He's a grumpy old sod," Prosser said. "You'd think he'd be happier with a successful business like he's got."

Jarvis laughed. "He's a bloody millionaire," he said. "He owns the Q pie-factory too. Why d'you think I keep

131

coming back here? It's not just for the fish. That's his daughter in the shop"

"I can't blame you there. She's a good looker."

"They all are, even the eldest sister, Francine."

Jarvis waved to Quiros, giving Prosser time to connect with the name. Quiros only nodded.

"I don't think you stand much chance there," Prosser said. When Prosser returned to the station, he displayed his famous temper when things were not getting done. He stood at the doorway to the CID Room and his voice reached to the partitioned offices beyond.

"Why didn't we know that Quiros, the Billingsgate fishmonger in the Constable Report, is Tyson's father-in-law?"

His question was met with silence. Even Val Franks, who was reviewing a stabbing incident, failed to answer.

"Why didn't we know that?" Prosser tried again, this time raising his voice further. A door opened at the far end and the Chief Superintendent looked out. "Mike," he called and disappeared back into his office, fully expecting Prosser to follow him, which he didn't. Instead he walked further into the room

"Two years. Two sodding years it's taken for me to find that out. And do you know how I found out? DI Jarvis had to tell me, as though it wasn't important."

Still the news failed to get a response. The Chief Superintendent appeared again in the doorway of his office. This time he thought it wiser to address Prosser and not demand his presence.

"Who is DI Jarvis?" he asked, demonstrating that Prosser's voice had been loud enough to penetrate the glass partition. Val Franks told him who Jarvis was as she could see that her guvnor was not in a subordinate mood at that moment – if he ever was.

132

"And am I right in thinking it was Poplar's case?" the Chief Superintendent asked. "So why would we have to have that information?" he asked Prosser

"Because it should have been in the Constable Report," Prosser answered without appearing to move his lips. "And other things should have been in that report that were not."

"Come in, Mike. Explain it to me." This time Prosser followed him into his office, ignoring Val Frank's sympathetic eyes as he passed. Reluctantly, he explained to the Chief  Superintendent how he had made his discoveries and how there was no description of a van picking-up the women and of a car dropping off another in the Report. When he had finished the other man opened his arms in a helpless manner.

"What can we do? Should I take it higher up and see if we can get an internal enquiry going?"

"No," Prosser said emphatically. "We don't want any more anodyne reports. We need  competent police work."

The other officer pointed out it was not their case. "If there is a link to Quiros and Tyson someone will have to authorise an investigation and it's not likely to be us who would get the job – especially given your personal involvement," he said.

Prosser's mood became more conciliatory.

"Look, Roger," he said, using the other man's first name which he had always avoided doing. "I know what you're saying and you are probably right. But this needs detective work; quiet, stealthy investigation. If it goes public we'll get nothing. Let me handle it. It won't cost money and I don't need a team – not yet anyhow. Let me dig a bit more. I won't make any waves"

The younger office considered the implications; he knew very well how damaging to an investigation personal emotions can be and he knew how desperate Prosser and his team were to put Tyson away. But he also knew that Prosser was as good as his reputation. He was no longer wary that the older man would try to usurp him, he had found no cause to complain of Prosser's attitude.

"All right, Mike. Take what time you need. Do it quietly. Don't upset other units and keep me onboard."

Prosser's first move was to visit the Food Standards Agency and two days later he and an FSA inspector, dressed appropriately, made a surprise visit to the Q Pie factory. Like baking, pie-making is mostly a night-time process and the factory manager was less pleased than usual by an enforced inspection in the morning just as he was about to go home to a good breakfast having already been delayed because the day-manager had gone sick and he was awaiting a replacement. He was quick to mention they had been inspected six months previously. The FSA inspector explained it would just be a tour of the facilities because his colleague was new to food-processing. "And we thought your factory an excellent example of the standards we require."

The factory was a modern unit on a small industrial estate. The process was divided into five parts – Intake, Preparation. Cooking. Packing and Distribution. Intake was the separate handling of the vegetables and the frozen chicken. The vegetables went through a washing, scraping and dicing process and ended up in the large steel vats for cooking. The chickens, which were still deep frozen, were put onto a conveyor channel and went under a crusher which broke the breast bone to open them up. The giblets were then removed and thrown into stainless steel bins and put into the cold store. The chickens continued through a steam-wash, meat removal and separation process. The main pieces of meat were cut manually and were then sterilised before being transferred to the cooking vats. The carcasses and the bones were cooked separately to make gravy and when cooked, the meat and vegetables were combined and put into the pastry shells and baked.

"What happens to the giblets?" Prosser asked and was told they were kept in cold storage and then went to a pet food company. He asked if they could see the cold-stores and they were shown into the steel-lined rooms where hundreds of frozen chickens were stacked in trays ready for processing. Prosser indicated four wheeled, baskets which seemed to contain lumps of frozen packets stuck together and was told they were the giblets.

"How long do you keep them here?" he asked.

"They are picked up every Saturday by the pet food people.

"What company is that? I don't know of one around here?"

"You would have to ask Miss Quiros about that."

"Miss Quiros?" Prosser asked innocently

"Anne Quiros. She's the boss."

"It's a lot of chickens. Where do they all come from?"

"Poland," he was told. It was not the answer he expected. They thanked the manager for his time and left him to go home to his breakfast.

As soon as he got back to the office, Prosser made a call to his daughter's friend Paul Richmond who worked with the Drug Squad based at Harwich. He told him he wanted to use his contacts with the Harbour Authority to inspect their manifests. Paul didn't ask questions as he knew one didn't do that with Prosser. He said he would have a bed for him. He knew how far Prosser would want to go back in the manifests, he knew he would be starting with the day Janet took her fateful decision to get into the Estonian truck and that could take days.

Beaumont was at its best, the tall beeches were pools of shade in the midday sun. Geraniums and Busy Lizzies cascaded from the many urns along the terrace and the herbaceous borders waved their colours in the cooling breeze like bunting at a festival. The family were gathered about the lily-pond where an old gazebo offered shelter should the sun be too hot. Dave Tyson was putting Porterhouse stakes and whole lobsters onto spits above the barbecue. George Quiros was watching him, and his wife and two daughters were sitting in a group of deckchairs like macaws in their multi-coloured summer dresses, their voices equally reminiscent of the birds. The children, including Tyson's twin eight-year old daughters, were playing hide-and-seek among the shrubbery while Jason hovered with one of the permanent security staff a little distance away.

To an unknowing observer it was like a scene from a Sargent painting, a privileged class enjoying their English garden. But to Detective Superintendent Prosser or to Val Franks or any of their officers, had they been there, it was a gathering of an East End mafia, as deadly as the beauty of a sidewinder snake.

"We ad a visitor the other day," George Quiros was saying to Tyson. "That copper who's daughter got burned in that 'ouse"

Tyson paused and looked at the older man. "Prosser?"

"That's who that wanker Jarvis said it was."

He explained how Prosser had found out about the Vendace they saved for Jarvis.

Tyson laughed. "Ee finks Jarvis is bent I'll bet."

"One of our porters said ee was talking to one of the truck drivers for some time," Quiros continued. "Ee said he was

136

in overalls then, like the porters."

Tyson put down his implements and took hold of his father-in-law's arm and led him a little farther away from the women. "Which driver was ee talkin' to?" he asked.

Quiros said he didn't know, the porter hadn't noted which truck it was. "But ee 'ung around for hours. I saw 'im wiv Jarvis about ten when I went over to the shop but ee was asking me about the Vendace just before seven."

"Ee won't let go. Ee's like a fuckin' terrier," Tyson said.

"Wot d'you expect. Ow would you feel if your kid was burned alive?" Quiros asked.

It was the first time he had ever referred to the incident. Tyson looked to where his daughters were playing.

"I'd do the same to ooever did it – and to all their breed."

Quiros raised an eyebrow quizzically. "Yeah. Right."

"Are we goin' to Barbados with Anne and the family?" Francine Tyson called

"What the fuck do I want to go to Barbados for when we've got our own place in Spain?" Tyson called back.

"Watch your language," Mrs Quiros told him

"Sorry, Doris," Tyson apologised. "They don't 'ave f… flippin tornadoes an' 'urricanes in Spain," he added.

"Nor niggers," Quiros said. Tyson turned back to his father-in-law.

"Don't worry bout that copper, George. I'll do somefing about the git. I'm up to ere wiv im," and he put his hand to his throat.

"Can ee know anyfing?" Quiros asked

"Course ee can't. They would 'ave done somefing abaght us by now if they knew anyfing. Ee's a maverick. Jarvis would tell you if there was anyfing to worry abaght."

"Just don't cause any more fires," Quiros answered.

When the Tysons went to bed that night, Francine wanted to know what her husband and her father had been talking about. Tyson dismissively explained Prossers' snooping. Francine was more concerned than her husband appeared to be. She wanted to know why he was snooping.

"Because 'is bloomin daughter 'appened to die in a fire at an 'ouse I 'appened to own 'an ee won't let it go."

Francine was well aware of the incident but, like many things, she preferred not to know too many details.

"Why does that involve Dad?" she asked

"Because a truck involved was delivering to 'im. You know all this. Why go over it again," he added tetchily.

Francine tried to remember whether or not she had known that the truck involved with the incident in Billingsgate had anything to do with the fire in Stepney – for which she had given an alibi for her husband not being there She paused in the process of cleaning her nail polish and considered asking her husband further questions about it but then decided that she did not want to know.

"I don't want my family involved," she told him. You can deal with these things, they can't?"

"Don't worry," Tyson told her. "It's only bloody Prosser pokin' abaght. Ee's not a problem. In two years they've found nuffink"

"Let's retire," his wife said as though the idea had just occurred to her. "Let's go to Spain. We've got more than enough."

"Retire? Are you bleedin nuts? What would I do in Spain? Play golf and drink meself to death? This is my bleedin country, my bleedin manor and I'm not being chased away by some tight arsed weasel of a copper. I'll take care of Prosser. Ee's a man on a mission."

"Don't do anything stupid, Dave. If it hadn't been for Marcus you'd be doing a life sentence now."

"Yeah. Marcus does a good job, I'll give 'im that."

"And he's the last person you want to fall out with."

"Why would I do that. Why would I upset Marcus?"

"You already did," she reminded him

"What? The uvver night? That was just a bit of banter. Marcus don't mind that. Ee was awright abaght it."

"No he wasn't. You broke an agreement. He's an honourable man, he expects people to keep their word."

"Wot's this place worf? Five, eight mill? D'you fink I'd give 'im that much dosh for doin 'is bleedin job?"

"If that's what you agreed. What's twenty-five years worth? That's what you would have got only for Marcus." Tyson stopped undressing and flopped onto the bed. He stared at his wife. "Are you serious, Fran?" he asked

"Yes. Like I said, he's the last person you should upset."

"Wot does Marcus know?" he asked. "Ee only knows wot we tell 'im."

"He's part of the family. He knows everyone. He talks to Dad, he talks to my sisters, he knows all the clubs and the clients, he knows everything about Jason. He even knows about Andy and Marek – whatever that is. He's a bloody encyclopaedia on us."

"Yeah. You're right," Tyson agreed. "But as Marcus says 'imself, if it's not written dahn or witnessed it's not evidence."

"All I'm sayin is he's smarter than any of us. You shouldn't have upset 'im like that. We need Marcus more than he needs us."

"You really fink that 'ouse fing upset 'im then?"

"Of course I do. And what Jason did to that poor kid. Didn't you see his face when you told him?"

"No. I didn't notice that. Yeah, you could be right, girl. Ee always said ee didn't want to know if ee didn't 'ave to. I'll tell you wot, Fran, you find out 'ow ee feels. Do wot you 'ave to. Find out wot ee 'as on us."

"How would I do that?" she asked

"With them tits you can do anyfink. We're a team, Fran. Between us we can deal with any shit."

Francine's approach to Marcus was to phone him and to apologise for her husband's behaviour. She said she needed to see him because she needed his advice.

They met for dinner at her hotel. "I'm staying in town because Dave's gone to Holland and I want to visit the girl's school for prize-giving," she explained.

It was a good hotel with a good restaurant which, she knew, would always interest Marcus. She looked her best in a red dress with a low neckline which complimented her tanned skin and black hair. It was tight at the waist and showed, even seventeen years later, why she had been chosen for a Playboy centrefold. They had reached the pudding stage before she got to the point of their meeting. "I'm thinking of leaving Dave," she told him. She waited for Marcus' reaction but he chose to wait for more. "The girls are getting older," she explained. "I'm not sure they are going to want a father like Dave around when they know what he's like."

Marcus immediately saw the problem. "Dave's not the sort of person to let go of anything," he reminded her. "There is no way he would let you divorce him and there is certainly no chance he would let you take the girls."

"Why not?" she argued. "He doesn't love me. I'm just a part of his business."

"A very important part of his business – and that is why he would never let you leave. You are too valuable."

Francine looked miserable. "I know. He would never leave us alone, would he? What can I do?" she pleaded.

Marcus took a sip of Sauternes. "Kill him," he said.

Francine jumped back in her chair as though the words carried an electric charge. She stared at Marcus until a

140

slight smile played about his mouth and then she laughed, not completely reassured that he was joking.

"Sure. How would I do that?" she asked. "Little me? Stab him, shoot him, poison him? It was you who said murder was not an easy thing to get away with."

"You could throw him off a bridge," he suggested.

A shadow went across her eyes. She thought she would be in control but Marcus seemed to be dealing the cards.

"Did he really do that?" she asked, not wanting to know.

"According to his son," Marcus said cruelly.

"That's awful. That temper of his…"

"He wasn't in a temper when he instructed Jason to drown the boy. He did it by telephone, with a code that I was naïve enough to pass to Jason."

The answers and Marcus' manner were not what she expected and their effect was showing on her face, tightening her mouth and deepening the lines.

"Or you could arrange a gas explosion," he continued.

"What do you know about that?"a touch of panic in her voice. "Dave wasn't involved with that."

"I rang him that night. I needed to speak with him because one of his girls had been arrested and had given my name. She was threatening to tell the police about the sex-trafficking and to tell them where the house was. I thought Dave needed to deal with it. He told me he was busy and it would have to wait. I asked him where he was and he said in Stepney."

"He was with me at home," she insisted.

"Then he must have flown into London because he arrived at Edgware Road police station very quickly.

"What time was that?" she asked

"Midnight," he said. "He talked to the girl, persuaded the police to let her go by promising a large donation to their fund, persuaded her client to drop his charge of assault and then he and Jason took her away with them."

He let the information have its effect. Things were not going as Francine had anticipated. His attitude was not what she had expected. She knew he would be angry with her husband but she had not expected to find such deep-rooted hostility and despite the suppressed smile that accompanied the worst of his comments, it did nothing to mitigate them. They ate their puddings in silence, Francine taking only specks of the praline and whisky sorbet onto her spoon.

"So there's nothing I can do," she said eventually. "I should have married you, Marcus."

"That would have been a wiser choice. You would not now be so financially endowed but you would have been endlessly amused and appreciated."

She managed a smile. "Now it's all too late," she said. "Why do we need all this money anyway? I don't even know why those girls are in that posh school. They don't need special education or to be able to talk like you if they're rich – and we are rich."

"They are there to be civilised," he said. "That means hiding you away from their friends. Wincing every time Dave opens his mouth. Making up stories about what you do for a living and being ashamed of you at their weddings unless they marry into the East London mafia."

"I thought you would cheer me up," she complained.

"Francine, you came to me for answers, not for platitudes.

"I know, I've made my bed and now I have to stay in it."

"Not necessarily," he said.

"A gas explosion?"

"Let me ask you, Francine. How would you have felt if Dave had gone down for that boy's murder?"

Francine didn't want to, had not done so, but now she considered the question for some moments.

"I don't know," she said thoughtfully "Frightened. Uncertain. Relieved. Yes, I think I would have felt relieved." She seemed surprised by her discovery. "Free." she suddenly concluded.

"Free to be yourself," he said. "Free to take the girls away and to become what you are capable of becoming."

"And what's that?" she asked, inwardly resenting the implication that she was not the finished article.

"A nice, normal human-being."

"Would you come with me?" she asked

"I would go anywhere with you if Dave was out of our lives."

"You said there's another way," she reminded him

"I could get Dave and Jason put away for life – of course, I wouldn't, unless that's what you wanted," he added quickly.

She reached across the table and put her hand on his and for a moment the gesture recalled a vision of Dominique, causing him to smile a distant smile.

"Could you do that? Would you do that for me, Marcus?"

Marcus refocused his thoughts. The vision of Dominique disappeared and he saw Francine's older but still attractive face instead. "If that's what you wanted."

"How. How could you do that?"

He answered only with a knowing smile.

Francine played with her praline, her large eyes pleading to his, hoping he would elaborate but he left her question hanging in silence between them.

"Don't you trust me, Marcus?" she asked

"Of course I do. But can you trust yourself? Can you really leave Dave and do what you would need to do?"

"I don't know. If Dave knew about this conversation you realise what he'd do to both of us don't you?"

"I have a reasonable picture," he said.

143

She reflected for a moment. "Can we really do this?"

"We can."

"Do you want to stay with me tonight? I need to know you mean what you say, Marcus." She reached across for his hand. "I need to be sure we're together in this. We need to trust each other."

"I have a recording," he told her. "A recording that proves that Jason killed Robbie and that Dave told him to do it."

Francine let go of his hand and sat back in her seat. "You have a recording?" she gasped before recovering her composure. "Is it enough to get them put away?"

"Oh, yes." Marcus answered. "Would you like a Cognac or should we have something in your room?"

It was seven am when a taxi dropped Marcus outside his house. He stepped from it lightly, his mind and body energised by the pleasures of the night. Francine had awakened his more youthful fantasies when he had dreamt of undressing her slowly, revealing those Playboy breasts, of putting his face into her stomach and squeezing her buttocks against his crotch. It hadn't been quite like that but it had been sedately sexual. She had seemed to welcome the tenderness of his attentions, the slowness of his kiss, the gentle exploration of his hands, the willingness to hold her after the consummation of his "fine instrument." So it was a cheerful man who paid off the driver and turned towards his new life – to find Leroy Winstone blocking his way.

"Hey, Marcus. Where you bin, man?" Leroy asked as though Marcus had no right to be coming home at such an hour.

"Leroy. Dear chap. I've been having a rather pleasant time," Swift smiled at him.

"Yeah? Well you better start unpleasantin' it man, cos I

found your dog inspecting all de trees along the Old Kent Road in de early hours of de mornin'."

Leroy was right, the pleasantness vanished like a mirage. He brushed past his friend and hurried onto the path of his small front garden then stopped as he saw three black youths sitting on the  steps.

"That's Licky an Donnie an Marvin," Leroy told him. "They're guardin your pad cos it's open house to anyone." Leroy explained that when he recognised Archie, he got hold of his collar and took him home,  and then he found the front door of the house open.

"I pushed Archie inside de house and called your name, then this feller suddenly came from behind the door an rushed past me an knocked me on my arse an' by the time I'd got up he was gone."

"Mother," Marcus said and started  towards the house. "She's all right, man," Leroy told him. "I done checked 'er out. She was sleepin' like a baby."

Marcus stood and got his breath. "Leroy, good friend, dear neighbour. I am eternally grateful."

"No sweat, Marcus. You goin' to see if they took anyfing? I didn't see nuffing when that feller came rushing out."

"What was the man like?  Did you see him?"

"Ee was tall an' sort of slinky, but I didn't see 'is face."

*Jason* Marcus told himself. He thanked Leroy and his friends and insisted they take a twenty pound note and buy themselves a deserved bottle of something. When they had left he inspected the front door. There was no sign of it having been forced but the lock seemed to have been  dismantled and he could not be sure whether or not he had fastened the mortise before he'd left. He went inside and was greeted by Archie who had probably enjoyed the attention of the boys and kept them company as they waited for his return. He then went downstairs and found his mother in her dressing gown, making a pot of tea. She told him she had slept well and hadn't heard anything unusual – but as she was getting a little deaf it was unlikely anyway. He decided not to panic her by telling her of the incident.

He went upstairs. He could immediately see that many of his books had been examined and had been replaced incorrectly. He could also see that papers on his desk had been disturbed and he found the desk-drawers open. He swept his eyes quickly around both rooms and then hurried up to the next floor. His bedroom had been searched without any attempt to disguise the fact, his suits were crumpled on their hangers, their pockets creased, and his shoes were scattered from their shelves. His shirts and jumpers had been rifled and the bed mattress disturbed. Then he remembered and rushed back down the stairs to his desk. He pulled open the full-width drawer. Gone. The pocket recorder was gone. He was certain he had left it in the top drawer. He fell onto a chair and slumped forward onto the desk, holding his head.

*"Company, villainous company has been the spoil of me...But love is blind and lovers cannot see the pretty follies that themselves commit,"* he declaimed into his hands. He wanted to cry but no tears came.


Francine Tyson had risen sleepily. She had not heard Marcus depart and thought again how graceful he was for a large man – graceful of touch, graceful of movement, graceful of manners – and she found herself smiling. He had surprised her during the evening by his incisive, ungilded solutions to her posed problems and she had found in them problems she had not realised existed before. His whole demeanour had been a surprise, there was a directness and authority she had not seen before – but then she had never seen him in a courtroom – and she realised there was more steel in him than either she or her husband had been aware of. Physically too he had surprised her. She knew nothing of his social life but, over the years, he had shown no interest in the many opportunities to take advantage of the girls who worked at their clubs, yet she instinctively knew he was not gay and she had always known he was attracted to her. In the early years, if he had insisted, she might have succumbed to his charm, but he had always held back from taking their flirtations further, conscious of the difference in age she supposed. Because of this she had expected him to be a clumsy, hasty lover and had been not only surprised but seduced by his expertise. There was also a large element of excitement about their love-making. She had not been with anyone but her husband since they had married - despite his known interview techniques with the lap-dancers and hostesses of their clubs, where a test-bed was part of the office furnishing – and she had seldom been tempted by any of the clients – who had found her as attractive as any of the girls they had paid to watch. She had developed an early business ethic which she found more rewarding than any physical encounter that might have been, and there was also the fear of her husband's temper; she knew exactly how he would react to any hint of infidelity on her part. So it was with a feeling of utter freedom that she had made love with Marcus, she was like a dog let off a leash for the first time and it all added to the enjoyment of the night. She serviced her husband regularly, but his love-making was like the sexual assault of an orang-utan. Marcus had been attentive, gentle and kind, not a physical kindness, he had been robust enough, but a feeling of him wanting to please her more than himself, and that was something she had never experienced from her husband.

So her smile remained in the shower then over breakfast and she arrived at her daughter's school without the usual feelings of apprehension and inferiority.

It was a faith school in south west London and she had never quite managed to dress like the other parents despite her efforts to conform. But M & S skirts and jackets were not individually cut to enhance her breasts and curved hips.

She had selected a sober Armani jacket and skirt which was more conservative than her usual taste but emphasised rather than hid her natural qualities and only managed to make her look overdressed and overspent. After the prize-giving and during tea she answered a call from her husband.

"Where the fuck 'ave you bin?" he demanded.

She excused herself and walked out into the cloistered garden, her smile sinking deep into her body. She explained where she was, a fact he had obviously forgotten. He was conciliatory only for a moment before he rushed into an expletive-laden description of a search of Marcus' house "You sure ee said it was at 'is 'ouse?"

She assured him that Marcus had told her that he must remember to put it somewhere safe and would do so as soon as he returned home.

"Then we'll 'ave to do it anuver way," he told her.

She could not prevent herself asking, "What other way?"

"I'll 'ang 'im by 'is toes so ee can watch Jason cut 'is Mum to bits – an. I'll slit 'is dog's froat first."

Francine returned to the tea-room. She looked at the parents and the children talking excitedly around them. She saw her daughters standing alone, waiting for her with frowns on their faces and she thought of Marcus. She forced a smile but her inside felt like crying.

Marcus Swift sat at his desk for some time. His eyes took in the whole room, the furniture, the pictures, his beloved book collection and then he went into the next room. The baby-grand and all the memories of friends gathered around it, his theatre programmes, the Bukhara carpet, his favourite photograph of his father on the piano, his accreditations, Oxford degree, his scholarship award, Middle Temple membership, a school prize for the best oration in Latin and his most satisfying award; a framed certificate for the best English language epic poem from the Llangollen International Eisteddfod.

*"Let's talk of graves, of worms and epitaphs, make dust our paper and with rainy eyes write sorrow on the bosom of the earth. Let's choose executors and talk of wills."*

Archie came trundling in at the sound of his master's voice, tail wagging and tongue lolling. He licked the hand that went down to greet him.

"Dear friend, loyal comrade. Let us go and talk to Mummy."

His mother was nursing a cup of tea, watching the morning news, still in her dressing-gown.

"Mother, it's going to be a beautiful day. Why don't we go to the seaside," Marcus suggested.

"What do we want to do that for?" his mother responded

"Because it is a beautiful day. Because we haven't been to the seaside for a long time, and because Archie would love it." Archie showed his enthusiasm by barking in a surprisingly strong voice.

"There, he approves. Come on, Mother. You know you love to be driven into the countryside."

"I 'aven't 'ad any breakfast yet. And I 'ave to wash and get dressed." his mother protested.

"There's no rush. Have some toast. We'll stop for lunch

149

en route. I've got one or two letters to write and by the time you've done what you have to do, I will be ready."

Marcus finished his writing then showered and changed into a striped linen blazer and flannels. He stood in front of a mirror but saw only briefly his physical reflection before his mind took him beyond the glass to another place. His mother's voice, asking what she should wear, had the same effect as might the shattering of the glass.

"Something light and pretty," he called down to her. "And that nice straw hat. It is going to be rather hot."

"We'll 'ave to take lots of water for Archie, then – and his dinner. What time are we coming back?"

"Let's not think about that. We have all the time we need."

They headed south in his Jaguar ("Father always wanted a Jag"). His mother, soon losing familiar streets, fell back on old memories of when her husband had bought a second-hand Austin. "Are we going to Margate to 'ave some whelks?" she asked.

"No, Mother. We are going to Eastbourne."

"Isn't that where people go to die?"

"It's where people go to live a little longer."

Being a Londoner, Marcus had always thought of the seaside as somewhere where one could be vulgar without offending anyone but not a real place to live. He was once temped by a friend to consider moving to Brighton until he suggested it to his mother whose comment, "Wot would you want to go and do that for? They're all queers an spivs down there," ended the idea.

They stopped at a pub to have an early lunch and to let Archie and his mother relieve themselves.

Both of them had slept for most of the journey and were surprised by the sight of so much greensward crowding in on them. Archie sniffed the air and ancient forces moved

150

his body so that Marcus was pulled along as he explored the grass like the retriever he should have been. The dog made snuffling noises and vocalised his pleasure and rolled on the grass and Marcus knew he had made the right decision.

Later, they drove along Eastbourne's smart promenade with the windows open to the sounds of the sea and the squeals of children and seagulls and sudden bursts of music from various entertainment arcades. They parked at the western end of the front and found a quiet shelter where they sat with ice-creams and watched the sea thrusting progressively up the beach.

"The sound of evolution," Marcus remarked

"You do talk nonsense sometimes," his mother laughed.

"Nonsense is all we have.    Everything else is unimportant."

"I wish you'd get married, Marcus. What about that girl you brought home the other day.  She was pretty – and she liked Archie. What was her name?"

"Dominique Harcourt," he sighed.  "She's French."

"Well, she can't 'elp that can she? She seemed a nice lady."

"She is delectable," he told her and a smile grew on his face, the same smile he wore on the occasion that he now remembered so vividly.

"Well then," his mother interrupted. "Why don't you do something about it?"

He was surprised; his mother had never before declared an interest in his love-life. "Would you like me to be married?"

"Of course I would. It's no fun being on your own."

"You were on your own," he reminded her.

"No I wasn't. I always 'ad you."

"But I was away at university for five years and then I

was away a lot  when I did the county circuits."

"Yes. But you were always somewhere weren't you?"

"You should have had grandchildren," he said. "I'm sorry mother. You would have enjoyed having grandchildren."

"Well, don't you worry about that, we've always got Archie," she said and Archie acknowledged the compliment "Don't you want to be married, son?"

It was a question he had never seriously considered. Nor had he considered why he had not considered it. Now he realised it had never arisen because he had never been in a long relationship. He had female friends, one or two of them, like Deirdre Hodge of the Shakespeare group, he knew would have been pleased to let the friendship become something more. But with the foresight that made him a very good advocate, he knew that more would not be enough and that friendship would be lost. He thought too that he must have a weak libido as he had only ever lusted over one person and that had been Francine Quiros. The thought of Francine brought his reflections to an abrupt end. It was a wall beyond which he did not want to go.

"Mother, have you been happy?"

"I don't know about 'appy. But I'm well content."

"Even without Father?"

"It's no good worryin about wot you can't change. You've got to enjoy wot you've got. Don't you enjoy wot you've got, Son?"

"Yes I do," Marcus suddenly realised. "Yes. I enjoy it very much," and he smiled at his mother and ruffled Archie's head. "Shall we go up on the cliffs and have a fish and chip dinner?"

They drove up the winding road to the top of Beachy Head and  on to East Dean where they bought plaice and chips from one of the oldest pubs in the country.

"I got some for Archie too," Marcus announced as he returned to the car. "I'll take the batter off and mix his tablet into the fish. You must take your tablets too," he told his mother. "I'll go and get us some tea."

They sat in the car and listened to nineteen fifty's dance music on the radio

"Can't beat them big bands," his mother said and reminisced how she and his father used to go to the Lyceum in the Strand on Saturday nights and dance to the Geraldo orchestra.

Marcus suddenly realised that dancing was something he had never tried to do – but he stopped himself thinking of what else he might not have tried to do.

"Is that Archie snoring?" his mother asked.

Marcus turned and smiled at his friend who was stretched out on the rear seat. He reached back and fondled Archie's ears. The dog acknowledged the gesture with a tired movement of his tail.

"I feel a bit sleepy myself," his mother said

"Look at the sun, Mother. Isn't that the most beautiful thing you ever saw?"

The sun was then an orb of shimmering orange settling into the sea and spreading a melon coloured haze across the sky.

"It's lovely," she agreed sleepily. "The end of a perfect day."

He reached across her to recline her seat. He kissed her forehead then started the car and drove onto the narrow road that skirted the cliffs and headed towards home. There was no other car in sight. Several people were on the cliffs, walking or sitting, enjoying the last moments of a memorable day. As he swung off the road onto the grass and bumped his way across it the sun was almost directly ahead and as he accelerated towards it, people stood still or stretched out their arms as though to impede his progress.

*"O, sun, thy uprise shall I see no more,"* he cried out of the open window.

High above, seagulls, spiralled on the thermals of the evening heat, wondering if this huge bird would fly as it left the cliffs, but saw only that it dived quickly into the sea six hundred feet below.

# CHAPTER FIVE

# COGNITION

Mike Prosser drove the tedious, traffic-laden route to the port of Harwich. It was the same route that Janet had taken as her last ride in life and every bend, every junction, every mile was a countdown to where she took the typically impulsive decision to put herself in danger and it brought the last two years rushing back to him like a rewound video.

His first surprise was to see how huge the port area was, and how many vehicles there were lined up neatly in blocks. He was also quick to see there were toilet and eating facilities. So why would the Estofish truck stop at the M11 services if it had to wait to clear the port? The obvious answer was that the women in the truck were willing but illegal travellers and needed toilets which they could not use at the port and that was how Janet's presence was discovered, as Val Franks had thought, and would discredit his theory that there had been an informer. But there was still the omission of the van in the Constable Report. Was that a cock-up or something else? He was there to find the answers. He was met by Paul Richmond at the Port Authority building and explained the purpose of his visit.

"I think the Estofish truck was accompanied by another that night and if so, that would explain how they knew about Jan. They might have been in tandem watching each other's back."

He then told Paul about the regular chicken deliveries to the pie factory and the conversation he had had with the Estonian trucker. "He said they delivered every other week but the fish truck only delivers every four weeks. That would mean that every four weeks the fish and the chicken deliveries coincide."

"But the fish deliveries are from Estonia and you said the

chickens came from Poland," Paul reminded him.

"I don't have all the answers, Paul. That's why I'm here."

"Okay. So we have to find a connection between the two. We'll start with the shipping company; They will have their copies of the Shipping Notes, which will show the name of the carriers. But they won't be very pleased for us to go back that far."

They were not. The commercial invoices were filed but not put into a database and it required a lot of sifting which the two officers did, starting with the ship time and date which they knew from the schedule of Janet's truck. Paul's advice was to find from the invoices the carrier's name and see if they could get a link to the Polish supply company. When they found the invoice for the Estofish delivery the carrier was named as, 'Wiewiorka Rozwoz'.

"It doesn't look Estonian," was Paul's comment.

"No. It looks Polish to me," Prosser replied.

"let's go with that name and see if we can find it on any other shipping notes for the same day," Paul suggested.

It was another hour before they found what they wanted; a shipping order to the Q Pie factory on the same day.

"That's the connection, the haulage company is the same. Do you think the Polish is someone's name?"

"Let's find out," Paul answered and searched his laptop for a Polish/English translator. 'Wiewiorka – squirrel. Rozwoz – transport.' Squirrel Transport," he announced.

"That's clever," Prosser said. "I must get into this computer lark a bit more. Can you see what Eekhoorn Vervoer means in Dutch, that's the name of the company delivering the chickens."

Paul repeated the translation process putting the Dutch words into the dictionary. "Bingo again. Eekhoorn means squirrel and Vervoer means transport. Squirrel transport," he announced triumphantly

The two men sat back, pleased with their efforts.

"So we know the Dutch fruit and veg company and the chicken deliveries company have the same name as the Estonian fish deliveries," Prosser enthused. "let's find out if the fish and chicken deliveries coincide every four weeks." They did. "That's how they knew about our infiltration; the two trucks looked out for each other."

"And no inside informer," Paul told him pointedly. "What we need to do now is to find out when the deliveries coincide next."

"And why," Prosser added

After returning from Harwich, Mike Prosser went home briefly. He showered and changed then packed a small bag with two flasks of coffee and several wrapped food items he had bought, then he drove to the industrial site where the Q pie factory was located. He had chosen a small electrical wholesale unit across from the rear of the factory as a point of surveillance. The electrical supplier did not open on a Saturday so he was unlikely to be challenged for parking outside. He arranged the car so he could see the loading bay of the factory through his rear-view and side mirrors. It was very early on Saturday morning and he knew the factory had been supplied with a delivery of chickens the previous day. He settled down and supped his first cup of coffee. He was safe just to doze, knowing the sound of any vehicle would bring him upright. There were several false alarms as shift workers departed or arrived and it was nine am before he saw a dark transit van pull against the loading bay. A mouthful of salmon and cucumber sandwich almost choked him as he saw that one of the men who emerged from the van and jumped up onto the loading bay was "shortish and fat," the description the woman who lived opposite to the house where Janet had died had given of one of the men she saw. After some time the two men reappeared, each wheeling a bin of what he assumed to be the giblets he had seen in similar bins on his inspection. Wearing plastic gloves, they took the contents of the bins and put them into plastic crates and slid them into the van. They repeated the operation five times, two bins a day, five days a week, he calculated. When they had finished they chatted to someone supervising them from the factory and then got into the van and started the engine. Prosser dived sideways as he saw the fat man look in his direction but the van drove out into the short service road and disappeared round a corner. Prosser started the car and followed. The site was directly off a main road and he approached the junction cautiously. Being Saturday morning the road was quiet and he could see the van heading east. He followed some distance behind, keeping it in sight and he annoyed a bus driver who thought he was travelling too slowly although he was doing the regulatory thirty miles per hour. He saw the van make a turn, heading south. Now it was not so easy as they were into shorter streets with many junctions and once he panicked as he thought he had lost it. He guessed which turn it had made and was relieved to see it again and even more relieved to find a car between them. He held back as he saw the van pull into a petrol-station. They continued in an easterly direction before the van turned again off the main road and he was suddenly following it through residential streets, mostly of old apartment buildings that Victorian philanthropists had built for the poor. He had not expected to be following it in such streets, he had assumed a pet food factory would be in an industrial area like the pie factory on bus routes and with other traffic to hide behind and he became nervous as the van turned south again towards the river and he was trying to remember any likely place in that direction for a food manufacturing outlet. They had turned onto what used to be the dock road and he slowed right down as the van was held up at red traffic lights where road repairs restricted passage to a single lane, but he could not help but catch up with it. The van jumped forward as the lights changed and Prosser followed but the van stopped so suddenly that he could not avoid hitting it from behind. He saw both doors of the van open and he was quickly out of the car, holding out his arms in submission.

"I'm really sorry, chaps. All my fault," he was saying when the fat man hit him in his stomach. He collapsed forward to ease the pain and opened his mouth wide to allow the compressed air to deflate his lungs. He was about to collapse onto his knees when a second blow to the back of his neck quickened the process and his face hit the cobbled road with a crack.

He regained consciousness with difficulty and with severe pain and discomfort. His face felt swollen, pressing into his eyes and the pain stabbed his ears in waves and went up into his head. He attempted to open his eyes but he gave up as the attempt increased the agony. He tried to open his mouth to get more air into his body and he thought his lips were stuck together until he realised his mouth was taped shut.

As his brain awakened the nerve receptors to the rest of his body he was aware that he was lying on his back with his arms behind and underneath him. He tried to move his legs but his ankles refused to part. Slowly, painfully, his body reacted to the messages and recognised that his mouth, ankles and wrists were all fastened securely, probably with sticky tape. He bent his knees upwards and turned onto his side. He tried again to open his eyes and after several attempts he made them focus on his surroundings. There were no windows in the room and the daylight coming from under the door was very weak. He seemed to be in a small room and the wall now facing him was shelved to the ceiling and stacked with what looked like sardine-sized tins. He heard voices and closed his eyes again and tried to concentrate on the sounds. There were two males speaking in either Polish or Russian and they seemed to be arguing but then foreigners often seem to be arguing he thought. The voices stopped and then one of them was speaking English.

"Yes, it's me, Andy. We have a problem." Andy was obviously using a telephone. He described the event of Prosser's detention and then answered questions, "I'm at the plant. No, he was unconscious. We were outside your place, coming to see you as we arranged, then we realised he was following us. No, no one saw us. He's taped up, he's not going anywhere. Okay, Jase, we'll wait here until it gets dark. We've still got plenty to do."

Then the voice was again talking Polish, Prosser had decided there was too much swishing of vowels for Russian, and the other man sounded argumentative again. Turning onto his side had eased the excessive pain in Prosser's head and face and the relief was like a balm and he found himself losing consciousness again. When he wakened it was darker and he realised his eyes were working better and the light coming under the door was now electric and not natural. He could still hear the voices but further away. He tried to move. The pain was now a constant throbbing around his face and his back and legs were aching. He turned onto his other side and moved his legs from the knees to get the blood into them and did what he could with his arms by pressing his shoulders back and forth and moving the arms outwards. He heard the ring of a mobile and heard Andy's voice again. "Yeah, Jase. You spoken to Dave? He wants us to take him to your place? Is that safe? Sure, you know best. Okay. In about an hour then." Andy spoke in Polish to the other man and then Prosser heard their footsteps on a stone floor getting nearer. He pretended to remain unconscious. The door opened and electric light filled the room.

"Come on, wake up," a voice said and someone kicked his legs. Prosser groaned and was kicked again. He turned his head as best he could and opened his eyes.

They lifted Prosser to his feet and one of the men produced a knife. Prosser flinched away.

"Not yet," the man laughed and cut the tape from Prosser's ankles. They held him by his arms and pushed him forwards. As they turned him in the narrow room the shelves were knocked and several of the containers fell onto the floor. "Pies" Prosser read across the top of one of them as he was pushed through the doorway. 'Small pies,' he told himself.

They emerged into what was obviously an industrial unit with the only daylight coming from skylights in the roof. It was only light enough for them to walk through the unit safely without putting on any lights but he could see there was light machinery and some boiling vats similar to what he had seen at the pie factory. There was no one else in the building and as the sliding doors were opened and he was pushed out into a yard, the fat man activated an alarm system which, Prosser noted, looked more complicated than usual and he saw too that the man locked the door in three places. He found the yard was high-walled with a wire on top of it and he noted a CCTV camera covering the yard and the high, steel gate protecting the entrance.

He was frog-marched to the same van he had been

following when he was assaulted. He had already used mnomics to remember its registration, PR54; Police Radio $5 + 4 = 9$. He was pushed into the van and the doors were locked behind him. As the van started, he started counting, one and two and three... He was up to two thousand when the van vibrated over a cobbled road. He knew where they were and wondered if anyone had found his car or whether it had just been stripped and his jacket, which he had left on the seat, containing his ID had been stolen. They stopped, two thousand, three hundred and eighty seconds, divided by 60; thirty eight minutes at about twenty two miles per hour. He was still working on the sum as the doors were opened and he saw they were in a small underground car park. He recognised Jason's voice,

"Bring 'im up. Me and Marek will do it. Move the van Andy before some arsehole complains." Then he was looking at Jason.

"Prosser," the tall man said. "Fuck me."

Prosser thought he would love to but couldn't tell him. Fear showed on the other men's faces when Jason told them who he was. "A copper?" Marek said.

"Why didn't you know? Where's his coat?" Jason asked. He was told it must be in his car. "Fuck!" Jason commented. "Where's the car?"

When he was told it was just down the road at the temporary lights, Jason's impatience exploded. "Great. So now the cops will start knockin' on our fuckin' doors."

"We had to get him into the van quick before anyone saw us. We didn't have time to mess about with his car," Marek responded.

"There was no sign of the car when I passed there earlier," Jason said. "Someone must have moved it or had it away. Let's hope it's wasn't the fuckin' cops. Okay, let's get him up to the flat."

Jason and Marek dragged Prosser to a small lift as Andy went to move the van. Prosser noted the lift stopped at the third floor. Jason looked cautiously along the small, plush carpeted corridor before saying. "Okay. Let's be quick," and almost dragging Prosser along the corridor by himself. A door was ajar and they entered an apartment. Jason closed the door behind them and the Pole was about to push Prosser onto a chair.

"Not there," Jason told him. "He smells like ee shit 'imself. Take 'im into the bedroom an dump 'im on the floor. Fuckin' Prosser. You're a pain in the arse. Dave is going to love this though, ee'd already marked you. Now we don't 'ave to worry about snatchin' you."

The two men dragged Prosser along the laminate flooring into an adjoining bedroom. They dumped him on the floor against a wall and retaped his ankles together.

"What are we going to do with him?" Andy asked.

"Kill 'im," Jason said as they returned to the kitchen

"Here? Won't it make a mess."

"No mess," Jason said.

"What did Dave say?"

"He wants it done. But how much does Prosser know?"

"Nothing," the fat man said. "He was out like a light. We had to carry him into the unit. He didn't see anything."

Jason answered his mobile. "Yeah, Dave. Yeah, we've got 'im at my place." He answered questions and then, "No mess. I've got a way. No problem," and rang off. "Let's 'ave some grub. It's too early to do anyfing yet."

"Shouldn't we make him talk?" Marek asked.

"Naw. We can't make any noise in 'ere. It's a respectable pad. Don't worry, ee's not goin to talk to anyone."

Prosser knew his jaw was broken and was grateful for the tape over his mouth as it prevented him from damaging the joint any further. The pain in his head had eased and if he made no sudden movement it was tolerable. He looked around the room and appraised his situation. He wondered if he could sidle over to the far side of the double bed where a table lamp was lit next to it. If he could knock it over and break the bulb… no, they would hear him moving across the floor. He looked sideways and saw the curtains went down to the floor and guessed the window was full length – even a door. What was outside it though? Could he get up and throw himself through it? No, he would have no momentum and he wouldn't get very far with his ankles taped together and, besides, he knew he was on the third floor. But he did shuffle along the wall next to the curtain. He worked his throat and blew through his nose until he felt some sputum run down it. He turned his head and worked his nose against the curtain but had to stop as the pain returned like darts to his face. He rubbed his head against the wall, hoping some hairs would come away or that his sweat would stick to it.

He could smell cooking coming from the other room and he realised how hungry he was and, oh, what would he give for a cup of coffee? He went back to his sums. Thirty eight minutes at twenty two miles an hour? 38 x 22...eight hundred and thirty six  divided by sixty...about thirteen miles north. Tottenham perhaps?  But if they were back on the dock road, probably Wapping where he had been accosted, that would be almost directly north. But they had gone east for a while before turning south...

He was still working on the problem when the door opened and Jason returned followed by the other men. Jason walked past Prosser to the window. He opened the curtains and revealed double French doors. He opened them and stepped onto a small  balcony and Prosser heard the sound of a ships horn and he knew his last calculation had been accurate and suddenly he realised how serious his predicament was. Oh, Jesus, he thought. That's why they're waiting. He thought of Edna and Val Franks and Janet and David. He thought of Miss Hardcore and Robbie and young Danny Murphy and Marcus and Tyson. Tyson! Was the devil in control? Was paradise lost? Did it ever exist? The meek will inherit the earth. Like fuck, they just get eaten. He wondered if anyone had found his car yet. There was ID in his jacket which he had left on the passenger seat, not his Warrant Card, only his name and number, he knew not to have official ID while working undercover. Undercover? Christ! he was rubbish at that. Then he thought again of Janet and knew how guilty and foolish she must have felt when she was found. But we tried, he told himself silently. At least, we tried.

Outside on the balcony, Jason looked across the wide expanse of river towards the Isle Of Dogs. He could see the spiked towers of the millennium dome. Pleasure craft were moving on the far side of the river, lit like ballrooms, their music blasting across the water. He looked down the three floors and could see the tide was up, lapping the walls of the building. He looked up and sideways, inspecting the balconies around him. There was no sign of them being used. It was Saturday evening and all the upwardly mobile residents were out and about in the Chinese restaurants and pubs and clubs. He stepped back into the room.

"Okay," he said. "The tide's up. Let's do it."

The men pulled Prosser to his feet and dragged him to the French windows. Jason again inspected the neighbouring balconies then nodded and the two Poles pushed Prosser forward so that his chest hit the rail of the balcony. He had a brief view of the expanse of river and he cried into the tape across his mouth and struggled then Jason bent down and lifted his legs and tipped him over the rail. Jason quickly pushed the other men inside the room and he was closing the doors behind him as the splash of Prosser's body hitting the water reached up to them.

Val Franks walked into the Chief Superintendent's office. She was holding a sheet of fax paper

"Hello, Val," her chief said. "What have you got there?"

She handed him a fax. "Do you know what the DS is up to, sir? I've been trying to get hold of him?"

The CS was hesitant. "He wanted a few days off," he told her curtly and looked at the fax she handed him.

"Interpol have identified that girl who was killed with Mike's daughter,"she told him.

"Natalia Kovalova," he read. "Seventeen years old from Minsk? She was Russian. That would make more sense than Estonian, Estonia is part of the EU, Russia isn't. She must have been smuggled into the country."

"I ran the name through our data-base," Val told him. "She was arrested for demanding money with threats and for affray – on the same night that Janet and she were killed."

She explained how the girl had been taken to Edgware Road police station after a complaint from a hotel. She had asked for her solicitor, "Marcus Swift."

"That was stupid if she was illegal. What happened?"

"She was released with a caution after her American client withdrew the charge. I spoke to someone I know at Edgware, they remembered Marcus but said it was two other men who came and took the girl away."

"We need to know who they were."

"Haven't we got enough to get Marcus in for questioning under caution, sir?" Val suggested.

166

The CS stalled. "What about that Chandri business, did Forensics get anything on the money or the envelope?"

Val Franks had not realised Prosser had told him about it. "No. They said the money was too well used, " she said.

"Still, it's a serious charge we can throw at Swift. With this evidence we can say he was the last person to see the Russian girl alive," the Chief Superintendent suggested.

"That's why I wanted to run it past the DS," she said.

The CS decided to come clean and told her why Mike Prosser had not been around. "If the Russian girl was not one of the women in the truck there would certainly appear to be more questions to answer about that night – as Mike has always believed."

"What should I do? I've been ringing his phone but it's not switched on. Should we get Marcus in?" Val asked.

"Not yet. Let's give Mike a bit more time. He'll be in touch."

Jason had been right about Prosser's car. It was soon discovered by an irate motorist who honked at it when it didn't move after the lights had changed to green and it was only after the motorist had reversed and squeezed past it by going onto the pavement and shouted abuse as he passed that he saw the stationary car was unoccupied and the front was damaged and from an angry young man he changed into a concerned citizen and stopped and walked back to Prosser's vehicle. He saw the jacket on the passenger seat and the mobile phone next to it and called the local police.

At home, Val Franks was about to settle in front of the television with a Chinese take-away and a glass of Chardonnay when her mobile rang and she saw with annoyance that the call was from her Chief

Superintendent. He told her how Prosser's car had been found. Yes, they had checked the Ambulance Service and the hospitals but no unidentified patients had been admitted. "I thought you would want to know," the CS told her.

Want to know? Of course she bloody well wanted to know. She had been well pissed-off that Prosser had been conducting an investigation by himself and had not trusted her to know what he'd been doing. But underneath her anger there had always lurked the fear that his obsessive nature would get him into trouble again. And now it had.

She tried to eat but soon pushed the food away. She got her coat and drove to the office. She made straight for Prosser's desk and studied his note-pad. She started to ring the recent numbers written on it in his flowing, rounded hand. She reached the Department of Environmental Health and the Pet Food Manufacturers Association and the Harwich Port Authority but only got answering machines then she rang another number and Paul Richmond answered. She had met him at Janet's funeral and remembered him because he was attractive. He was at first evasive to her questions after he had recognised who she was but then she told him about Prosser's car being found and nobody knew what he was up to.

"Oh, Christ!" His reaction did nothing to alleviate the churning in her stomach. "Okay, Val. I'm coming to London. I'll be with you in a couple of hours."

It was less than that when he walked into the office looking even more attractive in jeans and a leather jacket and a two-day growth of stubble. He sat down with the coffee she handed him and she was annoyed at herself for wondering if he was married. He told her about Mike's visit and about the connections between the fish and chicken deliveries to the two Quiros outlets and of the Polish connection of the trucking company to the Dutch company associated with Tyson. He told her of Mike's inspection of the pie factory and how he had been unable to find a pet food manufacturer in London. "That's what he was working on. He was looking for the factory."

Val Franks was hurt and angry in contrasting waves of emotion as she listened to the Drug Squad officer. Why hadn't Mike trusted her? Then she remembered her reaction to his obsession with the Constable Report and the anger and hurt were replaced by guilt. "Right,"she said and stood up decisively. "We'll start with that pie factory and find out where this pet food place is."

"That's not a good idea, Val," Paul Richmond told her and explained the enormous significance of Mike's suspicions should he be right. "He won't thank us for barging in before the two deliveries coincide again next week. If we show our hand now it won't happen and Mike's efforts will be for nothing."

They argued Val's concern for her boss' safety against a possible major drugs bust. She wanted to arrest Tyson and the whole Quiros family and when he asked what good that would do she realised she was acting emotionally and her frustration suddenly brought tears to her eyes.

Paul got up and drew her into him.

"We'll find another way. Trust Mike, he's the best."

The Chief Superintendent surprised them by arriving, still in his weekend clothes, and Val Franks was impressed by his hands-on concern. Paul repeated all he had told Val and the CS agreed they should not do anything yet to jeopardise Mike's investigation. He had already put Scotland Yard on stand-by should they need any legal warrants signed quickly and he had authorised two more detectives to be brought in to help with the house-to-house enquiries that the local force had already started near to where Mike's car had been found. He had also called in a non-uniformed staff member to extract from the electoral roles the names of all residents in that area to see if there might be a clue as to what Mike was doing there. They agreed the most likely scenario was that Mike had been shadowing a vehicle and had been spotted but they had to cover all possibilities.

"If he's been snatched they must have thought he had found something serious," Val Franks said. "His life could be in danger. If it's about drugs we know they won't think twice about killing him."

Paul Richmond told her that if that was the case he was already dead, his experiences failing his diplomacy. "But," he added quickly when he saw Val's face, "If Mike was still following someone that means he hadn't found anything, so they might just want to know what he knows. We need to know where he might be taken to make him talk."

"We can shake a few trees," the CS said. "We can bring in all of Tyson's known associates, including the Quiros lot and Tyson himself."

"They'll all be at the Ladybird on a Saturday evening," Val Franks said.

"Then that's where we'll start," the CS told her.


Mike Prosser's ejection from the balcony was in a head-first position but the muscular thrust by Jason to his ankles kept his legs going outwards so that by the time he reached the water he was almost in a vertical position and his entrance might have been worth two points in a diving contest. His instantaneous assessment of his chances of surviving an inevitable death by drowning improved slightly as his feet quickly hit the bottom of the river and he realised the tide was still running in and his automatic thrust against the bed soon brought him to the surface. It is said that something learned is something gained and Prosser had learned a great deal about water during his years of holidaying in Cornwall. Both his children had become expert surfers and that had been a factor in his son, James' decision to accept work in Australia, but although their father had never quite mastered the art of riding a surf-board, he had become an excellent swimmer and as soon as he had thrust off the bottom he instinctively felt the direction of the current. He knew that it is easier to swim with a tide than against it and as he came up he was already inclining backwards so that when he surfaced he was almost horizontal on his back. He straightened his legs and kept his head still and was soon floating upstream like the many pieces of flotsam around him. It wasn't easy, he could not use his arms to keep him balanced and he knew that if he was turned face-down he would not survive. His head was the critical factor, any sudden movement of that would unbalance him, but he needed no encouragement to keep it still as any movement of the neck stabbed it painfully even though the water had numbed the pain a little. He was able to turn his shoulders which gave him just enough sideways movement to negate the ebb and flow of the water and to maintain his balance.

He remained near to the building from where he was ejected and he could see the many lights and balconies of the apartments and thought hopefully that surely someone must see him? Or if they did, would he not look just like a lump of timber or an island of plastic that were common on an incoming tide? Gradually the buildings seemed to slip past him and then there was nothing but the blue-red sky. He began to notice the cold and had the urge to strike out to get the blood circulating through his body and he knew it was going to get increasingly difficult to maintain his position and the first impulse to panic threatened to destroy him. He swivelled his eyeballs sideways as far as they would go without moving his head and saw the spreading tide was keeping him near to its limitations and he was surprised to see a wall looming towards him. He knew that any collision would unbalance him and he bent his knees carefully and tried a dolphin kick, dropping his right shoulder like a rudder to steer him away from the side and he was encouraged by the effect. He tried several more kicks and remembered when his children had first taught him to use the painful motion to improve his butterfly stroke.

The wall soon became another building, another warehouse converted to luxury flats where once stevedores, draymen, rope and tallow makers and myriad other trades had earned their livings and lived in squalid houses which had long since gone. Surely someone would be on one of the balconies on this mild, late August night, guzzling their lagers or sipping their Shiraz? But nobody called. No voices spread over the conduit of space. Only the distant sounds of the occasional pleasure boat on the far side of the river punctuated the sinister stillness of his world and another block of hope seemed to pass beyond his view. His body was now numb from the cold. He tried another kick and found his legs reluctant to obey the signals from his brain and the extensor muscle behind his knees tightened and he knew that his body was closing down and soon he would be a floating corpse.

The buildings had once again given way to a wall and he wondered how far he had drifted upstream. He remembered there was a pier at the western end of

Wapping High Street which the river police used and their boat-house was next to it. Could he last that long and if he hit the timbers of the pier what could he do with his hands fastened behind his back? He knew the police did not operate from it at night. He was slowing down, the wall seemed to be stationary, was the tide on it's ebb? Then there was a gap in the wall and before he could register the fear that it might be one of the many little rivers flowing into the Thames, he had hit something with his left shoulder which swung him round away from the wall. Then he felt it again, painfully on his head. He thrust down with his hands as far as he could and felt something solid which he pushed against which brought his legs down into the water and he thought he was gone as his head went below the surface. He felt something at his feet and he kicked against it although he had no feeling in his legs to tell him he had succeeded but his head came up out of the water and he realised that his feet were still in contact with something solid and he pushed again and his hands too touched something and then he realised he had hit a set of steps set in line with the wall. He felt with his hands and his feet and tried to work his way upwards, then his feet shot off the slimy step and he was under water again. Again he tried and again he failed and he suddenly wanted the torment to end. Then he heard a voice, Janet's voice, clearly vibrating across the water, "Come on, Dad. You can do it." He felt again for the steps and graduated his hands and feet, being careful not to thrust. He worked his way upwards with the restricted dexterity of a crab until only his feet were in the water and then he lay back and lost consciousness.

The Ladybird club had once been a cinema and before that, a Victorian theatre. It had been closed for many years when Tyson bought it hoping to be able to sell it on to a developer to build a block of flats. But the council had put a Preservation Order on the façade and the internal decorations and he found himself with a useless building that was about to bankrupt him. Then someone asked if they could hold a rave in it and paid him for doing so and he realised the building had some sort of potential. He cleared the ground floor of the old seats and got a temporary alcohol licence and hired a small local band to perform on the stage and filled the place two weekends running. Then he tarted it up and opened a bar and ran it as a regular disco-club. But it was his wife, Francine who saw the real potential of the building. After her centrefold success she had worked in the Playboy clubs in the States and had seen how sex and entertainment never failed to make money if they were combined with style. She met Tyson when he approached her father to put money into his disco-club. Quiros was known locally to have invested his money in property and one or two pubs and he had known Tyson since he was a young tearaway with a penchant for violence and he did not want to get involved with him even though he admitted the younger man had a nose for business and he could see that music and booze was a winning combination. But when Francine saw the inside of the theatre she looked beyond its peeling stucco façade. She saw the ornate plaster work of the ceiling, the great chandeliers which still hung from it, the boxes and the upper galleries and she saw how it could be if it was all regilded and carpeted and the chandeliers sparkled again and she persuaded her father that it would be a safe investment even if they just renovated the ground floor with its stage and built an American long bar.

So her doting father did as she asked and the project was

soon making big profits and Francine then gave her attention to the upper floors.

The ground floor was still the popular venue for dancing and drinking but Francine separated the old foyer into two entrances, one for the dancing and the other for a members-only club and casino. The latter was approached up a red carpeted stairway to the dress-circle which had been walled in sound-proof glass to keep out the music from below and the floor levelled and extended. It was furnished with gaming tables and plush settees and topless waitresses served drinks to the many Arab businessmen and embassy staff and wealthy young Chinese who slipped the bonds of home and sipped expensive champagne and gambled their parent's money.

The old circle became a dining club where food was prepared by a top chef and served with expensive wines, and cabaret stars entertained the members. The whole was a testament to Francine Tyson's taste and ambition and she supervised it with the attention of a broody hen. She had named the venue The Ladybird after the American President's wife of that nick-name because she had met her as part of a Playboy contingent supporting an Aids charity to which the First Lady had given her support and Francine had been greatly impressed by her, the more so because she had been singled out for a long conversation because she was English.

When the two van-loads of police officers arrived it was midnight and the club was in full swing. A Scotland Yard commander had brought the warrant himself and was in charge of the operation. There were several armed CID officers including Val Franks and two units of uniformed officers. Val Franks knew the layout of the place as she had been with the team who had gone there to arrest Tyson after the explosion that had killed Janet Prosser and the other girl and it had been discovered that Tyson owned the house. She had briefed her superior officers on the layout and uniformed officers were strategically spread to cover the entrances and the rear where a carpark was controlled by a lifting barrier and supervised by a gateman. Paul Richmond had chosen that route.

As the senior officers led the way up the red carpeted stairs they first encountered Jason and another security man sitting on them. The commissioner waved the warrant at them and the party swept quickly upwards with Jason backtracking ahead of them and talking into a radio microphone clipped onto his shirt. They were met by Francine Tyson at the doors to the casino. "Do you realise what this will do to my business?" she asked the Commander who led the contingent of officers. He told her they were not there to interfere with her business but they had a search warrant and would exercise it.

"What are you looking for?" she demanded but received no answer and had to concede as the police party pressed forward.

Inside the casino, Francine Tyson ran up a short staircase into what had been the old projection room and now served as an office and a useful observation point for the gaming tables. An officer quickly followed her but inside she only grabbed a microphone and made an announcement to the effect that there was to be a routine police inspection of the premises and to carry on enjoying their evening. The police party quickly realised there was no hiding place in the casino area and continued their journey upwards to the circle restaurant. The diners showed signs of panic at the sudden intrusion of police officers, despite Francine's attempts to reassure them.

At the far end of the room Tyson rose aggressively from a large round table where George and Doris Quiros, their

176

daughter Anne and the two Polish men, Andy and Marek who had earlier taken Prosser captive, were seated.

"You've no bloody right," Tyson shouted and started to get to his feet but was told by the Commander they had every right and waved the search warrant in Tyson's face.

"Where does that door go to?" the Commander asked and pointed to a door behind Tyson's table.

He was told it led to an office and to the kitchens and store-rooms and was also a fire-escape. The Commander detailed four uniformed officers to search the area and then addressed everyone at Tyson's table.

"We need each of you to identify yourselves to these officers with proof of your residence and precise details of your movements since this morning. Anyone failing to do so or giving false information may be arrested and charged."

"What the fuck is this all about?" Tyson demanded and was told a police officer had been abducted and they had reason to believe he might be on these premises.

"We got rid of all the rats from 'ere years ago," Tyson responded. "Go ahead, be my guest, waste yer bloody time."

The office behind the restaurant was large and the top table guests were ushered one-by-one into it and questioned by the detectives. Francine Tyson told her husband she would ring Marcus but he told not to bovver as ee'd done a runner. "What do you mean. How do you know?" she demanded fearfully.

"Ee's bloody gone. 'im an 'is old-lady an that fuckin dog. They've disappeared. Ee's done a runner. The ungrateful sod."

His wife stared at him so hard there was no need to vocalise the accusations that were forming in her head. Tyson avoided her and raised his glass towards the

Commander and the Chief Superintendent.

"Cheers, constables," he said. "Do wot you 'ave to an then get off me premises so I can fumigate them."

Outside, Paul Richmond with three officers had entered the car park and explained to the gateman sitting in his little box the purpose of their interruption. One of the officers was left with the man so he was unable to use the telephone in the box as Paul Richmond and the other policemen picked their way between the Maseratis and Ferraris and Bentleys to the far end where a utility block protruded from the main building and was the bottom of the area Francine Tyson had just described as housing the kitchens, store-rooms and fire-escapes. Richmond stopped short of the building as he saw, in the dark corner beyond it, overhung by trees, another vehicle, totally different from those behind him. He walked to the dark-coloured van and examined it, one of the rear light-clusters was broken and the bumper collapsed inwards. He tried the rear doors and found them unlocked. He shone his penlight around the inside of the van which appeared to be empty and then he concentrated on a dark patch on the floor. He put his face to the patch and sniffed.

"Not oil," he told one of the officers. "Could be blood."

He walked back to the gate box. "Who owns that van?" he asked the attendant and was told it was Andy's "Who is Andy?"

"Andrzej Dudek. The Pole." Richmond's interest quickened.

"Where is he now?" He was told he was inside the club "With Marek. Marek Majewski, Anne Quiros' husband."

Further questioning found that the van had arrived just as the gateman came on duty at eight pm and that Jason was following the van in his car.

Paul Richmond walked away from the box and phoned Val Franks' mobile. He told her about the van and the two men.

"They're here. They've just been questioned," she told him. She closed her mobile and whispered to the two senior officers, telling them of Paul Richmond's discovery.

The two Poles and Anne Quiros, having given their details, were again seated at the table. The Chief Superintendent had been handed a notebook with the results of the questioning He now read from it. "Andrzej Dudek, Marek Majewski?"

The two men looked at him. "I am arresting you on suspicion of the abduction of a police officer," he told them and motioned to two uniformed officers who stepped forward and began to pull the men off their seats as the CS continued to read them their rights. As the officers began to handcuff them, Anne Quiros jumped to her feet and started pulling at the police officer trying to put the handcuffs on her husband.

Val Franks pulled her away as Doris Quiros and George Quiros returned from the interview room. Doris Quiros hit Val Franks with her handbag and was aiming another blow at her head when the CS grabbed her arm and pushed her roughly onto a chair, then George Quiros pushed the CS with so much force that he fell across the table, scattering dishes and glasses onto the floor. Dave Tyson sat away from the table watching the mayhem with a grim expression on his face but even he knew not to get involved. Francine Tyson looked on with more concern and Jason hovered, waiting for Tyson to tell him what to do. Order was restored when two other officers intervened and George and Doris Quiros and Anne Quiros were also unceremoniously handcuffed.

"Take them away," the Commander told the officers.

"We need Marcus," Francine Tyson suddenly screamed at her husband. " What have you done with him?"

"I told yer Fran, we aint done nuffink wiv 'im. Wot's that uvver geezer's name, you know, that friend of Marcus'. The solicitor bloke. Grimes or Grumble, somefing like that?"

"Grimshaw," his wife said.

"Yeah, right. Find 'is number an give 'im a call."

In the car park, Paul Richmond had put the uniformed officers to guard the van. He then phoned in the registration and asked it to be ID'd with the DVLA data-base. While he was waiting Val Franks appeared and told him of the arrests, then the senior officers joined them and gave permission for the attendant to allow customers to remove their cars and they watched the steady exodus of clients and waited for a low-loader to remove the van for forensic examination. The two Polish men and the Quiros family were bundled into the police vans.

"Why take them to the station?" one of the detectives asked. "Give us ten minutes in the van with them, sir and we'll soon find out what they've done with the guvnor."

Both the senior officers silently sympathised and felt the urgency too and the Chief Superintendent even ignored the reference to Prosser as "the guvnor."

Paul Richmond answered his phone and started to scribble in his notebook."We've got a registered owner for the van," he told them. "Smakosz Pies, an address in Tottenham."

"Pies?" the CS said. "Another pie factory? Right. Let's get a team there, that's maybe where Mike's being held."

Before they could move, the Commander answered his mobile. They all watched and waited as the concern grew on his face. He closed the phone. "They've found him," he announced. But the look on his face failed to cause any jubilation. "He was in the river," he told them grimly.

"Is he..." Val Franks couldn't finish the question

"They're not sure. The medics couldn't revive him, but they said there is a pulse. He's been taken to the East London Hospital."

"The bastards," one of the detectives said and kicked an Audi.

"Look, they didn't say he was dead," the Commander said. "If he survives he will be a target so this news must not go beyond us. We still haven't found him. Understood?"

They all agreed

"What about this pie factory?" Paul wanted to know.

"Well, it's not urgent now," the Commander told him.

"I think I should check it out, if that's okay with you, sir?"

"It can't do any harm. Take another officer with you."

Paul Richmond turned to Val Franks.

"I want to go to the hospital," she told him

"I'll do that, Val," her CS said. "You go with Paul. I'll let you know as soon as I've got any news."

Paul Richmond put a hand comfortingly on Val Frank's back and gently moved her towards the street where she had left her car.

"I found this in the glove-compartment of the van," he told her as they walked, hoping to take her mind off Mike Prosser. "It's a petrol receipt from a garage and it was paid with a credit-card at 10.30 yesterday morning. It will prove who was driving the van at that time, so they can't say it was stolen or anything."

Val Franks found it difficult to be enthusiastic and she drove in silence to north London. The address was hard to find. It was a long U shaped street with industrial units backing onto a railway embankment at the bottom of the U and an island of small estate houses in the centre with a surrounding wall so they were only accessed from one end.

It was the perfect situation for a clandestine operation, not overlooked and each unit detached with their own entrance and their loading yards divided by a high wall. The unit they wanted was situated at one end of the U backed by the railway embankment. They pulled up short of the entrance and Paul Richmond walked forward, careful to keep close to the wall. Like Prosser had done previously, he soon took in the CCTV cameras on a corner column covering both the steel gate of the entrance, the yard and the doors of the unit. He peered through the steel slats of the gate and saw the industrial building had no windows, only skylights on the low-angled roof. He returned to the car and they drove back to the beginning of the street.

"I can't chance the front," he told Val Franks. "It will be alarmed and there are no windows." He started to rummage in the boot of the car.

"What are you looking for?" she asked. He explained that the only way of getting into the factory was via the roof.

"There's a tow-rope there that's never been used," she said.

He found it still in a plastic bag then he took out the wheel-nut spanner and tucked it inside his leather bomber-jacket.

"Okay. Let's go," he said and led the way through a wire fence where the street turned away from the units and protected a disused gorse-covered plot leading up to the railway embankment. They picked their way carefully through the bushes and climbed to the top of the embankment where the walking was easier. They could then see all the units were built hard against a ten-foot-high retaining wall and the guttering of the sloping roofs was only a further five feet above the top of the wall. They walked to the end unit and then descended the embankment to the wall.

"Feeling strong?" Paul asked.

He explained how he wanted her to brace her back against the wall and cup her hands in front of her. With a hop he had one foot in her hands and she pushed upwards so that he was able to grip the top of the wall and then pull himself up and swing sideways until he got one foot and then a knee on the top of the wall. He balanced himself in a crouched position before jumping to grab hold of the guttering and scrambling onto the roof. It was too dark to see into the unit and he only had his penlight torch but he was able to see the skylights were not opening ones which made his next task easier as they would not be fastened by any internal mechanism. He took out a military-style knife contraption and selected a spiked blade. He judged the point where the bottom of the moulded plastic windows sat into the heavy-duty PVC frame and began to knock the spike into it using the wheel spanner. He hoped none of the units employed night security staff as the noise echoed from the corrugated roof alarmingly. When he had made a hole through to underneath the bottom of the window he then worked on it with a knife blade until he had gouged a hole big enough to insert the end of the wheel spanner. He then put all his weight onto the spanner until he heard the window part from the frame with a loud crack. It was then easy for him to force the rest of the window from the frame.

There was enough night light for him to see the roof construction was of A frames set on horizontal steel joists which were approximately eight feet from the bottom of the skylight opening. He unwound the tow-rope and fastened it around the bottom frame of the skylight and threw the end into the building. He twisted a wrist around the rope and, holding onto the frame with his other hand, lowered himself inside then grabbed the rope with his free hand and lowered himself onto the steel joist. He walked along the four-inch joist to the wall and dropped the twelve feet onto the ground. He worked his way inside the building, using the penlight and as his eyes adjusted to the night light filtering through the many skylights, he could see the factory seemed only to be used at one end. He could make out the cooking vats and a long, steel-covered table. He saw boxes of small foil containers with lids packed separately and unused. He then found two doors at the far end of the building and had soon picked one of the locks with a selection of small needles he carried in a wallet. He found a light switch and as soon as the room was lit he recognised the glass heat-jars, the evaporation tubes and steel trays and burners of a drugs laboratory. He examined the storage jars of powders and chemicals and his fatigue disappeared in a rush of adrenalin.

He locked the door and opened another to an adjoining room which was the room where Prosser had been held many hours before. He switched on the light and was confronted with the shelves of sealed foil containers and as he picked one from the shelf and read the word 'Pies' emblazoned across the lid he had a similar feeling of puzzlement as Prosser had experienced earlier. He then saw a smaller word above it, "Smakosz." He picked the tab and peeled back the foil lid and flinched away at the smell that rose to meet his nose. He took out his knife and scraped away what looked like a meat and jelly mixture and found a small plastic sachet beneath it. He smiled but really wanted to jump around and scream. He put the container into his handkerchief and zipped it into a pocket. He closed the door and retraced his steps to where he had made his entrance.

The roof construction was supported by vertical T members and it was no problem for him to grip them and to shuffle his way up to the joists. He replaced the skylight and hoped the damage would not be noticed from below and that it would not rain before they could impound the building. He ran up the embankment and hugged a patient Val Franks and told her of his discovery.

"Mike was right," he said.

"He usually is," she replied as they picked their way to the car.

As soon as they entered the police station she asked the important question of the Chief Superintendent. "How is he?"

"They're operating," he told them.

"So he's alive?" Val said and leant against a wall.

"Only just. His jaw was broken and he has a complicated fracture of the skull and they think a nerve is torn and needs repair and he was seriously hypothermic. But he's alive and they think they can repair him but they don't know if there is any organ damage. He will have a body scan as soon as he's stable." Val Franks went quickly into her office.

"Best leave her," the CS told Paul Richmond as he started to follow. "What about you, Paul. What did you find?"

Paul Richmond took the foil container from his pocket and unwrapped it. He folded back the lid and repeated his previous act of scraping away the filling to reveal the plastic sachet beneath as though it were a precious jewel.

"Heroin?" the Chief Superintendent asked excitedly.

185

"Yes. Probably with additives. There are hundreds of these tins. It's a massive operation. We're talking millions."

He told the senior officer how he had entered the factory and hoped his visit would not be noticed. "We need to get everyone connected to this," he emphasised. "We need to know how they distribute the drugs, who their customers are, who their supplier is. We need the Drug Squad involved, sir, and possibly SOCA too," he said, using the acronym of the Serious Organised Crime Agency.

"I think you're right, Paul. What do you think we should do first?" the Chief Superintendent asked.

"We need to put the factory under surveillance. From the railway embankment you can see the main gate through the gap between  the units. From there we could film anyone visiting and any vehicles entering or leaving the yard."

"I suspect there won't be much action for a while as we seem to have the main antagonists in custody, but I take your point. I'll have a word with the Commander. We'll need to talk to a few more people to decide how we handle it. Well done Paul. Mike will be bloody pleased, it almost makes his suffering worth while. Get some sleep – and take Val with you. We won't be interrogating anyone until Monday and then I hope we'll be charging them."

Paul Richmond found Val Franks  at her desk.  He put a coffee in front of her and told her what the CS had decided.

"Come on, Val, let's go to your place and get a few hours sleep. There's nothing more we can do here." But she wanted to go to the hospital. "Okay," he agreed. "Let's do that first."

The CS had already arranged for armed officers to guard the Intensive Care ward and the detective's ID's were closely inspected. A surgeon explained what they'd done. "He's in an intensive care bed now and we'll see if he improves in the next few hours," he told them. Val asked if they could see him. "Only to look at."

They looked through a window into the ward but all they could see was a contraption holding Mike Prosser's head in position and another on his jaw and a jigsaw of tubes and wires around him. His face and head were bandaged under the metal frames and only his eyes could be seen, deeply closed and surrounded by yellow and purple bruising.

"Try again in twenty four hours," the surgeon told them.

They drove to Val's flat. She made coffee and put a generous tot of whisky in the mugs. They sat on opposite settees, their fatigue keeping the silence between them and they were soon asleep.


At the Ladybird club, the customers had begun to leave as soon as the police had entered the casino – despite Francine Tyson's assurances – and the exodus had increased in momentum after the arrests and the mayhem in the restaurant. Dave Tyson had sat for some time at the round table after the restaurant had emptied but then he suddenly stood and lifted the table and heaved it across the floor then stamped on it until it split across its length.

"Fuck you, Marcus," he screamed. "You disloyal bastard."

Francine Tyson knew that such moods were best ignored but her resentment smouldered and a sense of injustice and guilt made her yell back at him.

"How can you say that? He would be here now if you hadn't cheated him and sent Jason to rob him."

"That's bollocks," he told her.

"Then why has he disappeared?"

"Because ee finks I'll cut 'im up for wot ee told you."

The words articulated the fears she had suppressed in her own mind. She knew he was right and the stress of knowing and not knowing and the arrest of her family were too much for her mind to deal with and she was near to tears.

"He's out there with this evidence which he will probably send to the police," she said.

"Wot fuckin evidence?" her husband scoffed.

"For one thing, that you were in Stepney on the night those girls were burned alive," she almost screamed at him.

The effect was immediate. "Marcus told you that?" he said.

"Yes. And if you've forgotten that, what else have you forgotten?" she demanded. But her husband's brain was already wondering the same thing.

"I'll 'ave to find 'im an do somefing abaght that," he said. "My family's been arrested. We have to do something about that first. Why Andy and Marek? What's this got to do with them?"

"Don't worry abaght them. They'll keep their moufs shut."

"What about. What have they done?"Francine demanded, "Did you get hold of that Grimshaw geezer?"

Francine's face showed her frustration with his continued reluctance to tell her what the raid was really about.

"No. There was no reply. I left a message. He was probably asleep as it was one thirty in the morning. Why have they arrested Andy and Marek?" she persisted but before her husband could reply the doors at the far end of the room opened and the car park attendant stood there, holding a set of keys towards them.

"Wot the fuck do you want?" Tyson shouted at him.

The man explained that everyone had gone and the police had taken the van away.

"Wot van?" Tyson and his wife asked in unison

"Andy's van," the man replied and told them how the police had found the damage to it and asked what time it had been put there.

Tyson sat down heavily. "They brought the van 'ere," he said disbelievingly. "How fuckin stupid is that?"

"Can I go now." the attendant asked and Francine nodded permission. When he'd gone she turned on her husband. "What about the van?" she asked threatening to lose control completely. He told her how the two Poles had abducted Prosser.

"And what did they do with him?" she demanded.

"You don't want to know, Fran," he answered

"Of course I want to know," she yelled at him

"Fuck me, Fran. Why d'you want to know the details. They dealt with it. Awright?"

"No, it's not all right. They have been arrested. They were singled out. That means the police have some evidence against them. So it's not bloody all right, Dave."

"Look, Andy and Marek know wot to do. They know they just have to keep shtum. If the cops knew anyfing they would 'ave arrested Jason too," and he nodded at Jason who had entered the restaurant and was now standing beside Francine Tyson. "Ee was wiv Andy and Marek an no one's arrested 'im. Right Jase?"

"Yeah, boss."

"The van was damaged. So it 'ad an accident. So wot?"

"So what?."

Francine threw up her arms. "I've had enough. I'm going home," she announced. "Are you coming?"

"No. I'll stay 'ere an sort fings out," Tyson answered.

"Suit yourself," she said and walked away.

Tyson gestured for Jason to sit. "You wanna drink?"

He poured two brandies. "There's no problem is there Jase? You did take care of that copper proper like?"

"He'll be fish food by now, boss."

"Good. Good. Then there's no problem, right?"

"Right, boss."

# CHAPTER SIX

# GETTING BACK

Val Franks opened one eye and for a moment had no recollection of where she was. Something had wakened her, a laugh, a man's laugh. That's ridiculous she thought. Then she remembered and sat up from her cramped position on the settee too soon. "Ahh!" she cried as her neck cracked and she remembered how Dominique had dealt with it and quickly moved the image from her mind. She could smell coffee. She got up and went into the kitchen. Paul Richmond was sitting at the table playing with a laptop. He smiled at her. He was not wearing a shirt and she was surprised at the amount of tattoos on his body.

"Morning," she said. "Were you laughing?"

"I was," he told her as she poured herself coffee from a percolator he had filled and freshly made. "Do you know what Pies means in Polish?"

"Sandcastles?" she suggested

"Dogs," he told her. "And Smakosz means Gourmet. Gourmet Dogs. That's cool eh?" She wanted to know why. "That's why Mike couldn't find a pet food factory in that part of London. And why the company is not registered with the Association. They will only be known to Poles."

Her brain began to catch up "How?" she asked.

"That's a good question. I've been online and put in Smakosz Pies and got a few hits in Polish. We need a Polish speaker."

"Justine is Polish – or at least, her parents are." she told him.

"Who is Justine?" he asked and was told she was a WPC.

"She's good, very bright."

"Then we'll use her," he said. "Do you want to ring the hospital?" Val Franks remembered and the tension returned to her face.

"It's no use, they won't tell me anything over the phone. Can we call in on the way to the Station? They might let us see him."

He smiled at her, a very appealing smile, she thought.

"I'm your guest, Val. We do what you want."

"Do you need to borrow a shirt?" she asked.

"I always carry a spare with me," he told her. "I never know when I'm not going to get home," but he didn't ask her how she would have a man's shirt.

"My ex" she said. "He didn't dare come back for them. If they fit you, be my guest. What does your wife think about you not getting home?" she added as innocently as she could

"No wife. Had one, sort of, when I was in the army. Didn't last long. She shagged my best mate."

At the hospital they looked through the window of the Intensive Care ward again. He looked no different. He did not seem to have moved or opened his eyes but the nurse told them his pulse was stronger and his heart-rate was stable. Val took a call from the Chief Superintendent, calling them both into a meeting at Scotland Yard.

It was the first visit to the Yard for both of them. They were escorted to a fifth floor suite where the Commander, who had supervised the raid on The Ladybird, was chairing a meeting of several officers that Val Franks didn't know apart from her own CS, but Paul recognised two of them, a Chief Superintendent Myer of the Drug Squad and another Drug Squad officer, a DI he had worked with once before. Myer congratulated him on his discoveries but was told it was all down to the persistence

192

of Detective Superintendent Prosser.

Myer wanted to know about the connections with the trucking companies and the Dutch company. Paul told him he had contacted a Dutch Customs officer he liaised with regularly and had requested more details about the Dutch company, its directors and their contacts with other companies. He also told Myer that his Super in Essex was liaising through the Polish consulate for the Polish chicken farms supplying the Q Pie factory to be investigated.

"Yes, I've talked to Barney," Myer said. "We go back a long way. He's happy for you to stay here and work with us."

"Thank you, sir. I'd like that. What's the plan for next Friday when the fish and chicken shipments coincide?"

"I think we monitor them into London and pounce when they unload."

Paul Richmond looked doubtful. He explained it was best not to let the drivers know they were compromised. "If the news gets back to Poland, or wherever, before we know who the suppliers are, where they come from, what the route is we'll never find out. I think we should hit the pie factory after the delivery is made and at least just shut down the UK operation and try to keep it quiet until Interpol and the other customs people have done their jobs," he said and added a "Sir" as he realised he was not talking to his usual team where ideas were exchanged openly, regardless of rank – like his previous life in the SAS.

After more discussion it was agreed that Richmond's plan should be adopted.

"I'll get the authority we need at this end to deal with the international situation," the Commander said.

"And my team can work out with Paul the best way to

handle the situation from here," Myer said.

"What if they find out we know about the dog-food cover?" someone asked.

"If that happens we'll just have to move in and shut it down and hope the news doesn't get out I suppose?" the CS said and explained to his opposite number how they had arranged for the surveillance temporarily but hoped his boys could take that task over. Then Paul Richmond told them about the name of the dog-food.

"It's got to be an internet outlet," he said and mentioned how Val had suggested a WPC could help with the translations. Val's CS said he would organise it.

"Have you interrogated the Poles yet?" the Commander asked and was told they would be doing that the next day but were waiting for the forensic report on the van. "Otherwise, we've only got circumstantial evidence until Mike Prosser can give us more," the CS told him. "Thank God Marcus Swift doesn't seem to be around, he would soon have them out," he added.

"Strange that," Val Franks ventured. "Do you think he knew we might be going to pull him in for questioning?"

"I hope not," her CS told her. "Only you and I knew about that."

"And Mike. But he would never have talked," she said quickly.

"Perhaps Swift had just had enough of Tyson," the Commander said, knowing Tyson's history as most of his Yard colleagues did. "Tyson's not the sort who would let him retire though. He'll turn up sometime."

There was some discussion between the Commander and the CS as to how best to interrogate the Poles and the Quiros family. Interrogation is not the ad lib questioning of suspects as it is usually portrayed. When done properly there is the same preliminary planning that a good QC would use before a cross-examination, based upon known evidence, unknown detail and possible expectations. With the two Polish men the evidence so far was only that they had used a van that had been in an accident, without proof of when that accident occurred and where it occurred and the best defence shot would be that they could be charged only with not reporting an accident and would have to be charged or released within twenty four hours.

If forensic examination showed that the stain Paul Richmond had observed inside the van was blood and especially Mike Prosser's blood, then charges of abducting a police officer, aggravated assault, causing injury to the person and illegally disposing of a person could be made even without Mike Prosser's evidence and the two men could be remanded indefinitely until Mike was possibly able to give evidence. It was with that hope that the Commander had used his authority to request an urgent diagnosis from Forensics but as it was unlikely they would even start their diagnosis until the following day. the time-line for charging the men was a problem. They had been arrested just after midnight on the Sunday morning and the normal twenty four hours could not be extended until the courts opened for business at 9 am on the Monday. Because of that they had to either charge or release the men within a six-hour extension beyond the time when the courts opened. That gave them only until three pm to deal with the Quiros family and to question the Poles. A further thirty six hours could be granted if they could prove further investigation would reveal evidence for a more serious charge and it was unlikely Mike Prosser would be fit in that time to give evidence – or ever. Their only hope was forensic evidence from the van to prove a link to Mike Prosser.

The assault charges relating to the Quiros family were

less of a problem. They would be hauled before a magistrate and certainly fined within the six hours after the magistrate's court sat on the Monday. However, there was no evidence they were aware of the dog food factory being a blind for a major drugs laboratory. Paul Richmond had remembered that Mike Prosser had told him that Anne Quiros was in charge of the Q pie factory but that did not mean she would know what her husband might be up to. The same applied to her parents. Without evidence of their involvement did they want to risk alerting them to the fact that they knew about the laboratory?

That was the main source of argument when the interrogation team of four detectives, including Val Franks and Paul Richmond was assembled. Paul argued that it would be counter-productive to let any of them suspect they knew about the drugs operation even if that meant delaying any investigation into the involvement of the Quiros family. His argument was conceded and it was decided only to charge the Quiros' with assault and to let them be baled. Paul Richmond and Val Franks were detailed to interrogate the Poles and Val wondered if she would be up to it, knowing the best person to do it would have been Mike Prosser.

"What is depressing about all this," her CS said when they had returned from Scotland Yard "Is that none of it is sticking on Tyson."

Val Franks felt the irony of the words in that they echoed the feelings that had for so long depressed Mike Prosser and she smiled that her two superiors were in agreement.

On Sunday morning, at home in Kent, Francine Tyson was relieved not to have her husband and Jason and his other cronies around. She was concerned by many

196

things, the most obvious concern being about her family and especially about her sister Anne. She had never liked Anne's husband Marek and she had liked him less when he brought Andy into their lives. The Pole was a mini version of her husband, aggressive, domineering and arrogant and she could not understand why Tyson put up with him but had suspicions as to the reason and those suspicions made her concern for her sister the greater because of Andy's authoritative attitude towards Marek. Marek was a nice looking man and she could understand why Anne had been attracted to him, the more so because he seemed immature and Anne liked to be in control, as did all of her family, but Francine had always felt him to be untrustworthy because he was basically a weak person. He had been a plumber and her sister had met him when he came with a team of Polish builders to build an extension to the family house. Soon after they were married, the home her father had bought them was invaded on a regular basis by her husband's Polish acquaintances and at first, Andy had just been one of them but then, when the others had suddenly disappeared, Andy had become a regular, dominating presence. Then Marek had suggested that, rather than waste the giblets and unused vegetables from the pie factory, they could start a pet food retail outlet. Everyone thought it was a good business idea but only Francine doubted that Marek had the brains to think of it and she suspected that it was more likely to have been Andy's idea and she instinctively felt uneasy about him. Marek had introduced him as someone with business experience and internet connections to the Polish community where they could sell the pet food exclusively as it was only a small-scale undertaking, so he had been accepted on that basis. But Francine had then been surprised when first her husband

and then her father had seemed to treat Andy as more than a minor business associate of her brother-in-law. Then her father had sacked the manager of the pie factory and put her sister in charge. He had said the reason was the manager had been creaming off some of the chickens and selling them on and that it would give Anne something more to do than to look after their child when they could afford plenty of domestic help.

Then there was De Haan. The urbane Dutchman, who had until recently been only an anonymous supplier of the vegetables used in the pie factory, had suddenly visited their Kent home and spent a weekend to which her father and Andy and Marek had also been invited. The Dutchman had flown in by his own helicopter and his bearing, manners and natural authority had reminded her of Marcus but there was a steel about him that Marcus lacked – or so she had thought at the time – and he did not in any way portray the image of a market gardener, even a Dutch one.

So all those questions that had slopped about in her sub-conscious surfaced again when she got up late on Sunday morning and reviewed the events of the previous night. It was all about a van and a missing police officer, but to Francine it was all about Andy and Marek and what her husband knew of the affair and what he was not telling her. She had become an expert at shutting out the repercussions of her husband's nature, what she didn't know she didn't guess, but now her family were involved it was different, especially as she did not know how they were involved.

Her mobile phone disturbed her thoughts. It was her youngest sister, the one that worked in the Quiros' shop, to say that their parents were not answering her calls and she thought they might be visiting Francine. Francine told her of the events at The Ladybird and her sibling became alarmingly angry, accusing Tyson of all the ills that had threatened their family since Francine had married him.

"He's a thug, a gangster, he has the morals of a feral tom-cat," she said.

Francine might have agreed with her assessment had she not been seven years older than her sister and she began to tell her to mind her manners but her sister's bile had been brewing a long time and she concluded her assault by saying, "You only married him to get that club because you wanted to be the female Hugh Hefner. Now we all have to suffer because of your ego."

It was a brutal awakening to the unspoken feelings within a family and it left Francine scarred.

She walked into the garden as though the house had captured the animosity. The day was warm and the heat soothed her body and she didn't move from a deckchair as she heard the telephone ring inside the house. She closed her eyes and thought of Marcus Swift and added another pain to her deep collection. What Shakespearian epithet would he quote to describe her treachery she wondered. Where would he go? Why has he not been in touch – even to articulate the depths of her deception? And then her brain began to calculate the possibilities of his disappearance. She knew Jason had not found the incriminating recording Marcus had confessed to having. She knew Jason had been disturbed in his search and Marcus would have guessed the purpose of a burglary. She knew he would also have guessed the source of that purpose and that Tyson was the instigator of the intrigue. But why disappear? Why not just phone Tyson and warn him that he had enough evidence to get him a life sentence and that it was in a safe place should anything happen to him or his mother? She was shocked that she had not asked the question of herself before and, despite the views she had expressed to her husband earlier, the answer she found shocked her even more; Marcus was out to get revenge; he had disappeared in order to give the evidence to the police. My God! That's what he is going to do. He's going to get his revenge on all of us. On me.

She got up quickly from the chair and went towards the house where she had left her mobile. She would phone her husband and warn him. She saw on her mobile that the missed call had been from her youngest sister, probably wanting to apologise for her outburst. She rang her back but her sister was no friendlier. She demanded to know what Francine had done about getting a lawyer for her parents. Francine said she had put a call in to someone but they hadn't got back to her.

"I know someone," her sister said. "Should I ask him to help?" Francine didn't know how long, or even if ever, Grimshaw would get back to her.

"Yes. That's a good idea," she answered. Her sister rang off without another word.

Francine thought again about phoning her husband and warning him what Marcus was likely to do. "So what?" she suddenly asked herself. So what if Marcus has sent the evidence to the police? Hadn't Marcus promised twenty five years of freedom for her and the girls?

The one stipulation her father had made for lending Tyson the money to convert the old cinema was that the club would be owned jointly with Francine. It had been a shrewd move considering that he did not then contemplate they would get married. Now it seemed especially important. She sat in a chair and felt the comfort of the silence around her. She took a deep breath and exhaled it slowly and sat back in the cushions and a smile played about her face. Twenty five years? The smile grew broader. 'Thank you, Marcus,' she told herself.

The next day she received a call from Robert Grimshaw. He apologised for not getting back to her sooner, he was in Manchester and his secretary had told him of her message. She was driving into London when she received the call on her hands-free phone. She told him she had wanted to get hold of Marcus Swift but it was not now so urgent.

"Haven't you heard?" Grimshaw said and related the demise of Marcus, his mother and his dog.

There are usually fifty suicides a year from the cliffs of Beachy Head so they rarely make more than a paragraph or two in the local newspaper but a car driven over the cliff makes better copy than usual and when the car contained an eminent barrister and his mother, and especially when it involved a family pet, it was the stuff of local headlines and relayed to the wire services.

It would not be surprising that someone of Francine Tyson's character would not read a newspaper but most of the millions of people like her do manage to find it almost impossible to avoid television or radio news items in their efforts to find suitable music or visual entertainment in order to avoid thinking about more serious aspects of their lives. But Francine's schedule was such that she rarely found herself being at home long enough to watch television and when driving between her various locations of club, home, school and family, she listened to her selected MP3 bands and, like millions of other people, she never read a newspaper, so it was not surprising that Grimshaw's information about his friend came as a devastating shock.

Although the story had appeared briefly on the local television channels over the weekend, it was not until the national media outlets had picked it up that morning that even the police and the legal establishment had learned of Marcus' dramatic end.

Francine's shock was physical. Although her heart was unaffected, her body seemed to lose all feeling and went dramatically cold and she pulled her pashmina tightly about her torso and began to shake.

She had pulled onto the hard-shoulder when she had received Grimshaw's news and now she fell out of the car and was violently sick onto the cow-parsley and daisies that nodded at her. A female driver pulled in behind and hurried to her assistance, wanting to know if she should call an ambulance as she saw Francine's obvious distress. Francine told her she would be all right but then she began to cry and the stranger put her arms around her and held her like a child. Francine sobbed for what seemed to her to be a long time and then she suddenly felt better and thanked the Good Samaritan as though she was making a fuss about nothing and the bemused woman left her and drove away.

Instead of driving to the club as had been her intention, Francine found herself driving on into the West End and checking into the same hotel where she had so tragically seduced Marcus Swift.

She did not get the same room but as they all looked similar, the effect was the same. She had no idea why she had done such a thing and she lay on the bed and stared at the ceiling in the middle of an afternoon and a kaleidoscope of emotions defused her eyes so that the ceiling was only a haze of reflected daylight. She eventually slept and it was dark when she opened her eyes again. She switched on a light and looked at her watch then remembered she had turned off her mobile. It rang as soon as she activated it.

"Where the fuck are you?" her husband wanted to know

"Did you hear about Marcus?" she asked, ignoring the question.

"Yeah. Someone phoned me. Wot the fuck did ee go an' do that for?"

"Don't you know?"

"Why should I?"

"Because you sent Jason to break into his house knowing he had made love to me."

"Ee did wot?"

"How do you think I got to know he was keeping some evidence on you Dave? Do you think he just told me like it was unimportant?"

"You fucked Marcus?"

"Yes. And I enjoyed it."

She closed the phone and switched it off. She rang her daughters from the house phone. The girls were allowed to make or receive one call each evening before bedtime and Francine, like all the parents, tried to do so every day. Just before the allowed ten minutes were up she asked them, "Are you happy there?" There was a silence from the other end. "I don't mind what you say," she continued. "Josie, Pippa, tell me. I want to know what you really think?"

One of the girls started, "Well, Mum, it's quite nice," then the other interrupted. "It's awful," and a torrent of complaints poured from them both.

"All right, girls. We'll do something about it," she told them and her voice reflected  her newly discovered resolve.

She showered and redressed and went out and bought some underwear and toiletries then she walked along Piccadilly and looked at the faces of the people as they passed. She noticed what they wore, how they walked and how they talked, as though they were alien to her. She passed long queues for buses even though the commuting rush was over, then she walked on to Leicester Square and had something to eat then went to a cinema. It was late when she got back to the hotel but she had a drink in the lounge before going to her room and sleeping heavily for the rest of the night.

In the morning she was up early and drove to Wimbledon. She went into the council offices and enquired about day schools in the area then she went into estate agents and studied their lists of houses for sale. She saw three that afternoon and put a deposit cheque down on one of them. It was unoccupied and had been on the market for two years. It had a large garden and a tennis court but was of modest size with only four bedrooms.

Her business brain was unimpaired and she offered ten per cent under the reduced asking price and said that would be her only offer and waited with the agent for an immediate response; the offer was accepted. She went to her children's school and told them what she had done. They jumped around and hugged her and stuck out their tongues at a group of girls who disapproved of their behaviour.


The young solicitor found by the boyfriend of the youngest Quiros daughter performed the easier part of his task well; he advised the parents and Anne Quiros to plead guilty to the charge of assault, and just after lunch on the Monday they were fined five hundred pounds each and George Quiros also received a suspended three month sentence for violent behaviour. But the solicitor's second task was beyond his experience.

Still awaiting the result of forensic analysis of the stain inside the van, the police only had the physical and circumstantial evidence that paint marks on the damaged bumper of the van matched that of Mike Prosser's car and that the two Polish men had together arrived in the van at The Ladybird just before 8 pm. The detectives' task was complicated further by the Poles deciding at some stage to only speak Polish and the WPC Justine, was used as a temporary interpreter to get the solicitor over this first hurdle. It was explained to him that formal charges were awaiting further forensic evidence and if necessary another thirty six hours would be sought by a magistrate's warrant to keep the men in custody pending more serious charges.

The solicitor was on uncertain ground and not wanting to give the police further authority he demanded to know the evidence they already had to hold his clients as he would certainly oppose any further detention and, as it was, would apply for a Release Order that day.

The police team knew that without the forensic evidence they had little legal justification for holding the men and they knew the decision of the men to only answer in Polish was designed to use up the precious detention time before charges could be made.

Andy was the leader of the two and they had marked Marek, Anne Quiros' husband, as the weak link. They told the solicitor they would question the men under caution starting with Marek. The solicitor immediately argued that the WPC was a hostile interpreter and would not agree to questioning under caution. Then Val Franks asked Marek if he only spoke Polish at home. He mumbled an unconfident agreement.

"Good. Then we'll get your wife in and she can act as your interpreter," Val Franks said and got up to make the call.

"Okay. Okay, I do speak English," Marek confessed,

much to the annoyance of his friend Andy.

"Good. Then we'll proceed in English and you can interpret for your friend," Val Franks said, resuming her seat.

It was an unusual situation for the police to question both men together and conceded possible advantages but they had very little time left to question them and both the solicitor and, they suspected, Andy knew it. The detectives knew they had no chance of being granted a further extension unless they could come up with strong evidence with which to charge the men.

Val Franks started the interview by explaining to the Poles they had been arrested on suspicion of abducting a police officer and that the van in which the men had arrived at The Ladybird was damaged and forensic evidence had matched paint on the bumper of the van to that of the missing police officers car – even though they had not yet received any forensic evidence. She addressed the young solicitor.

"Inside the van we found blood stains and if forensics match that blood to the missing officer your clients are facing charges of abduction by force and possibly more serious offences depending on when the officer is found. We expect the forensic report within the next few hours and on that basis a magistrate will not release your clients."

The effect of the information was clearly visible on the faces of both the defendants, and the solicitor said he wished to speak with his clients privately.

"Be our guests," Val Franks told him cheerfully. "There are two cells empty. We'll wait to hear what they have to say."

Within an hour the solicitor and the two Polish prisoners had returned to the interview room. The solicitor pushed a writing pad across the table to the detectives.

"My clients have made a statement," he told them.

The detectives quickly read what had been written. The men admitted to being involved in a motoring accident with an unknown person. The said person had driven into the rear of their van at temporary traffic lights on Wapping High Street. When the men had got out of the van to inspect the damage the other driver attacked them, hitting Marek in the stomach. Andy had then hit the man thinking he would next be attacked. The man fell against the back of the van and cut his head and then fell to the floor. He seemed to be unconscious and they decided they should take him to hospital. They lifted him into the back of the van then he suddenly came round and attacked them again. They pushed him onto the street and drove off. They realise they should have reported the incident but neither of them had a mobile phone and afterwards they decided the incident was not serious enough to waste police time.

Val Franks smiled at the solicitor and wondered if Marcus Swift had been as good at his age. Paul Richmond asked the questions.

Where exactly did the accident occur? Where had they been before the accident and where were they going to? What were their movements for all of that day from when they took out the van to when they arrived at The Ladybird?

The solicitor argued that the questions were irrelevant but Paul Richmond said the veracity of their statement would have to be checked and they could only do that by proving there were no other factors leading to the confrontation with the police officer. The solicitor relented by telling his clients they need only give details of their movements up to the time of the accident.

They started with the time when Andy picked up Marek at his house in Camden and they then drove to the Q Pie factory arriving there at seven am. They loaded the waste food products from the factory into the van and then drove to their dog-food plant in Tottenham where they unloaded the van and put the food products into cold storage. They then drove to Wapping, stopping for petrol at a garage which the police could verify, and the accident happened when they got to Wapping High Street.

"Why did you go to Wapping?" Val Franks asked and was told they were visiting a friend hoping he would be available to have a lunch-time drink with them. "What is the friend's name?" she persisted. The Poles hesitated to answer and then Marek told her it was a Mr Bolton. "Address?" she asked and the solicitor interrupted and told the men they didn't have to answer the question.

"We need to know his address so we can verify their statement," Val Franks told him but then Andy spoke rapidly in Polish and Marek interpreted.

"We never went there," he said. "Because of the fight with the man we didn't want him to see where we were going."

"So it is not relevant," the solicitor repeated.

"Where exactly did the confrontation occur?" Val asked, trying a different tack.

"If you found the car you know where it was."

"It might have been moved."

The solicitor nodded permission for Marek to answer. He told them approximately where the temporary lights were.

"Tell me about this plant where you took the waste food to," Paul Richmond said.

"It's a dog-food factory. Very special dog-food. Do you have a dog?" Marek asked, getting more confident.

"No. But my colleagues have quite a few."

208

"Then you should try our dog-food, it's the best. Give me your address and I'll send you some," Marek smiled.

"Thank you. Is it your business?"

"It's jointly owned with my wife," Marek answered.

"And was anyone working there when you delivered the waste-products – by the way, what are the waste products?"

Marek caught the look his colleague gave him. "No one was there. We don't work Saturday except to pick-up the food, we buy the unused veg and chicken bits from the pie factory.

"The same factory your wife happens to own?"

"My wife only works at the pie factory. Her father owns it," he told them and they noted the glare he got from Andy.

"Thank you for that information," Val Franks told him. "So, in all that you have said there is no one anywhere, apart from a petrol station attendant, who could possibly verify your movements before and after the accident and support your statements?" Marek shrugged his shoulders.

"All right," she continued. "So this is your official statement of what happened. We'll get it typed up for you to check and sign." She lifted the papers and got up to end the interview but all the time she was wondering how Mike Prosser would handle it. Everybody was on their feet thinking the interview was over as she reached the door. She turned to the solicitor.

"Thank you for this," she said indicating the pages of the statement. "We'll let your clients know what we think about it when the officer they attacked has recovered sufficiently from his injuries to tell us exactly what happened." She watched their eyes closely and saw Andy actually smile for a second. "Didn't we tell you we had found him? Yes, the river police rescued him. He's in a

209

bad way, his feet and hands and mouth were taped together. He's very lucky to be alive – but we hope he will make a complete recovery soon and then we'll see if your clients have to face a charge of attempted murder."

The two Poles and their solicitor stared after her as she turned and led the way out of the room.

She crumpled as she entered the observation room where the CS and two other detectives had been watching.

"Mike always said, if it's not going well, make something happen," she said as she saw the concern on the CS's face.

"You've certainly done that. We'll have to move Mike as soon as we can to a safer unit now they know he's alive."

"And we'll have to put the boys watching the dog-food factory on alert," Paul Richmond said. "If they think we know about it they might try to move everything."

"I'll get on to it," the CS told him. "Things are certainly going to happen."

They walked together into the squad room and as they entered the CS was saying. "Bolton. How do I know that name?" A non-uniformed officer nearby told him.

"It was one of the names the criminal register threw up from the electoral roles, sir."

The CS looked at her blankly.

"The roles you asked me to check on Saturday night. I checked the residents around Wapping High Street with the criminal register data-base. I highlighted all the names with records. A Bolton was on the list I put on your desk, sir."

"Thank you Philips. Well done, " the CS said and went into his office. He reappeared with a file of papers.

"Yes. J S Bolton. Ivory Wharf," he read

"Jason," Val Franks said. "Of course, that's where they were going. And Ivory Wharf is right on the river. That's where they threw Mike into the river," she said.

"You're right. There may be forensic evidence in Jason's apartment," the CS said with enthusiasm.

"Mike would make sure there was," Val said.

"We'll get a search warrant and get a forensic team over there, the senior officer said. "Val, can you liaise with the hospital and see when we can move, Mike. He's too vulnerable where he is?"

At the hospital, Val Franks spoke to the surgeon who had operated on Mike Prosser. She told him of the increased danger and that they would need to move him to a private, secure unit. "Well, he's doing a lot better," the surgeon told her. "We were going to move him out of intensive care tomorrow and put him into a private room but there's no reason why he couldn't go somewhere else by ambulance as long as it's not going to be a long journey."

"Can I see him? Just to say hello – I promise," she pleaded.

"Certainly. That would be good, we need to get his brain stimulated a bit to start making the right connections – but don't ask him any questions, that would be too stressful."

Prosser looked more restful and the bruising about his eyes was paler. He was connected only to a pulse monitor and a saline drip and still wore a head restraint. She sat beside him and took his fingers in her hand and started to tell him everything that had happened over the weekend. She talked for almost an hour and her throat was dry and getting sore by the time she had run out of information.

"I didn't tell David or Edna," she told him. "I thought it was better if you told them in your own time."

She felt the faintest movement from a finger onto her hand. "Do that again," she said and he did. She lifted his

211

hand to her face. "I'll tell the doctor. We're going to move you out of here and get you somewhere safer."

The solicitor rang George Quiros as soon as he left the police station. He had been asked to report to him on his efforts to get the two Polish men freed. He started to tell Quiros the reasons why he had failed to get the men baled but the older man interrupted.

"Can you meet me at The Ladybird club so you can tell this to Mr Tyson at the same time?" he asked.

It took George Quiros twenty minutes to get to the club and the solicitor arrived ten minutes later, looking around him like a child in a sweet shop as he was led up to the fourth floor office. Tyson rose to meet him and shook his hand.

"Call me Dave," he told him as he introduced himself. "George says you done a good job. 'ave a drink." He gestured for the young man to sit in one of the high-backed, sprung, leather armchairs and gave him a generous measure of Scotch. "Now, tell us all that 'appened. Every word those coppers and Andy and Marek said to each uvver."

The man enjoyed his own voice and if Val Franks had been there she might have again wondered if he was like the young Marcus Swift. He told them every detail of the exchanges. He had a good memory and related everything to the point of pedantry. Tyson  interrupted at times, checking he meant exactly what he had said,

"They definitely mentioned the dog-food plant? An' this uvver geezer asked who owned it? An Marek told them his wife?Are you sure nuffin more was said abaght it?

an' they mentioned Mr Bolton, but they didn't give 'is address?" The solicitor confirmed the questions.

"Right son, you done well. We'll be able to give you

212

plenty of work," Tyson said. He took a bundle of bank notes from a drawer and threw them across into the startled man's lap.

"See yerself out."

"I hadn't finished," the man said and looked less comfortable. He told them of Val Frank's bombshell as she ended the interview.

Tyson and George Quiros said nothing for some minutes then Tyson said, "Awright. Thanks son."

The young man got to his feet and left the two men sitting, not looking at each other and not speaking.

Eventually Tyson said, "It's all going shit-shape, George."

"They could be bluffin," Quiros answered.

"We don't know, do we? They could be right too." He lifted the phone. "Jase, where are you? At'ome? Good. Get what you really need togevver an' then get across 'ere an' do a Stepney on your pad. Awright? Yeah, that's wot I said, a Stepney." He put down the phone and looked at the older man. "I fink we need some 'elp. I'd better call DH."

"Do we 'ave to do that, Dave?" Quiros asked.

"Yeah. I fink we do. If those two are facing an attempted murder charge we don't know wot they'll say to get off the 'ook, do we? If they start  grassin' we're all  in the shit, aint we?"

George Quiros sighed then nodded agreement. Tyson opened a wall safe and took from it a mobile phone.


Jason looked about the bedroom then lifted the case from the bed and carried it to the door of the flat. He then walked back into the sitting-room and through it to the kitchen. He opened the oven door and turned on the electric grill then he turned on a gas ring on the hob next to it. He closed the kitchen door then picked up his case and left the apartment. At The Ladybird he found Dave Tyson alone.

"What's up, boss?" he asked and sat down as their years together had made their relationship one of accepted familiarity.

"Did you do it?" Tyson asked

"Yeah. We might 'ear the bang if we open a winder."

"No. I'm not talking abaght that, Jase. Wot I meant was; is it right, you dumped Prosser in the river?"

"Yeah. That's right"

"An' ee was bound 'and an' foot?"

"Yeah."

"So ee couldn't swim?"

Jason seldom laughed but now he almost did. "Course not."

"Then 'ow the fuck did ee get out of the fuckin river?" Jason looked at him. He was not a stupid man but he saw no logic in the question. Then he made a joke, "Wiv a fish 'ook?" he suggested. But Tyson was in no mood to appreciate humour. He beat his great fist onto the desk and made several items jump into the air.

"Alive, Jase. Fuckin alive."

Jason shook his head. "No way."

Tyson then told him what the police had said to their solicitor.

"No way. They're bluffin," Jason said. "Ee's well drowned."

"Then 'ow did they know ee was taped up 'ands, feet and mouf?"

"Someone fished 'im out. But but there's no way ee's alive." Jason even thought the idea funny.

The logic of the answer had not occurred to Tyson who was always quick to assume what he wanted to believe.

"So they might be bluffin," he admitted. "We've got to

214

find out bloody quick like 'cos DH is sending someone over to take care of Andy an' Marek."

"Ow do we do that?" Jason asked.

"Check the morgues, see if anyone's been fished out of the river." Tyson said. "There's the East London an' one in Greenwich. It's most likely if they did fish 'im out ee'd be taken to the London 'ospital. Take some dosh wiv yer, say your old man's missing."

"What if I don't find 'im?"

"You'll 'ave to check all the 'ospitals. But that'll be risky. If ee's alive they'll 'ave coppers around 'im. Be careful."

"If they've found 'im, that bird of 'is will know where ee is. Franks. DI Franks."

"Yeah she would. Good idea, Jase." Tyson agreed.

"It'll be the quickest way," Jason said.

"But be bloody careful, you can't slip up on this. I've got to tell yer, mate, if that geezer Prosser is still alive you've 'ad it. You've eiver got to do 'im or scarper abroad."


The gas fell to the floor and pushed the light air ahead of it and some seeped under the kitchen door but not quickly enough to prevent a build-up in the room. It took an hour to reach the hot grill where it ignited. The kitchen door flew across the sitting-room and split against the outside wall. The brickwork of the internal walls was shredded and flew about like missiles and the window-doors of the sitting-room were forced from their frames and projected into the river, much as Prosser had been forty eight hours previously. That alleviated the force of the explosion but combustion occurred first to the ceiling tiles, which fell semi-molten onto the worktops and tea-towels, and then to the gas still flowing from the severed pipes. The fire spread to the living-room furniture and curtains so the blaze was soon seen from the river and a fire-boat was quickly onto the scene as the residents vacated the building in panic.

Jason drove down to the wharf after he left The Ladybird. It was just getting dark and he could see the glow in the sky as he left the club. All the emergency services were there and the area had been sealed-off and people were standing in groups wondering if they would still have somewhere to live as they returned from work.

"Wot 'appened?" Jason brazenly asked a policeman.

"You should bloody know," a woman, whom Jason vaguely recognised, said. "It was your bloody flat that blew up."

"You are Mr Bolton?" the policeman asked. "Come with me please, sir. My guvnor would like a word with you."

Jason followed him to a police control unit van. He was interrogated for over an hour. He admitted to having used the gas and the grill to make some cheese-on-toast and then he got a phone call and had to rush away. Eventually he was allowed to leave saying he would stay at The Ladybird club until he sorted something out with the insurance company. He looked around the scene hoping to see DI Franks but it was not in her manor and he really didn't expect to see her. But he knew how to find her and she would now become the main focus of his attention.

Val Franks drove a yellow sports car. For a plain clothes officer it had both advantages and disadvantages. Psychologically it was good for her as she could feel like something other than a policewoman as she drove it to and from the station and she would not have done had she chosen a black or silver saloon. It also had the advantage of not being suspected as belonging to a police officer and was especially useful when she had to do any surveillance of suspects, but the disadvantage was that people remembered it. So it was with Jason. He knew Val Franks

216

well from Tyson's many indiscretions and his run-ins with his nemesis, Mike Prosser, and he was easily able to identify the car leaving or arriving at the police station's garage.

The station was a large detached building on a main route but its garage was located behind and underneath the building and access to it was via a one-way side street on one side of the building and egress from it was also one way on the other side. So from a vantage point in a street leading off the main road and opposite to the police station, Jason was able to observe all police vehicles entering or leaving the premises. He knew he could not risk leaving his Mercedes near the building for long periods as it was well covered by CCTV cameras and he knew it was no good confronting Val Franks while she was on duty, so he chose to park on a yellow line after six pm in the street opposite. It was after eight when he saw the Mazda exit the car park and he was able to follow it to Val Franks' home in Greenwich. She lived in a small private estate of one-up, one-down maisonettes set in blocks around landscaped gardens of trees and shrubs. Her ex-husband, feeling the guilt of his infidelity, had agreed to her sole ownership, which, considering they had only been married for less than two years, was little financial loss to him.

She lived in the top maisonette at the end of a block and having seen her car pull in to the estate and having parked outside and entered on foot, Jason was able to observe her park her car and select a communal door and enter by way of a security code. He also observed that the door was covered by a video link.

He waited behind shrubbery until he saw lights go on in the upper floors of the two-floored building and then he moved closer and examined the entrance and the back of the block. He retraced his steps to his car and drove back into London.

It was nearer to ten o'clock the next evening when he saw the Mazda exit the garage. He overtook it as it neared the Greenwich location and he had parked safely out of sight and was waiting behind a clump of viburnums as Val Franks parked and walked to her front door.

She had entered the security code and had pushed the entrance door a foot inwards when Jason's left arm went over her shoulder and clamped her against him and his right hand held a  retractable blade to her throat. She could feel the steel pressing into her and knew not to struggle.

"Where's Prosser?" Jason demanded.  She could feel the heat of his breath on her neck.

Val Franks' brain was immediately quantifying the chances of escaping being raped and was almost relieved by the question. She did not recognise the voice as it was the same as thousands of other cockney-bred men's voices but she knew instantly it was Jason, she knew her assailant was tall enough to be able to reach easily over her shoulder onto her chest and his chin was pressed against the top of her head and as her right hand had gone instinctively upwards to protect her throat, it could feel the iron muscle of his wrist. Once it had dismissed a sexual predator, her brain didn't take long to find another motive.

"Prosser's dead," she answered.

The knife blade moved a little across her throat and although she felt no pain she could feel the blood quickly begin to trickle down her front and into her blouse.

"You've got one more chance. I'll find 'im wiv or wivout you, dead or alive. It's your call." he told her.

She forced her brain to keep calm – but  her voice

surprised her, it was much lighter than normal and not how she was thinking.

"He's almost dead," she said. "He was in a coma for two days. He's only just out of intensive care."

"Where?"

"Here," she said and felt the top of the blade press harder so that she could hardly breathe. "It's true. We knew he wasn't safe in hospital. We brought him here." The pressure was relaxed and she took a deep breath, wondering how badly she was cut.

"Show me." Jason said and his left arm suddenly swept downwards and gripped her left wrist and bent her arm behind her back.

"Please," she pleaded. "He probably won't ever be able to talk again."

"Yeah. You've got that right," Jason said and pushed her forward into the hallway and up a short flight of stairs in front of them. On a small landing Val's hand went towards her shoulder bag.

"I have to get my keys out," she told him in a normal voice.

"Careful," he told her. She noisily fiddled with the two locks and then pushed open the door. She switched on a light to show a small hallway that led into a larger room. "Hi, Mike," Val called. "It's only me." Jason closed the outside door quietly behind them then prodded her forward and examined  the sitting room

"Where?" he said and Val Franks indicated one of the doors off the hallway. "I'll make us some tea, Mike," she called again. Then Jason hit her and she fell unconscious onto the carpet. Jason turned the handle of the door she had indicated and stepped quickly into a bedroom.

With the light from the hall just reaching into the room and the light from outside coming through a large window, he could see a shapeless pile of duvet and pillows on the bed and it took him a second to realise there was no one under them. He turned to go back into the sitting-room when Paul Richmond stepped from behind the door and palm-butted him on the chin. Jason staggered back towards the bed but as Paul was coming forward to press the attack he managed to step sideways and Paul's momentum carried him onto the bed, which was the one place he did not want to be. His arms pumped downwards and his legs kicked upwards and he executed a perfect hand somersault which took him over the bed and against the large window on the other side. Jason quickly followed around the bed and lunged at him with the knife. Paul swayed sideways and turned and elbowed the tall man behind his neck sending him against a wall. Paul followed with a kick to the small of the back and Jason slashed backwards and cut Paul across his bare stomach. They both retreated to a momentary stand-off with Jason again probing forward with the knife and Paul backing away waiting for the thrust that might kill him. Jason's height was a problem and the knife, held from his waist and probing forward with a piston movement of the arm, was almost level with Paul's chest and attacking a knife arm from below was never a successful manoeuvre. Paul feigned a kick towards Jason's groin and the big man instinctively pulled his pelvis back which lowered his knife arm. Paul's leg had continued the movement forward but instead of aiming a kick it had gone between the big man's legs and planted firmly on the floor. At the same time Paul turned his back into Jason and gripped the wrist holding the knife in both hands and forced it downwards and as Jason's head came lower Paul smashed the back of his own into Jason's face. Jason roared and bit into the back of Paul's neck but the movement loosened

Jason's arm and Paul smashed the knife hand against the end of the bed and the knife flew under it. Jason had reached over Paul's shoulder to grip his throat but Paul fell to his knees and sent the big man over his shoulder onto the bed. There was a desperate struggle for supremacy but Jason's uncultured violence was no match for Paul's trained techniques and several elbow smashes and then one big kick sent Jason crashing through the window in a shower of flying glass. Paul staggered forward and looked down. He saw Jason pick himself up like a drunkard and weave his way across the lawn towards the road. Paul went into the living-room where Val Franks was trying to pick herself up from the floor. Her face was swollen and blood was running down her chin and joining the blood from a superficial cut to her throat and running onto her chest. He helped her to her feet and they supported each other into the kitchen. Val switched on the light and saw the blood still oozing from Paul's stomach wound. She soaked a tea-towel in cold water and held it to his stomach and they leaned into each other.

"I don't think much of your house guests," he told her.

She tried not to laugh as any facial movement hurt.

"You knew I hated tea," he added

"I'll try to get us an ambulance," she mumbled and picked up the phone.

"I'll do it," he said, pressing the wet towel into his stomach  which continued to bleed through it onto the floor. "They will just think you're some drunk wasting their time."

Jason reached his car and eased painfully into the leather seat. He picked pieces of glass from various parts of his clothing and some that had penetrated into his skin.

He felt like he had received a serious beating, which he had, and the uniqueness of the thought was almost as painful as his ribs, back and face and the various cuts to his body. But the greater pain was to his self-respect; he had failed and it was not an isolated failure, it was possibly terminal. Val Frank's reaction to his demand to know where Prosser was, even allowing for her experience of threatening situations, had confirmed that Prosser, unbelievably, miraculously, had survived and Jason might soon have to face a charge of attempted murder. Before his assault he had time to retrieve the situation but now he would be a hunted man with nowhere to hide. He could not go back to The Ladybird or to any of his known locations and even if he could he knew that Dave Tyson would not want a wounded stag bleeding around him as the hounds gathered to hunt him down. He could not even check-in to a small hotel in his state without arousing suspicion. Fortunately, he still had his suitcase of clothes, his passport and a considerable amount of cash in the boot of his car. He knew London as well as a taxi-driver and had hundreds of acquaintances, many of whom owed him favours, but he also knew the police would soon be all over them and his face would soon be all over the television news as the wanted instigator of the dramatic explosion and fire which would make equally dramatic pictures on the evening's screens and in the morning newspapers.

There was only one other place beside London that he knew intimately, Tyson's estate in Kent. He started the car and headed in that direction before the police put out an APB.

He stopped at Maidstone Services and cleaned up in one of the toilets before continuing his journey but it still only took him just over the hour to reach the Eurostar terminal at Ashford. He drove into the long-stay car park then carried his case into the terminal building. He went first into a toilet and changed into a different jacket then he stood in a small queue and bought a ticket for Brussels. He bought some Euros from a bureau de change then purchased a newspaper and a pair of sun-glasses and held the rolled-up paper to his face as he negotiated his way across the terminal building and out of a side entrance.

He saw a bus leaving for Canterbury and jumped on it. From Canterbury he caught a train back to London.


Francine Tyson had avoided speaking to her husband for twenty four hours and she had not returned to their Kent home. But she knew, attractive as the separation was, she could not leave him to stew without some kind of emollient. She rang him and told him their daughters were very unhappy at their boarding school and she was arranging to find a suitable day-school for them in Wimbledon.

"Just like that?" was his comment. "Wivout any discussion abaght it?"

"Since when have you been interested in your daughter's education, Dave?" she shot back at him.

"I need you 'ere Fran, there are fings 'appening I 'ave to deal wiv an' I don't want to 'ave to run the club an' all." She told him she would be back for the weekend and he didn't have to worry about the club.

"If I fought Marcus was still alive I'd be worried wot you was up to," he said "You fucked, Marcus. That's a laugh Fran. Ooed want to fuck 'im – unless it was some choirboy," and he was still laughing as she shut down the phone. How she would love to tell him what a good lover Marcus had been.

She had booked into a small hotel near Wimbledon and

visited three schools in the area and was beginning to like the experience of being in a small village so near to London and was amazed to find what seemed like a different country only a few miles from the East End where she had spent almost all of her life.

She had seen the girls each evening and had taken them out one afternoon, much to the displeasure of their headmistress, but as she had already given the school notice of their leaving she was not worried by the careful lecture about parental support and rather enjoyed the experience. So she was in a better place when she received a call from Robert Grimshaw wondering if she could call and see him.

His practice was in the Middle Temple of the Inns of Court, the fascinating, unspoilt part of eighteenth century London which was the heart of the legal profession. Like so many native Londoners, Francine had never been there before and as she wandered through the labyrinth of court yards she was thinking about Marcus and this world of which he had been a part.

She found Robert Grimshaw to be a small, bony man with a surprisingly strong, expressive voice.

"Please have a seat Miss Francine," he said which made Francine wonder if he knew she was married. He sat at his desk and smiled at her, his blue eyes studying her from behind his spectacles as though in admiration of what he saw. He handed her an envelope.

"It's from Marcus," he told her and her heart hesitated.

Her hand shook as she took the envelope from him. She knew it could not contain anything more than a letter and she dreaded what Marcus would say in it.

"You heard from him?" she asked rather pointlessly.

"He sent me that letter with a sort of will," he explained.

"Marcus did not make a proper will but he wanted to

convey his wishes upon his death and in a letter has authorised me to execute them."

"When did he do that?" she asked.

"It is dated Friday morning, the day he and his mother died."

"Did he leave anything for the police – like a recording?"

"No. Why do you ask? Did he have some unresolved evidence of some sort?"

"It was something he was concerned about. We had dinner together the night before he died."she explained.

"Well, he has said nothing about it in his letter of intent. It is really rather simple, he has left his house and its contents to a Mr Harry Meadows, he's chief clerk at Kerry, Bryce and Tomkins; I believe he and Marcus were at school together. But he has made a proviso that the house should be made available every last Thursday in the month for our Friends of Shakespeare Group – it is a reading group to which I too belong. It was typically considerate of Marcus to think of us."

"And that's all?" she asked

"And two thousand pounds to go to a Mr. Leroy Winstone for he and his friends to 'Have a splendid memorial bun fight at which I will be there in spirit.'

Francine looked again at the envelope in her hands.

"Should I open it?" she asked.

"If you so wish," Grimshaw told her and handed her a paper-knife. She slit open the envelope and pulled from it a sheet of notepaper.

*'My Dearest Francine,'* she read and had to stop and check herself. She handed the letter to Grimshaw.

"Could you read it for me, please?"

Grimshaw took the letter and read aloud.

> *No longer mourn for me when I am dead,*
> *Than you shall hear the surly sullen bell.*

*Give warning to the world that I am fled*
*From this vile world with vilest worms to dwell*
*'Nay, if you read this line, remember not*
*The hand that writ it' for I love you so*
*That I in your sweet thoughts would be forgot*
*If thinking on me then should make you woe.*
*O, if, I say, you look upon this verse*
*When I perhaps compounded am with clay,*
*Do not so much as my poor name rehearse,*
*But let your love even with my life decay,*
*Lest the wise world should look into your moan*
*And mock you with me after I am gone.'*

"It's a Shakespeare sonnet, seventy one I think," he told her.

"What does it mean?" she asked

"Many things, but basically it is a plea to a lover to forget their love for fear it will do her harm."

Francine could not prevent a tear seeping from an eye and she accepted a tissue from Grimshaw and dabbed it dry.

"I don't wish to pry into your affairs Miss Francine, but I think Marcus is telling you he loved you and not to worry."

She nodded agreement but was unable to speak. She rose and held out her hand to thank him. He ushered her gently through his secretary's office and onto the small landing and watched her descend the stairs, her high heels picking a careful route upon the wood.

Chief Superintendent Myer of the Drug Squad was reading a fax sent to Scotland Yard from Holland.

'De Haan, Alexsander. b Krakow, Poland. 12.Nov.1963 Father Kogut, Bernard (Polish). Married,

Tengizerkek, Gulmina (Kazakh Name change by deed from Kogut 1985..
Owner Eekhoorn (squirrel) Prieel (garden house). 400hect. Market produce company Reg office. Utrecht.
Also owns Eekhoorn Vervoer Trucking comp. Reg office, Utrecht.
Director, Wiewiorka Rozwoz. Trucking comp. Reg. Office. Szczecin (Stettin), Poland.
Father Bernard Kogut owns several farms with two brothers in and around the Szeczin (Stettin) area including intensive chicken factories. Interpol have requested police monitoring from the Polish Ministry. The name of his mother, Tengizerkek, means seaman or seafarer in Kazak. Interpol investigating possible shipping link to Turkey via the Caspian. All your suspects, including de Haan, would seem to be Polish and your focus might need to be the Polish community in London. Haan means "rooster" in Polish.'

The fax message arrived as Alexander de Haan's helicopter was landing at Lydd airport, a few miles from Tyson's estate. He had cleared through a customs officer and was about to take off again to fly on to the green lawns of Beaumont when he took a call from Dave Tyson asking him to meet up in London at the Waldorf hotel. He requested clearance to Battersea Heliport.
Tyson and George Quiros were at the hotel to greet him

and his two associates. De Haan displayed all the power of his financial success in every part of his personality, from his lean, healthy physic, his tailored suits and hand-made shoes to the ease of his walk and the calm of his voice. He dined with top police officers, gave generously at many charity events and lent his yacht to politicians. Tyson and Quiros were, to him, no more than cogs in a vast engine of enterprise and inwardly he winced at their vowels but recognised their value. The UK operation was productive and profitable for all of them and he cared enough that it should not be jeopardised to answer personally Tyson's call for assistance.

Tyson apologised for the change in venue.

"The cops are all over me clubs an' Beaumont, looking for Jason," he explained.

"We heard about it, even in Holland," de Haan said. "They seemed to think he had got over to the continent."

"Yeah. 'is car was found at Ashford an ee bought a ticket apparently, but, oo knows? Jase is a pro."

De Haan then listened without interrupting Tyson's account of the arrest of the two Poles and the attempt on Prosser's life, then he asked questions. Have they checked the factory since Saturday? Do they know for sure the officer is alive? Has Jason been in touch since he disappeared? When he received all the answers in the negative he considered them for several minutes.

"We'll take care of Andy and Marek," he said. "It does not make me very happy, Andy is my cousin and his old mother is going to be very upset."

"And Marek is married to my daughter," Quiros reminded him.

"I understand. But we have no choice," the Dutchman explained. "We cannot risk them being charged with attempted murder and going to trial. They know too much. We sometimes have to do things we don't want to do. But Jason is a different problem."

"Jase would never grass," Tyson said. "ee'd rather die."

"Would you stake your life on it?" de Haan asked him. "You may have to." Tyson didn't answer. "But where do we find him?" the Dutchman wanted to know.

"Ee'l be in touch," Tyson said with confidence. "If noffing else, ee'll need money sooner or later."

"I hope you're right. While he's on the run he's not a problem, we can't do anything until he's found. Now, about the factory; you will need to check whether the police suspect anything. Pay someone to go there. Someone who knows nothing about you. We need to know if the police are watching it." Tyson nodded agreement "Good. I'll stay at the Savoy for two nights."

The Dutchman rose, shook hands and ended the meeting.


At the police station in south London, the duty officer received a call saying the Law Society had been asked to find a Polish speaking criminal lawyer to represent a Mr Marek Majewski and a Mr. Andrzej Dudek and they were sending a solicitor, a Mr Grzegorz Pajewska to speak to them. The officer asked them to spell the name and he recorded it in the Day Book and informed the CID.

Mr Pajewska eventually arrived and was briefed by Val Franks as to the charges against the two men. He was asked to take off his coat and to empty his pockets before being shown into Andy Dudek's cell. He explained to Dudek that de Haan was taking personal charge of their case.

"What time do you have your main evening meal," he asked and was told they were both given a tray at the same time, usually six-thirty. "Good, then it will be getting dark soon afterwards," the other man told him. He then took from his ear a small pill. "Take this just before you eat," he said. "After eating you will feel ill. You will feel some pain and want to be sick. You will call for help. You will be taken to hospital by ambulance. Don't worry, you will soon feel better. We will take you from the ambulance and fly you to Holland." Andy understood and shook the man's hand. "Thank Alexsander for me," he said.

The man then repeated the message to Marek, taking another pill from his other ear. Marek was not so enthusiastic. "What about my family?" he asked.

"Don't worry. They will join you when we get you to Poland," the other man assured him.

At six-forty-five the men were given a tray with soup, chicken-pie with mashed potato and broccoli and apple pie with custard. They both obediently took the pill with a mouthful of tea before they ate. They immediately felt distressed, had difficulty in breathing, felt their body temperature drop and they both wanted help but by the time they realised their distress was getting worse they were unable to call for help and they were unable to get enough oxygen to counteract the loss caused by the cyanide.

By the time someone came to see if they had finished eating they were both dead.

At four thirty that afternoon de Haan and his two companions, including Mr. Pajewska, had lifted off from the Battersea Heliport and were en route back to Holland.


Paul Richmond had thirty six stitches to treat his stomach wound and with it taped up to prevent stretching, he was soon back with the other Drug Squad officers on surveillance of the dog-food factory. They operated from

230

a van parked outside the wall surrounding the housing estate where residents of the estate parked at night when their normal parking spaces were full. They used a three-shift system, one on the embankment with night-vision glasses, one in radio contact in the van and one sleeping. Paul Richmond had just settled to get his head down in the rear of the van, having just finished his boring shift on the embankment, when his companion's radio receiver was activated. "I think there's someone at the gate," the surveillance officer's voice said. "Can you see a vehicle?" he was asked. "No. Hang on. He just looked through the gate, now he's gone...No, he's still there. I think he's using the entry console in the wall. Yeah, the gates are opening."

The other man started the engine of the van. Paul Richmond was up quickly and his stitches told him he should not have done so.

"Wait," he said. "Switch off the engine." He went forward and took the microphone from the other man. "What's he doing, Jonesy?" The voice at the other end told him a man had entered the yard. He seemed to be alone. He was walking towards the factory unit. Can't see him now, he's hidden by the building. Should we call up the cavalry?

"No." Paul Richmond answered. "Let's wait."

They waited ten minutes and the surveillance officer reported no further movement. Paul's companion was getting nervous.

"He might be burning everything," he protested and Paul's nerves were not much better.

"They won't do that unless they have to, it might be a test," he said, hoping he was right. The surveillance man called again.

"I can see him. He's walking towards the gate."

"Is he carrying anything?" Paul asked and was told he

wasn't. "Is he hurrying?"

"No. He doesn't seem to be. He's at the gate, closing it. He's gone right, away from you."

The other men breathed easier. "It was a test," Paul announced to his companions. "Okay, Jonesy. Be alert. If they think they're not being watched they may arrive to clear the place tonight."

They spent a fitful night, half-expecting to be disturbed but nothing further occurred and Paul Richmond knew the deadline of the Friday deliveries was that much nearer.

Val Franks, her mouth still uncomfortable from having four stitches to the lower lip and chemical stitches to the shallow slit across her throat, attended the meeting at Scotland Yard with her CS. It was presided over by Chief Superintendent Myer of the Drug Squad but the Commander and a Deputy Commissioner also sat in on the meeting. They went over the offensives they had suffered, from the destruction of Jason's flat and his disappearance to the murder of the two Polish detainees and the assault by Jason on two of their officers. Flak had been flying from all directions.

The explosion and fire had already drawn interest from the national media but the deaths of two suspects whilst in police custody had intensified the interest so that Scotland Yard's press office was stretched to deal with it. The inevitable internal investigation into the murders of the two Poles also added to the stress levels of Val Franks and the other officers involved.

But it was not only the police who felt the heat of the media interest. When they linked Jason to the explosion at his flat, his known association with Tyson reawakened their curiosity with the deaths of Danny Murphy and

Robbie Birch and the tragic results of the carnage on the motorway, knowing Tyson had been involved, and it wasn't long before they discovered that one of the Poles who had been murdered was married to Tyson's sister-in-law. So the press hounds gathered around the Quiros family.

George Quiros was not easily intimidated and he attended his market stall as he had done for forty years, his size and invective sufficient to deal with the interruptions to his routine from the many reporters. The other stall owners and porters did their share by bustling the intruders with fishy clothes and hands and accidentally dropping ice on them so that their interest around Quiros soon waned.

But Tyson had other ways of dealing with the media frenzy. When the cries about Tyson's involvement could not be ignored because they could not find him as he had chosen to sleep at The Ladybird and not to venture out, he suddenly invited all of them into the disco area and had several of his scantily clad girls serve free drinks from the American Long Bar. Then he perched in a chair on the stage and invited them to ask their questions. It was a bold, daring move and typical of Tyson's natural instinct of when threatened, to go onto the offensive.

He fielded all the questions with chummy openness, making jokes where he could, showing remorse and concern for all those poor people killed because two kids were doing what he used to do when he was their age and living in poverty on a South London estate. He then turned that into a diatribe against politicians for not caring about young people and against the police who harried them for getting into "a little bovver 'cos they 'ad nuffink to look forward to."

He was asked about his friend Jason. "Aw, mate," he

233

addressed the questioner. "If there's anyfing that breaks me 'eart it's when someone you love, someone you trusted, let's you dahn. Ee was like me bruvver. I 'ave no idea why ee tried to kill that copper. Oo knows? All I can say is ee must 'ave bin provoked 'cos ee wouln't 'ave done anyfing like that otherwise. Ee was a nice feller an' I wish ee would get in touch so I can 'elp 'im."

It was a clever ploy. He knew the police had not revealed the attempt on Prosser's life. When they had issued an appeal to trace Jason it was only to say he had attacked and injured two police officers and was dangerous and should not be approached and they had not provided an explanation as to why the explosion occurred in Jason's flat which left the general idea that it had something to do with drugs. So Tyson's suggestion that he had been provoked put more pressure on the police rather than on himself. The press went home happy with many amusing quotes and anecdotes and plenty of free drinks and the impression that Tyson was a character and wasn't doing anyone any harm.

But his wife was not so amenable to the interference in their lives. For one thing, the publicity was not the best introduction to the school she had selected for her daughters and she was grateful the new term was several weeks away and hoped the furore would then have subsided. But coming on top of her emotional reaction to Marcus Swift's death, the events of the last three days had increased her feelings of isolation and pending disaster. She had gone home to her parents, knowing that Anne would be there.

Despite the sibling rivalry between the girls there had always been a strong family unity, welded by their mother and bolstered by the doting father. Anne was distraught by the death of her husband – surprisingly so as she had tended to bully him – and she wanted to know why it had happened.

The younger daughter focussed the blame on Andy, for which Francine was grateful having had to fend off a similar offensive about her husband the previous weekend, and they all found him a convenient target for their suspicions. George Quiros and his wife encouraged the direction of their ire; George to emolliate his own guilt and Doris because she knew that their sudden influx of wealth had coincided with the introduction of Andy to their family.

"Did Andy and Marek kill that policeman?" Francine asked bluntly in the manner of her recent conversion to wanting to know everything.

"Of course they didn't," her sister Anne responded angrily.

"That's why they were arrested," Francine pressed, knowing more about it than her sister.

"So who killed Marek and Andy?" the younger sister asked.

George Quiros attempted to steer the conversation away to less controversial subjects but Francine would not let go.

"I would like to know what Andy and Marek were up to on Saturday," she said. The question went unanswered and added to the tension. "Dave knew what they were up to but wouldn't tell me."

"Of course he bloody knew," the youngest sister said,

"Just leave it alone, Fran," her father told her. "What we don't need to know we don't want to know," he added and Francine knew from where she had got that philosophy which had helped her endure her marriage.

"And just let things jump up and bite our arse?" she answered and was admonished by her mother.

"I would like to know what Andy and Marek were up to in that factory of theirs," she persisted.

"Fran, I've told you, leave it alone," her father shouted, so violently that the women reacted physically..

"Just go home to your old-man and behave yourself," he added in a calmer voice. Francine embraced her mother and her sisters and left without another word.

At Scotland Yard the nerves were almost as tense. Having gone through a de-briefing after Jason's attack, Val Franks was then questioned again by the Commander. Even though the questioning was more of personal curiosity than of official concern, it was not easy for her to relive again the circumstances, knowing how very close she and Paul Richmond had been to being killed. 'Thank God for the SAS,' had been her comment to Paul Richmond in the ambulance. But she felt that even the Commander's mild enquiries were probing. It was she who had authorised access for the phoney solicitor to see the Poles. Even though it had not been her job to check his ID, she had the same feeling as when Robbie Birch's birth certificate had not been checked, with almost similar results. She thought of Dominique and suddenly, in the midst of a group of males, she wanted to hold her again. Chief Superintendent Myer was discussing a report from the WPC Justine who had been trawling the internet for connections to Smakosz Pies. She had found the reference to the dog food opened normal sales information, the price depended on the quantity ordered and included free delivery for boxes of more than twenty tins.

"But she has highlighted references in the text which she has translated," DCS Myer was saying. "For instance; Klaps – smack, slap or clout. Kuter - smack. Smek – taste or flavour. Despite the obvious association of the words

236

they did not seem out of context, but when she clicked on them they opened up a box asking for agents to sell the dog food and in that text there were words such as, Kraina Snow – dreamland and Wielka Nadzieja – white hope. The text asked the customer to leave their number on a reply website. So it seems that is the way the drugs are marketed. We have someone watching Dudek's flat and also Anne Quiros' to make sure no laptops are removed and at the appropriate moment we will exercise search warrants to confiscate all electronic equipment including phones. They have to have a list of clients somewhere and we need to find it."

He then took them through the information he had received from Interpol and the Dutch customs investigators.

"We may be at the end of a trafficking network from Afghanistan through Kazakhstan and Turkey and into Europe," he told them.

"You really think it's that big?" one of the junior officers asked.

"Yes. Why else would someone take the incredible risk of poisoning two witnesses in one of our police stations?" the Commander answered tetchily.

"So they weren't killed because of Mike?" Val asked.

"We don't think so," Myer told her. "They would be facing a long gaol sentence. Someone wanted them dead so they couldn't offer us anything to mitigate that sentence."

"With the help of Customs investigators at Harwich and the co-operation of the Dutch and Polish agencies we are launching a major operation this Friday," Myer continued. "The Essex police and I will be finalising plans this afternoon to present to an operations board by the Commander and all of you will be briefed as to your parts tomorrow morning. We are calling it Operation Janet," he said. "We owe that much to Detective Superintendent Prosser. If it wasn't for him we wouldn't be where we are. Paul, where's Paul," he asked and was told Paul Richmond had been on night surveillance. "He shouldn't be working," Myer said. "But we need him because he's the only one with detailed knowledge of the drugs factory. Val, can you ask him to see me when he's recovered?"

She was surprised that everyone seemed to know he was staying with her and had not made any crude jokes or references to it. Do they think I'm gay? she wondered.

As soon as she was free she left for the private hospital to where Mike Prosser had been moved. She had not seen him since the move. He was in a single room at the end of a carpeted corridor. There was still an armed officer outside his door. He turned his head as she entered and his eyes were wide open. They looked at each other, speaking silently, and his eyes rather than his mouth smiled at her. He tried to raise an arm but only managed to get it a little way off the bed. He pointed a finger at her and his voice was weak and slurred as his jaw was still taped-up.

"What happened to you?" he asked through the side of his mouth. She pulled a chair next to him and told him. He shut his eyes as though to block out the pain of what she had suffered. His finger found her hand and she took hold of it and brought him up to date on everything that had happened since she last spoke to him. When she had finished she wondered if he had gone to sleep as he had closed his eyes again and it was some moments before he opened them and tried to speak.

"So if Marcus was called to Edgware by the Russian prostitute he knew who took her to that house," he said with difficulty. "And now he's dead. And Jason's gone. Only Tyson is still around, doing what he does." His voice was not more than a whisper.

Then she told him about the weekend's operation and what they had called it. He attempted to smile. "I think we'll get Tyson in that net, Mike," she said hopefully. He looked at her and his brow creased quizzically, he didn't have to speak it but the doubt was graphic. She stayed until a doctor told her Mike's brain had done enough work for that day.

Operation Janet began at 14.30 hours on the Thursday afternoon when the ferry left the Hook Of Holland for Harwich. The ferry company had been alerted by the Dutch customs service and one of the Dutch investigation team travelled on the ship. With the sailing manifest he identified the two trucks, one Estofish bound for the Quiros stall in Billingsgate and the other of the Wiewiorka Rozwoz company bound for the Q Pie factory. He noted the drivers ate together onboard and he radioed their registration numbers through to the Customs officers at Harwich. At Harwich, an unmarked truck driven by one of their officers and carrying police from the Essex firearms unit waited for the arrival of the ferry at 2000 hours. The two trucks were aligned to disembark together and it was 21.30 hours when they cleared the port and were followed closely by the Customs vehicle. They stopped at the rest point on the M11 for twenty minutes which was the schedule observed by the police two years previously when Janet Prosser was part of a similar operation. It was thought to be no more than a toilet stop and they soon continued their journey into London along with many other trucks and the Customs vehicle.

At Billingsgate there were no more than two detectives to

identify the arrival of the Estofish truck. It did not start to unload until 3.30am and it was noted that George Quiros, despite his age, was there to supervise but the detectives reported nothing unusual about the operation.

At the Q Pie factory there was a stronger police presence. An armed response unit was parked nearby in an unmarked van and Chief Superintendent Myer, Val Franks, a third detective and four uniformed officers were in three cars spread along the road of the industrial estate surrounding the factory and the detectives were in sight of the loading bay as Mike Prosser had been on his fateful surveillance operation.

The truck carrying the Essex Police unit had pulled back to a position on the A12 after they reported the two East European trucks had diverted to their respective venues and they waited there for further instructions.

At Ilford, outside the Quiros family home, police officers were also awaiting instructions. Likewise in Camden, other officers were positioned outside Anne and Marek Majewski's house and in Tottenham officers had joined the surveillance team watching the late Andrzej Dudek's flat.

At the pie factory, the detectives watched the chicken deliveries being unloaded from plastic crates into steel baskets and wheeled into the factory, the process taking almost forty-five minutes. It was some time afterwards that the driver climbed back into his cab and drove out of the yard and the Essex unit was alerted to await the truck's return.

The night manager of the pie factory was as alarmed by the sudden influx of police officers as were Anne Majewski and her young son and his nanny and Doris Quiros and the youngest daughter when other police officers hammered on their front doors and rushed in brandishing search warrants.

At the Q Pie factory, the manager and his staff were immediately co-operative, showing no signs of complicity in any illegal activity. The processing of the new delivery of chickens was already begun with them being loaded onto the conveyor belt and going under the crusher to split them open. The Chief Superintendent pulled open a broken carcase and emptied the plastic bag of giblets onto a table. Val Franks handed him a knife and watched him hack it open and separate the contents, a small, plastic sachet weighing approximately twenty grams was heavily frosted and indistinguishable from the other frozen pieces. The officers smiled their satisfaction but the faces of the manager and his watching staff registered astonishment. They were instructed to split all the chickens and as they came off the conveyor belt the giblets packets were subjected to the same treatment with the same results. The staff were going to be busy that night and no pies were going to be made.

At Billingsgate market George Quiros and his staff had performed a similar unloading operation of emptying the crates of iced fish into their own containers and the empty crates were then stacked together by George Quiros himself and manoeuvred onto a sack-barrow to be transferred back to the truck which was parked some distance away. George Quiros was about to make the journey when a man, wearing the white coat, apron and hooded top of the market porters, stood in front of him and put his hands on those of George Quiros as though to take the barrow off him. Quiros was about to tell him where to go when he looked up into the eyes of Jason. A smile of understanding went between them and then George Quiros took his hands away and watched Jason wheel the barrow to the Estonian truck.

241

Simultaneously, officers entered all the houses of the suspects. Computers were confiscated and Andy's flat was subjected to a forensic search. At the dog food factory a team of detectives led by Paul Richmond had been given the go-ahead to gain access and in Kent a unit forced their way past the electronic gates of Beaumont to serve a search warrant on a furious Dave Tyson.

In Poland, near the village of Gorzow, one hundred kilometres south of Stettin, a ring of armed police officers from the anti-drug unit of the Policja Kryminalna, approached a chicken farm across the uncultivated fields surrounding a small lake in the dark mist of a damp night. They had no need of directions as the sound of the chickens guided them to the complex of long sheds rearing out of the mist like a prisoner-of-war camp from the recent past. An outer perimeter wire fence and the Rottweiler dogs patrolling behind it added to the illusion. They knew of the dogs and had prepared large pieces of meat dusted with anaesthetic powder and they were soon able to continue to another fence and cut their way to the sheds.

Their trespass triggered security lights and a siren alarm and they rushed the house set near the farm where lights had gone on and doors were already beginning to open with three men stepping out holding shot-guns. Strong spotlights were trained on the men and they were told to put down their weapons and lie on the sodden ground.

In the cellar of the house a sophisticated laboratory was found. It was equipped for the chemical process of distilling the brown cakes of morphine stacked in a locker into the 90 per cent pure powder known as No. 4 heroin. One of the men was identified as the local chemist and a relative of Andrezj Dudek and Alexsander de Haan.

The haul from the chicken carcasses at the pie factory

was 20 kilos of almost pure heroin and was estimated by Chief Superintendent Myer that it would have cost some £300,000 to the supplier alone and when increased with additives by seventy five per cent the street value would be ten times that amount.

"A nice monthly income," he told the officers.

The purpose of the house searches was to examine computers and phones for any relevance to the drugs operations but no evidence was found and no charges were levelled at the individuals who had suffered the police incursions in the middle of the night. Tyson was particularly vocal at this failure, threatening legal action, especially for damage to the electronic mechanism of the gates to the estate, but after the police had departed a phone call from George Quiros soon dissipated his anger.

He was quick to admire the balls of Jason's ploy and relieved to know he was still using his brain. Their long relationship had lasted because he had always been able to rely on Jason doing the right thing, keeping out of trouble and never opening his mouth where he shouldn't. It was the nearest thing to a friendship Tyson would have, similar to his marriage, based on a working relationship of mutual understanding.

"Good on 'im, George," he said. "Won't do any 'arm to 'ave an escort for the lolly. DH will look after 'im."

After prolonged examination of the dog-food plant, Paul Richmond's team discovered what the various police searches had been looking for, a laptop computer hidden in a ceiling panel of one of the offices. The computer revealed a network of agents, mostly of Polish origin, in many parts of the country.

The two delivery trucks were shadowed by the Essex police vehicle back to the port of Harwich for their return journeys to the Continent and as soon as they entered the

Port holding area they were accessed by police and Border Agency officers.

When the empty crates of the Estofish vehicle were examined, used bank notes totalling two million pounds were found in their false bottoms and Jason was hauled out from under the driver's bed. It was six am when George Quiros was about to leave Billingsgate for home that he was arrested on suspicion of laundering drugs money and harbouring a wanted criminal.

It was a massive result for all the agencies involved, including the police, customs and Interpol working in other countries and their enquiries would continue along the route of supply through Turkey and Kazakhstan to the borders of Afghanistan. The euphoria was felt in the many police stations and custom's buildings involved and was carried by Val Franks to Mike Prosser's hospital bedside as she was on the way home to get some sleep. He was much stronger and his voice was almost normal as he told her she looked as though she had been up all night. He listened to her account of Operation Janet and there were times when his eyes reflected her enthusiasm and excitement.

"So, we've got Jason at last – but not Tyson," he said.

"It's a great result, Mike, thanks to you. Don't be down on it. The Commander said he was coming to see you. I think there's talk of another medal for your collection."

"That's nice. But I think they should give one to Tyson; a long-service award for escapology," he said.

"Jason will be facing at least two charges of attempted murder," she reminded him. "We've got him on a spike, who knows what he'll give us for a few years off a long sentence," she said.

"He won't give us Dave Tyson. He's still out there, surrounded by dead bodies and not a scratch on him. You

should have let me run him down, Val."
Val Franks felt his depression and could think of nothing to say to lift it from him.

# CHAPTER SEVEN

# RETRIBUTION

Mike Prosser was right. Despite the falling debris around him, Dave Tyson was undamaged, but not unaffected.

He could not avoid the cries of anguish from the Quiros family at their father's arrest and his wife was not slow to add her concerns. Where did all that money come from? Where was it going to? Why did their father have to take the blame?

He had the urge to ask them where did they think the money came from to pay for their houses, their cars, their holidays abroad, their clothes their swimming pools, their booze, and their expensive meals? Did they think that was all fish money? But he didn't. He bit his tongue and told them it would be sorted.

His analysis of the situation at that stage was only that the Estonian truck had been targeted because of bloody Prosser's nosing about and a good lawyer would soon have George Quiros bailed as there was no proof the money that had been recovered from the truck had anything to do with him. But Jason was different. He was in gaol, a place he had managed to avoid all his life. Tyson remembered de Haan's prophetic question; could he stake his life on Jason not grassing him? He believed he could. Jason might even be a hero and say the money in the truck was his. After all, he was facing two long sentences for attempted murder, what would another three years matter?

But would de Haan see it that way? There was no way the police would fall for another stunt like the murder of the two Poles.

Tyson knew he had to tell him about the money, two million quid was not pocket money – even for de Haan. Tyson feared no

246

one in London, but de Haan was in a bigger league and he had more players in his team than Tyson could muster. Before he could resolve the problem de Haan phoned him.

"What have you got to tell me, Dave," was his question.

It was a Rubik cube. He must know something to ask the question, but how much did he know? And how did he know anything?

"Wot d'you want to know, Alex?"

"I want to know all that you know," the Dutchman replied.

"I don't know where to start. Tell me wot you've 'eard and I'll tell you wot I know."

"I've heard that our supply chain has been broken."

Tyson wondered if he knew about Jason but had to be sure. "Whereabouts?" he asked.

"In Poland," de Haan told him.

"Poland?" The answer was not what Tyson was expecting and suddenly moved his problems to a new dimension. "D'you fink Andy or Marek talked then?"

"Not according to Stefan. He said they were up for escaping when he saw them in prison – they wouldn't have wanted to risk that if they had traded information with the police would they?"

"I don't know. Probably not," Tyson delayed. "But ow did the Polish fing 'appen. Is there a leak your end, Alex?" he said and felt easier for suddenly shifting the spotlight somewhere else.

"It was an organised police operation, not an accident. And as far as I can ascertain, it was not a local police raid. So, you see Dave, my problem is that I have to know where this breach was made. I have to know how serious it is. I have to know whether I am now a target, and anything you can tell me to help me know those things would benefit me and might help you."

Tyson recognised a threat, even dressed in de Haan's careful vocabulary. He had to give the Dutchman something to chew on.

"They've got Jase," he answered instinctively but his brain was not as quick as his opponent's

"When?" was the immediate reply.

"Last night," Tyson answered and knew as he said it, it would not fit the time schedule of the Polish raids.

"Exactly when?"

"Early hours. At Harwich."

"Then that is not the cause of the leak. It had already happened by then," de Haan told him. "But continue, Dave. Now you are beginning to tell me things I should know. Why at Harwich?"

"Ee was in George's truck."

"The Estonian one?" Tyson confirmed that it was and he knew what the next question would be.

"With the money?"

"Yeah. They've arrested George for laundering."

"Dave, I now have many questions but it would be nicer if you didn't make me have to ask them so please tell me why the police searched the Estonian truck."

Dave Tyson had known only about the police raids on the houses and the Estonian truck and his analysis had not stretched beyond that. Apart from Jason's arrest he had felt only the satisfaction of being clever, of having escaped, but the news that there had been raids on their Polish supplier told him that those police operations might not be unconnected. If the tide had reached de Haan's front door it would soon wash back to London. Should he warn de Haan how serious it might be? Should he tell him about the police raids on their homes and, worst of all, should he tell him the police now knew about

248

the dog-food plant from Andy and Marek?

"That copper, Prosser was digging abaht George's place. I just fink ee suspected the trucks were used for smuggling," he lied and knew he had decided his future.

"So you don't think it was anything more than that, a spot check? But why would they target George's place at all?"

"They already 'ad those trucks lined-up since that uvver business. That bastard driver trying to do 'is own fing. We should've changed the system then." Tyson said, again trying to shift the fault lines..

"How much was in the truck?"

"Bout two mill," Tyson answered. Then he got bold. "Wen are you going to replace Andy?" he asked.

"Soon. We'll see what happens in a day or so."

"Yeah. That's a good idea, Alex. Give fings time to settle dahn."

"Meantime, you have to think how you are going to replace that money," de Haan told him

After their father's arrest, Francine Tyson. with her sisters, had assembled at the family home in Ilford where the recriminations continued along the lines of their last meeting, except that this time their mother was the subject of the ferocity of their frustrations as much as Tyson and Andy had been before. The sisters knew from their questions about why their father had been arrested for money laundering, that their mother knew more than she was willing to tell them. They had all been brought up not to question any decisions their parents made but their anxiety for their father's welfare overcame their training and they bullied their mother until she broke down and confessed that she thought it had something to do with drugs. Drugs, like cancer, is a word  that has an assumed finality associated with it when it hits an unsuspecting family. All the girls knew that wheeling and dealing had always been part of their parent's lives. They knew not to ask questions when goods appeared in their garage and were sold on for quick profits. They had got used to strangers coming to their house with wads of cash and doing deals for boxes of cigarettes and alcohol and had accepted the turnover of expensive cars as normal business transactions. They had even thought their father's propensity to buy  near-derelict houses was fulfilling a social need. But drugs was a subject completely absent from their lives. Francine had given strict instructions to the security staff at The Ladybird to ban anyone found smoking or using illegal substances of any kind. It was partly to protect her licences but subconsciously it was a limit that allowed her to profit unconscionably from the many other weaknesses of the human condition. So the word fell among them like a deluge of sleet.

What? How? Where? The questions were unanswered as their mother only suspected but had never asked them herself. It explained why the police had raided their homes and examined their computers and the suspicion became more believable as they talked about it. Francine rang her husband and asked him if he knew anything about drugs and was told she was talking rubbish. Then Anne said she was going to the dog food plant to see what Andy and Marek had got up to there. Francine and the youngest sister  went with her.

They were faced by two police officers on the gate and after making noisy protestations were joined by a detective inspector  who interrogated them without letting them into the factory.

"Is it about drugs?" Francine demanded to know and was joined vehemently in her request by her sisters.

"We can't give you any information," the detective told them. "But I can say it has nothing to do with dog food," he smirked.

The girls drove back to their mother in depressed silence. The silence continued over cups of tea and home-made scones until Doris Quiros attempted to break the feeling of helplessness.

"You'd better get hold of that solicitor again, Anne," their mother said. Francine rang her husband again.

"You still think it's rubbish that drugs are involved," she told him. "Why are the police all over the dog-food plant if it's not about drugs?"

Her mother and sisters were pleased  she was now on their side and venting their anger on her unpopular husband, but the depression could not be lifted and the three girls slept with their mother that night for the first time in years. They were a family again, united in grief.

Francine's phone call had stunned Dave Tyson. He could find no words in answer to her and he had closed his phone without attempting to make a response. Her news about the dog-food plant had been completely unexpected. He and Fran's father had done what de Haan had recommended, they had paid someone to enter the factory and to come straight out again and they had reported back to de Haan that the factory was clear. Jason's arrest was not the result of a spot-check as he had let de Haan believe. He had not told de Haan of the house raids and had hoped they were just a police assault in the wake of the Polish men's murders. The news of the raids in Poland had shaken that hope and Francine's call had nailed it; the police operation was of terminal velocity. His immediate feeling was to phone de Haan but his body refused to obey his head. He just sat and contemplated his future, swirling the red wine in his glass and staring into

251

the nuances of colour like a fortune teller.

Francine was up early after an almost sleepless night but even so, she found her mother and Anne already in the kitchen.

"I'll go home and see if I can get any more information out of Dave," she told them, more in the way of escape than hope.

It was still very early when she turned off the main road and wound her way towards the estate. As she came to the highest point on the road, she slowed habitually, knowing the best view of the house and the estate was from there but because it was so early and there was no other traffic on the road, she was able to stop and enjoy the view. The house was on high ground set well into the rolling grassland of the estate with a trout lake in between and a blanket of deciduous trees behind it. She remembered the first time they had seen it and the thrill of the perfection of the view was as strong now as it had been then. She remembered that she had then asked Dave how they could afford it and now she thought she knew the answer. She drove on, wondering if Marcus Swift would have been happy there with his mother and his dog but she also realised she had not included herself in that scenario. She entered the Great Hall and immediately saw the two large suitcases near the door. Her husband appeared, wearing pyjamas and holding a pistol.

"Fuck me, Fran. You triggered the alarm," was his greeting.

"The gates don't work," she told him and he told her the police had forced them, breaking the electronic unit.

"Why have you got that gun?" she asked

"You never know. You might 'ave been a burglar."

"Who'd burgle you? Everyone around here knows what

252

you're like. Are you going somewhere?"

"I fought I'd better scarper for a while 'till fings settle dahn. I was going to ring you later," he said unconvincingly.

"Are you going to the villa?" she asked and was told he was. "Why so much luggage. Haven't you got enough there already?"

"I don't know 'ow long I'll 'ave to stay. Fings are a bit naughty for me. De Haan's not 'appy on top of everything else."

"The Dutchman? So he's behind all this?"

Tyson nodded wearily. "Yeah."

"D'you want some coffee?" she said as he followed her into the kitchen. They sat at the breakfast counter and he asked about her family.

"They're worried sick," she told him. "How bad is it. Why are the police all over the dog food place. What will they find there. Is that where the drugs are kept?"

Her eyes were cold and hostile and her husband knew she was not going to accept his usual bluster.

"It's better you don't know noffing, Fran. That way, you can't be accused of bein' involved with the drugs fing."

"So it is about drugs?"

"Fran, I told you, it's not good for you to know anyfing."

"You've told me enough anyway," she said. "Just one more question, Dave; is Dad involved?"

"Yeah. Course ee is."

Verbal confirmation of what she already feared had a physical effect. She slumped on the stool as if her spine had suddenly succumbed to an attack of osteomalacia and her face crumpled towards the table.

"Sorry, Fran," he said and reached out to touch her but she shrugged him away and got up and walked out of the kitchen. She was in the bedroom changing when he came in from having had a shower. "Are you driving?" she asked.

"No. I fought I would fly."

"What will you do with the Range Rover?"

"I've asked Joss to come over, he'll run me to the airport." Joss was the son of the tenant farmer who worked the estate.

"You could come wiv me, Fran," he said.

"And leave the club to run itself?" she answered. "That's our main income. What do me and the girls live on without that?"

"We could sell-up.You wanted to do that a few days ago."

"That was when I thought bad things were going to happen," she answered. "Now they have, I need what we've still got to sort them out. How long will it be before they get you, Dave?" She emphasised the question by looking straight into his eyes and his reaction was submissive enough for her to realise that he had asked himself the same question. "Is Spain safe?" she asked.

"Yeah. I'll be okay there," he answered but again it was not with his usual confidence.

She watched from an upstairs window as Joss arrived and took the Range Rover out of the garage. She heard her husband call up to her but she ignored it and saw him carry the cases out to the car. He turned and looked back at the house then his eyes lifted and he saw her at the window. He hesitated, then waved and she waved back. She had an urge to run down to say goodbye but she didn't move and watched the Range Rover make it's way along the drive.

Mike Prosser was sitting in a chair when his CS, Chief Superintendent Myer and the Commander crowded into his room. They were all effusive in their praise of the

254

progress he was making.

"You'll be happy to know you'll be made back up to Chief Superintendent when you return," the Commander told him. "It's the least you deserve."

"Thank you, sir," Prosser replied. "But I'm happy with where I am. We wouldn't want to lose Roger to another station."

The CS was visibly moved by his endorsement.

"We've all got a lot to thank you for, Mike," the Commander told him. It's one hell of a result. The Polish police have traced the trafficking route through Turkey and the Dutch people are gathering around de Haan and his empire. Thanks to your tenacity we've closed down a big slice of the drugs trade."

"There's always another to take its place," Prosser said. "Like the thin red line, one falls and another steps over the bodies."

The Commander nodded his head in agreement. "Last year we estimated there were over three hundred thousand heroin users in this country, over fifty thousand in the rehabilitation programme. The cost to the tax payer is six hundred million a year. You may be right, we'll never stop it but, by God, you've had a bloody good try."

Prosser smiled weakly but his face failed to reflect the Commander's enthusiasm. "I wasn't trying to solve the drugs problem," he told him.

"I know, Mike. But Tyson is all wrapped up in the package."

"I think when you unravel it, sir. You won't find him inside." The Commander made encouraging noises but when Prosser looked sideways and saw Val Franks hovering beyond the door, he was relieved when a doctor said they should not overtire him. "Keep up the progress and when you get back to your desk I think you'll find

Dave Tyson won't be bothering anyone any more," the Commander told him.

"I didn't mean to break up the party," Val Franks told Prosser.

"You always knew how to please me," he smiled.

"I've brought you some mail."

"I don't think I want any work yet, Val," he said.

"It's just a little packet. It looked private," she said and handed him a padded envelope. "It's Dominique's writing," she added.

He caught the questions in her eyes. He reached for a dinner knife to slit open the package.

After her husband's departure Francine Tyson had set about making herself busy. It was an inbred reaction to offset depression which had been passed down through generations of her Spanish-Jewish ancestry. She started on her husband's clothes. Despite his ability to afford good clothes his upbringing of wearing what was handed down from an elder brother or stolen by an occasional father had made him immune to fashion and his preference was always to wear jeans and plain shirts rather than a suit and he tended to wear things until they were so worn that even he noticed. She began to sort them into two piles, those to be thrown and those to go to charity shops, before she realised how many suits and shirts he must have taken with him and when she gave her attention to his shoes she saw he had taken several pairs. Her inclination had been to throw everything away, with the finality of an aggrieved wife or lover, but when she realised how few were left her enthusiasm waned and she began to put what was left into black bags as her mind dwelt on the question as to why her husband had needed to take  so many clothes to Spain. She was still thinking

256

about it when she was surprised to hear a car. She looked out and saw that Joss was returning the Range Rover. She went down and called to him.

"That didn't take you long to get to Heathrow and back," she said. Whenever they flew to Malaga they always used the scheduled flight from Heathrow.

"He went to Gatwick," Joss answered.

She knew Gatwick ran cheap flights to Spain in the summer but they had never used them and certainly wouldn't do so if they had anything other than hand-luggage and Dave had two large suitcases. She went back into the house intending to go online for Gatwick departures – and then she noticed the laptop, used generally in the kitchen, was switched on. She opened it and the webpage for TAP, the Portuguese airline was immediately displayed. She ran down the departure list for the afternoon schedules and her eyes were drawn to a flight to Rio de Janeiro. It departed at 16.30 and her husband would have been at the airport at 13.30. She realised he must have been using the computer when she arrived home and disturbed him. She sat back and assembled her thoughts, then she quickly accessed their main, joint, bank account. It had been cleared, the money having been transferred to a bank in Belize. She didn't think she could be shaken any more but that is exactly what she did, shake. Her body had gone cold and she shivered as though a storm had blown into the house. She recovered and went through their various bank accounts in Spain and Switzerland. She stared into space for some moments and then took her mobile phone and scrolled through the Contacts until she came to the familiar number for Mike Prosser's police station.

Dave Tyson had been been processed through to

the departure lounge and was looking at a sports magazine when he noticed a uniformed attendant searching the faces of the waiting passengers. He buried his face but the attendant was soon standing over him smiling, as she had been trained to do.

"Excuse me, sir, may I see your ticket please?" Tyson showed her. "Mr Tyson, I'm afraid your wife's had an accident. Would you come and speak to our information desk?"

Tyson was wondering how Francine knew where he was, then he realised Joss must have told her he had taken him to Gatwick and then he was beginning to wonder why they had not used the public address system to contact him and by that time they had left the departure lounge and he was faced by two security staff and nearby, an armed police officer with an automatic weapon held across his chest.

"In here sir," the attendant said and opened a door. Inside there were three uniformed police officers. A sergeant stepped forward.

"You are Dave Tyson?" he asked. Tyson nodded. "Your wife contacted the Metropolitan police to say you were leaving the country and that you were responsible for the deaths of two people by burning down a house."

Tyson's mouth opened wide but he soon recovered and laughed.

"My wife told you that? She's 'avin you on, mate. She's just pissed off cos I'm leavin' 'er."

"If she's doing that she's in serious trouble," the officer said.

"Yeah, right. You tell 'er. She's bleedin bonkers, off 'er 'ead. I couldn't stand it any longer that's why I'm doin' a flyer. Look officer, I've got a flight to catch."

"You'll have to miss that, I'm afraid, sir."

"You're bloody afraid? So am I mate. It cost me free fousand quid an' someone's going to 'av to pay it if I don't get on that plane."

"We'll sort it all out when the Met officers get here," the sergeant told him.

The statement silenced Tyson and his great frame looked submissive as apprehension took hold of it. He was escorted to the airport detention centre and was locked into an interview room. His immediate response was to vent his temper on the door and he kicked at it and hammered it with his great fists until his enthusiasm waned, then he slumped onto a chair to contemplate what he perceived to be his wife's treachery.

He had been there more than an hour when the door was unlocked and Mike Prosser and Val Franks entered. Prosser looked weak and walked with a stick. Tyson stared at him, his mouth gaping as though frozen in a yawn. Prosser lowered himself carefully onto a chair.

"Surprised to see me, Dave? Well, it was a damn close run thing I have to admit. But, you know, I just had to survive to see you again. I couldn't go without saying goodbye, could I? Especially when, *goodbye* really means, *goodbye*."

Tyson's expression didn't change, he seemed oblivious to how stupid he looked. He watched Prosser take a small voice-recorder from his pocket and hold it towards him.

There was a delay as Prosser watched Tyson's eyes staring at the machine. Prosser smiled and switched it on. Marcus Swift's voice was instantly recognisable.

*"Dave told me about Spain,"*

*"Yeah?"*

*"It was a shame you had to do that to the boy."*

*"Yeah."*

*"Was he a decent chap?"*

*"Yeah. He was okay."*

*"I suppose Dave's weather forecast was a coded message for you to get on with it?"*

*"Yeah. It's a code we use sometimes."*

*"Poor Robbie. But I suppose Dave had to get rid of him."*

*"Yeah."*

*"You must tell me how to get some muscle on my arse dear boy; it is inadequate to support my weight on this step."*

*"Yeah." .*

*"Well, good night, Jason. Sleep well."*

*"Yeah. You too Marcus."*

Prosser switched off the recorder and waited for Tyson to speak but nothing came.

"There's no need for me to caution you, we'll do it when we get you back to London." Prosser said. "Anyway, you know it by heart. Come on, Dave, get on your feet. We'll take you home."

# CHAPTER EIGHT

# POSTSCRIPTS

**J**ason. "The Estonian driver was moonlightin' when ee brought in them girls an' the copper got in 'is truck. When the uvver driver saw the Estonian geezer let the girls out at the rest-stop to find their way into London, ee 'ad to interfere. Then the copper tried to arrest the Estonian bloke an' ee 'it 'er, knockin er cold. The Pole rung Andy an' Andy rung the boss. The boss told 'im to put the copper in the Polish wagon an' for the Estonian truck to carry on to Billingsgate but to take the copper's phone in case they was trackin' the truck wiv it. Andy an' Marek met the chicken lorry an' took the copper to the 'ouse in Stepney an' they started movin' the girls out of there as a precaution. Then the boss got a call from Marcus telling 'im the Russian prossy was makin trouble up West. So I drove the boss over there an ee sorted it. Then we brought the Russian prossy back to the Stepney 'ouse. Then Andy an' me took the Russian prossy an' the copper into the 'ouse an locked them in a bedroom. Then the boss told us to put some towels on the landing an' set fire to em, On the way out, Dave turned the gas an' the fire on in the kitchen. Ee said it would make a nice diversion in case they was watchin the lorry at Billingsgate. Ee said it would kill two birds wiv one stove an' ee laughed. That's it. That's wot 'appened."

**Francine Tyson.** "I know I did wrong by giving my husband an alibi for what he and Jason did to those girls. But I had no idea what he'd done until Marcus told me. I just want to bring up my girls properly so they can forget who their father is."

261

**Judge.** "I doubt very much if they will ever achieve that, Mrs Tyson. But because of them I am going to give you a suspended sentence. See that you spend the time wisely."

**Dave Tyson.** (After he had been sentenced to three life-terms for the murders of WPC Janet Prosser, an unknown Russian woman and Danny Murphy). "Firty years? You're 'avin a laugh aint yer, Judge?"

**Judge.** Not yet Mr Tyson. But, no doubt, when you have subsequently been convicted of complicity in the murder of Robbie Birch – your son – and the manslaughter of four others, I and many other good citizens might raise a smile or two, sad as that may be, to know that you have not enough time left in your body to be incarcerated for the sentences you will then receive"

**Mike Prosser.** "James? It's me, your Dad. I know I don't phone. I'm coming to see you. I don't care who you live with, you can meet me at the airport wearing a pink tutu if you like. I just want to see you and hug you. Is that okay with you? We can do some swimming together, I've been practising."

**Dominique Harcourt.** (W*atching a satellite newscast and seeing Mike Prosser and Valerie being bombarded with questions outside the High Court).* She wiped the tears from her face and heard her voice from somewhere deep inside her body, "I will be back, Valerie."

Thank you for reading my book. I do hope you found it entertaining. My next novel,
***The Girl Of Drovers' Hill,***
will be available very soon.

P K Davies

59843979R00149

Made in the USA
Charleston, SC
14 August 2016